The Forever Girl

Brandon's Inferno

by
Chris O'Grady

Eloquent Books
New York, New York

Eloquent Books
An imprint of AEG Publishing Group
845 Third Avenue, 6th Floor – 6016
New York, NY 10022
www.eloquentbooks.com

ISBN: 978-1-60693-993-2   1-60693-993-9

Printed in the United States of America

Book Design: D. Johnson, Dedicated Business Solutions, Inc.

This is for Michelle
who saw something here that I didn't
and, of course, for Patricia

The Forever Girl was first published serially in the online mystery magazine MYSTERICALE's Winter 2008–'09 and Spring 2009 Issues.

One

Off to the west, half a mile or more, a thousand neons along the Strip thrust a glaring varicolored canopy high up into the night sky. In the other direction, a climbing moon, almost at the full, spread a softer silver light on the desert floor.

Cutting across the sage and cactus-covered plain, I was on my way to the first night of that week's tour of the graveyard shift where I worked.

About halfway there, I saw them dump him out of a slowly moving car onto a dirt road that cut across my regular route, just ahead.

The car came bobbing its headlights along the seldom-used track from the southeast, on my right rear. I glanced at its approach over my shoulder, but paid no special attention to it.

The path I had beaten for myself over the past few months angled into the dirt road maybe a hundred paces from me when the car went past. A short distance before it reached my path, one of the left-side car doors opened while they tumbled him out. The car had slowed almost to a crawl, so he rolled loosely and then lay still. The door slammed shut and the car speeded up, its two red taillights getting closer together the farther off they went.

By the time I came up onto the county maintained dirt road, I could hardly make out the taillights in the distance. There had never been a hope of getting a look at the license plate.

There was no hurry. He was either dead or alive. As I reached the road, I hesitated for that small second.

I should tend to my own business, cross the dirt road and continue on the second mile of my hike to the aluminum windows and screens assembly shop where I worked.

The small second passed. I didn't tend to my own business. I turned and walked along the road, back to where he lay.

1

It was as thorough a going-over as any I had ever seen.

He lay on his back. For the first moment or two, I thought he was dead. Then I heard his breathing, harsh, rasping, bubbling in his throat.

Maybe he was dead, at that. Or as good as.

It wasn't a professional job. They had done too much to him, for pros.

Both his eyes were black, the left one swollen shut, the other just about.

I squatted beside him, not touching him, waiting to see if he died. He didn't. His struggle to breathe went on. He had to work at it, but somehow he kept it going.

The gentle night-wind stirred some of the light-brown hair at the top of his head. The rest of his hair was matted to his skull by blood.

Still squatting there, I raised my head and gazed across the level land to the big-money Strip, wondering what he had done. Welshed on a bet? Stolen somebody's girl? Tried moving in on someone else's territory?

There could be a thousand reasons. Or none. He had been pulverized, and here he was.

Whoever had done it had enjoyed doing it, no doubt of that. I shrugged. It wasn't my affair. He might live a couple dozen more years, or he might go out like a candle-flame a minute from now, but that was nothing to me, either.

All I had to decide right then was which of three possible paths I was going to walk. I could forget I ever saw this man, go on to work, and attach aluminum storms and screens till eight in the morning. Or I could get to a phone, make a fast anonymous call to 911 and then go on about my business. Or I could pack him on my back across the sage flats to the nearest lights and get him treated as quickly as possible.

I settled for the second of the three. In the shape this guy was in, to move him might be to kill him.

"Look," I said, bending over him, "can you hear me?"

I thought I caught a gleam from the right eye, the one that wasn't completely puffed shut. It may have been moonlight reflected from his eyeball. His labored breathing was the only sound he made.

"I'll get to a phone," I told him. "Don't move from here. I'll get some help as soon as I can."

He just lay there, his face a smashed-in blob washed by the cold silver moonlight. The gleam was still there in that one eye, or it was there part of the time, but I couldn't be sure if he was conscious or not. So I had to leave him like that.

"I'll be as quick as I can," I told him.

I was surprised at the thickness in my throat. I was even more surprised to find myself running across the desert, headed due west for the nearest lights, weaving in and out among the clumps of sage bushes and an occasional cactus.

It had gotten to me, the way whoever had given him the business had given him so much of it.

In the old days, I had started out in the muscle bracket. I quit it before I graduated into the leave-them-dead class. But we did what we did like pros. We broke a guy's arm, maybe a leg. We put a scare into him, according to what the contract called for. But we didn't go crazy and pound all of him into the ground and still leave him alive. Even the hit boys did it clean, most of the time. They left you a man. True, they left you a dead man, but up to that final second, you were still a man; you were still yourself; you could see to your pride, and try to go out right.

That must have been what got to me: whoever had worked on him had loved every second of it. One of those sick bastards, as sick as you could get.

I was shaking, sweating, my lungs screaming for air from the unaccustomed jogging, when I loped out of the sage flats into the first dark quiet street at the edge of town. There was a block or two of that before the lights of the Strip blotted out most of the night.

I kept going until I reached the brightness, where I had trouble stopping. Grabbing a power pole at the edge of the curb, I stood there panting, gulping air, peering around for the nearest roadside phone.

Maybe I looked out of place in my work dungarees and blue denim shirt, because a patrol car slid to a stop in front of me. The nearest cop got out and came over to where I leaned on the pole.

He might have thought I was drunk. Maybe they still had some empty cells in the drunk-tank downtown.

"A guy . . ." I gasped. "Back there . . . in the desert . . . beat up pretty bad . . ."

His hard little cop's eyes turned even harder.

"You beat up a guy?"

"Not me," I snarled. "Just . . . found him. He's . . . bad shape. Need . . . ambulance. Better hurry."

He took hold of my upper arm, the way they do.

"Okay, get in the back seat. Where is this guy?"

My breathing was returning to normal.

"On a dirt road, that way," I said, pointing back the way I'd come.

He slid in beside the one at the wheel and picked up the mike.

"A dirt road?" he asked over his shoulder. "Which one?"

"I don't know. It crosses from southeast of town to up ahead, where we're pointed now. It must come into this road . . ."

The cop at the wheel spoke.

"I know the road he means, Mike."

He pulled out onto the Strip and went barreling along it, lifting the siren to just above a growl.

The other cop, Mike, talked low into the radio, directing the ambulance where to meet us.

We swung abruptly to the right, leaving the lights of the Strip behind us, then slowed and made a half-right, bumped down a slight grade, and leveled off at the bottom. Then the buildings were behind us, and we were running along in the moonlight. The sage flowed past on both sides of the county road.

I tried to watch for my path. Away off to the left, I could see the row of light-industry buildings, where I worked in the one on the end of the string, nearest to the Strip. Far ahead and off to the right was the house where I lived in a furnished room with a hot plate. That house was easy to see on any night: it was the last building down that way.

But I had never gone along this dirt road, so I couldn't be sure where the path was that I had worn for myself across the desert getting to work and back, whenever I didn't have a ride home.

"Which side of the road?"

"Right side. Close to the road. Practically on it."

Now we drove slowly. The patrol car's headlights gave plenty of light, once the one at the wheel stomped the brights on.

There was no oncoming traffic at that hour on a forgotten dirt track like that.

No one was lying beside the road.

After we had gone along like that for awhile, I suddenly knew there wasn't going to be anyone.

"They must have come back for him," I muttered, half aloud.

I felt like kicking myself for getting mixed up in it.

Mike turned and looked back at me a couple of times. Then he would face forward and watch the right side of the road again.

I kept thinking what kind of damn fool I had been to open up to him, back there on the Strip. I should have found a phone, called it in, and let them find him or not find him. I'd be at work right now, not starting to sweat again.

Finally I had to say the obvious.

"We've come too far. We must have passed him."

The cop at the wheel swung the front of the vehicle off the road in a clear space, backed, turned, and started along the dirt road the way we'd come.

"Maybe he crawled into the brush," he ventured. He didn't sound loaded with confidence.

"No," I said. "In the shape that guy was in, he couldn't have moved a foot."

They grunted and kept quiet, but I had to stick to my story.

"Look, let me out here," I called.

Mike laughed.

"He wants us to let him out here. Playtime's over."

"I can't tell where I'm at, inside a car," I explained. "I've always come across here on foot. I can't get my bearings. You get out with me, if you think I'm trying to cut out."

"All right, I'll do that," Mike said. "Drop us here, Sam. Stay behind him. Keep him in your brights. I'll walk along on my side, out of the lights."

Sam stopped the car. Mike slid out and watched me as I got out of the back of the patrol car's caged section.

"Stay in front of me," Mike ordered.

Moonlight gleamed on metal in his hand. He was a tough, experienced cop in a fast-money gambling town, and he wasn't taking chances.

"And don't go off the road, buster."

"Okay, buster, I won't."

I walked forward into the beams of the squad car's headlights. I could hear the crunch of Mike's footsteps keeping pace with mine, back there, just off the road.

The car eased along, a dozen feet behind me. I looked off toward the shop where I worked. It wasn't in line yet.

A bit farther along, it was closer to the way it looked when I walked toward it at night. I began to watch the left edge of the dirt road, trying to spot where I usually came angling into it from where I lived.

Twice I stopped at spots that looked familiar, but after sighting both ways, decided each time they weren't right. So I went on.

Then I found the path. It lined up all right, both with the shop up ahead and the other way, with the house where I was staying.

Crossing the dirt road, I checked the other side. Over the weeks, my shoes had worn a groove in the relatively soft shoulder, and there it was.

Standing there, I peered back to where the injured man had lain. From where I was now standing, even with only moonlight to help at the time, I had been able to see him lying there, after he was thrown from the car. Now, with the squad car's brights full on, I saw we hadn't just missed him coming along the road, both times just now. He wasn't there anymore.

"This is the path I follow on my way to the job," I told Mike, pointing at the rut through the sage bushes.

Mike stood beside the squad car, his face reflecting the headlights dimly.

"Where's the guy?"

"He was back there." I went back along the dirt road, past the squad car. Sam backed up, the car purring quietly along beside me. Mike's footsteps crunched in the roadside grit and desert sand.

When I thought I had almost reached the place where the beat-up man had lain, I stepped to the side of the road and bent, watching carefully as I prowled along.

"Don't go off the road," Mike called.

"Don't worry."

A few steps more, and I stopped and bent closer to the ground. It might have been the place where the guy had landed.

"Have you got guts enough to come up here and take a look?" I called over my shoulder. "This might have been where he fell."

Mike came out into the light of the red taillights and stood beside me, watching where I pointed.

The ground was scraped. A sage bush was smashed in on one side. I was relieved to see that. When the guy was thrown into the bush, it had probably hurt him plenty, but so far it was the only tangible thing I had found to back up my story.

"He hit about here," I said. "Then he rolled over into the bush, I guess. He stopped about there."

"Stay here," Mike repeated. "Don't go off the road. I don't want too many tracks screwing things up, if this turns out to warrant investigation."

"All right," I agreed.

I watched Mike walk wide around the bent bush to about where the guy had stopped rolling and settled. He squatted, flash in one hand, revolver in the other.

Inside the car, I could hear Sam talking softly into the radio.

A pair of headlights came rapidly toward us from under the golden pink bowl of light reflected from the sky by all the lights along the Strip. A siren sounded.

Mike looked up as the ambulance approached, then returned his attention to the ground. He put his gun away, reached out, touched something, held his fingertips in the light of his flash. Then he straightened and stood there watching the EMS vehicle slow and stop, with its headlights facing the squad car's.

I went on standing where I was, in the middle of the dirt road, lit by the squad car's red taillights. I waited. There was nothing else I could do.

Mike spoke to the EMS worker who alighted from the vehicle.

"Guy was thrown from a moving car, hit there, rolled, and ended up here. Now he's gone. May have crawled away, may have been picked up by a passing car. If we don't find him nearby, you wasted a trip."

The EMS man grinned.

"No, you wasted a trip for me."

Mike shrugged.

"I'm going to make a circle or two. If I don't find the victim, we'll have to let it go for now."

Turning, Mike disappeared into the sage.

EMS stared after him a moment, dug out a cigarette and set fire to the end of it with a wooden kitchen match.

"You the one that found the body?" he asked me.

"Yeah. The body was still alive when I left it."

"Could it move by itself?"

"I don't see how. It was well worked on."

Losing interest, he went over to talk to Sam in the squad car. After a moment, I followed him.

"Okay if I go on my way? I'm probably late for work now. Supposed to be there at midnight."

"Better stick around," Sam said.

"Officer, I've told you all I can. He was dropped from a car, landed over there, I took off for help, and now the help is here."

"Only he isn't here," Sam pointed out.

"That's not my fault," I complained. "I didn't put him there. All I did was find him and report what I found to you. From here on, it's your baby."

"Better stick around," Sam said again. "We'll clear it with your boss."

I gave up. When they start saying the same things to you over and over, you might as well argue with a block of concrete.

"Okay if I crawl in the back of your car again? I'll be on my feet till eight in the morning, if I ever get to work. Might as well stay off them while I can."

He grinned.

"Climb in."

Crawling in back, I shut my eyes, opening them once in awhile to look around. I couldn't sleep, but I relaxed as well as I could.

Presently another car came out. Plainclothes cops got out of it, talked to Mike and Sam. They all wandered around for awhile. Then it began to wind down.

Sam climbed behind the wheel again and Mike got in beside him. One of the plainclothes cops had me go over it for him. He listened quietly, nodded once or twice, and said, "All right, thanks for reporting it." Turning to Sam, he said: "Get his name and address and where he works."

"He's late for work," Sam said. "Okay if we drop him off?"

"All right with me," plainclothes said, and went away.

"Name's James Brandon," I told Sam's notebook.

"Address?"

"Seventy, East Tonopah Street."

"Where do you work?"

"U-Kay Aluminum Products. I don't know the street number." I pointed north across the sage flat. "The long white building on the end there, nearest the Strip."

"Good enough," Sam said. "I'll get the address when we drop you."

It was almost one in the morning before I picked up the airgun and started bolting the heights, headers and sills together.

Mike went and told the foreman why I was late, but before he left the shop, I noticed him step into the little glass office, where he talked for a few minutes with the boss. Probably asking about me. I didn't let it worry me. Nobody there knew anymore about me than anyone in the world knew. The fact that I had been working there for two or three months would be enough. Nobody in that shop had been there long anyway, except a few old-timers who had cushy deals. It wasn't the kind of shop that paid enough to make anyone want to stay longer than you had to. Minimum wage the first month, then you got an obligatory raise when you were let into the Union: ten cents an hour.

Thinking about that, I laughed. I could hardly figure out what to do with that extra four bucks a week I was getting, less taxes and whatnot.

By quitting time next morning, I'd had to tell my story to the guys at work half a dozen times, but they finally stopped talking about it and went back to telling one another who they'd laid lately and how drunk they'd gotten.

Punching out at eight-thirty, I washed up and walked across to the diner and had breakfast there. When the guy I usually caught a ride home with was through eating, I almost went with him, but on impulse I told him: "No, I forgot. I have to report at the Hall of Justice."

"Okay," he nodded. "See you tonight, Jim."

I didn't have to report anywhere, that I knew about. Wondering why I hadn't gone along with him, I sat there over a second cup of coffee.

I was certainly tired enough. I wondered about it awhile.

Over on the Strip, trucks drove back and forth with supplies for the little city, so its hungry-eyed people could spend short intervals between working gambling games doing a little eating.

Presently I quit wondering why I had turned down the ride home, because by then, of course, I knew why.

I sat there and looked at it, the way a circus aerialist must gaze out over the void before him before he takes the first dive out, reaching for the swinging bar.

I had kept away from the grift, gotten this bacon-and-bean job, just to clear the stink of it all out of my nostrils for awhile, but I was beginning to realize that some of us are apparently born to what I had been kidding myself I was trying to get away from: snooping, digging into the mess of life other people made for themselves.

Now I could feel myself inching toward the near end of that high wire again. I watched myself doing it, and wondered why. Because I knew damn well I would be sick of it again, if I went back into the investigation line.

I lit a cigarette, shaking my head at myself.

Maybe there would be nothing out there. Maybe he had just crawled off somewhere and died. Or maybe he had been picked up and hauled away to a hospital, or to oblivion.

I shrugged. Whichever it was, I knew I was going to walk back across the two miles of sage flats.

The pathetic part was, I felt the old lift, the beginning of excitement.

That was why I shook my head. At myself. It looked as if I was hooked. Again.

Buying two quarts of milk and a couple of hero sandwiches at a delicatessen, I slipped between the deli and the coin-operated laundry next door, and started across the sage flats.

The wind soughed gently, whipping the bushes, tossing some of them.

Walking through it, I swung my gaze back and forth, but I saw no one. When I reached the dirt road, I stopped and looked around. No police stakeout. Maybe they had gone over the ground again, when daylight arrived. Or perhaps my victim had turned up at a hospital and that was the end of the little mystery, and of his disappearing act.

But I stood there anyway, in the middle of the dirt road, waiting.

I had a feeling.

If you had asked me then, "Do you think he's still somewhere out there?" I honestly wouldn't have known what to reply. Probably I would have said: "No. I don't think so. How could he be?"

But I had the feeling, and I went on standing there. Then I turned along the road until I came to where they had dumped him. I looked all around the area.

I knew I wouldn't be able to see him. If he was good enough to stay hidden in the desert this long, I wasn't going to spot him. He might be lying fifteen or twenty feet from where I stood, but if he knew how to sprinkle desert sand over himself the right way, he would remain invisible. To my eyes, anyway.

"Look, I'm not police," I called out.

The wind blew the words away from my mouth. The sage bushes tossed, the desert stank with memories of night-smells, but nothing else happened.

I guess I hadn't really expected anything to happen.

Far off, beyond the house where I roomed, a car streaked along a road, headed toward the southwest end of the Strip.

I began to feel foolish, but I still stood there. He might not be anywhere around, and any words I called were being said to nothing but the wind and the desert.

"Okay, man, good luck," I finally muttered.

Turning, I started to cut across to my well-worn path, but glancing down at the paper bag I carried, I stopped and went back to the dirt road.

Holding the bag way up, I called: "Here's some milk and sandwiches. If you need them, get to them soon, before the milk turns sour in the sun."

Stepping off the dirt road in among the knee-high sage, I put the bag down in the shade of a big bush, went back up onto the road and along it to my path.

All the way across that second mile of wind-tossed flat, I didn't look back once.

The room I rented was on the second floor of an old adobe building at the end of a quiet neighborhood street, whose pavement ended halfway along the house. A concrete sidewalk ran along the side of the windowless adobe wall that fronted that section of the street and ended at my front door. Beyond that there was nothing but a few feet of dirt path to the corner of the building and then the sage-spotted desert.

Going around the corner of the building out of the wind, I unlocked the street door, then stepped back to the nearby corner of the house, where I stared back across the sage flat.

At that distance, I couldn't expect to see a thing, and I didn't.

The mid-morning sun was hot, once you were out of that wind.

Gazing across the two miles of flat desert, I thought of all that had happened out there. Then I went inside and up the stairs and unlocked the door of my room.

That night, before starting across again, I crawled out the east window onto the narrow terrace, whose railing was the top of the outside adobe wall of the building. There was just enough room out there for two or three people to sit, between my window and the northeast corner of the building. For one person, there was more than enough space.

With my back against the outside wall of my room, I sat on the edge of the hip-high wall at the corner. Leaning forward a little, I could look past the corner of the building and see the string of lights bordering the Strip. I didn't even have to lean forward to see the area where I would be working an hour from now. Everything was dark between where I sat and that strip of light-industry buildings.

Sitting there, I smoked a long while before rousing myself to leave for work.

The wind had dropped.

I took a flashlight with me.

When I reached the dirt road, I turned back along it. The bag of food and the two quarts of milk weren't where I had left them that morning.

I prowled around for awhile, but I couldn't find a trace of anything, so I just went on along to work.

In the morning, I didn't even stop for breakfast at the diner, but started back across to the dirt road.

Near where I had left the food, there wasn't a trace of anything. I circled around, taking plenty of time and going slowly, but I still almost missed it.

One of the milk containers was partly hidden in the shadow of a sage-bush. Picking it up, I examined it. There was a streak of red at the top. It might have been blood, left there when someone had been drinking, and the mouth doing the drinking had been bleeding.

Then again, maybe it wasn't blood.

Holding onto the milk container, I kept searching, but that was all I found. When the radius of my last swing had gotten to something like an eighth of a mile, I knew there wasn't going to be anymore than that milk container. I was surprised there had been that much.

Finishing the final circle, when I cut my own footpath partway between the dirt road and my current rooming house, I went along home, without looking back.

While I ate breakfast, I noticed another wider streak of pink in the middle of one side of the milk container, and there was a very clear fingerprint.

I couldn't tell which finger had made the print, but it wasn't the thumb or the pinkie: it was too big for that. One of the other three fingers.

Probably the police forensics team could tell, and they might also be able to find out if the owner had a record somewhere. If they had a reason for finding out.

But they didn't have a reason yet. The owner of the print hadn't done anything. Someone else had done it to him.

Still, I ought to turn the milk container and its print in. For identification purposes. Maybe the blood would provide DNA information. If the pink smear *was* blood.

That night, the police sent for me, while I was at work.

"Where should I go?" I asked whoever phoned. "I forget where your morgue is located."

"Not the morgue," he corrected me. "County Hospital."

So much for saving the milk container with the fingerprint. If he was in the hospital, they could get all the DNA and prints they needed from the guy in person.

Two

I went to the County Hospital in the morning. It sprawled on a machine-made knoll surrounded by bright green grass, which needed lots of water to stay that green. An occasional royal palm stood tall, here and there on the lawn. High up, the wind clashed the palm fronds.

None of the wind reached me as I went up the path that bisected the front lawn. When I went inside the hospital out of the sun through the main entrance, I felt the cool shady difference, even that early in the morning.

An aide at the receiving desk told me to wait. I sat on a bench and watched people pass.

I'd gone home from work, taken a shower, put on slacks and a sport shirt before coming back uptown. I'd gotten my usual ride home from the shop, but had to walk to the hospital. I wondered if I had enough money yet for another car. After I left here, I might do some looking in used-car lots.

A youngish-looking man crossed to me from the desk.

"You Brandon?"

"Yes."

"This way."

I followed him along a corridor until he stopped outside one of the wards at the rear of the hospital. A uniformed police officer sat on a chair beside the door.

With one hand on the doorknob, the plainclothes cop said to me: "If you could have gotten here last night, before they treated him . . ."

I stood beside him, waiting.

"I'm Detective Sergeant Brode," he went on. "This may be the man you reported, the one left in the desert a couple of nights back. I say may be, because while this one is pretty banged up and the doctor claims he got it several days ago, he was found in an alley in the northwest section of town, a short distance this side of that new casino out there, Florian's. You know it?"

I shook my head, no.

He shrugged.

"Half casino, half country club. They even handle yachts, farther north on the lakeshore." He grinned at the quizzical look I gave him. "Yeah, haul the high-rollers' yachts up to the lake and back, if they've got enough of that old stuff."

"As soon as I get enough of that old stuff," I said, "maybe I'll have them haul my yacht, too."

"Yeah," he grunted. "Anyway, he was found in this alley, not as far out as Florian's. As I say, he might not be your guy, but . . . how did that line go? . . .he's the only one we've got. See if you can make some kind of identification."

His hand started to turn the knob.

"What about his papers?" I asked. "Do you know his name yet?"

His hand stopped turning the doorknob. His eyes watched me thoughtfully. He sighed.

"I'm glad you asked that question . . . I think." He seemed to hesitate before going on. "He was clean. No identification of any kind. Nothing in his pockets but three blood-soaked handkerchiefs and a couple of . . . well, no papers, anyway. Sound usual?"

"No."

"That's what we thought, too."

"He might have been robbed," I suggested.

I tried to recall if I had felt the bulge of a wallet in his trouser pocket against my knee, when I squatted beside him on the dirt road that night. Maybe I had just imagined it, or assumed it was there.

"He might well have been robbed," Brode agreed, watching me closely. "Well, come in. See if you recognize him."

His head was heavily bandaged. Almost his entire face was covered by thick swathes of gauze. I could smell the medicine odors coming from him in waves.

There wasn't much to recognize . . . that I could see, I mean. He lay under clean white sheets at the far end of a long, very crowded ward. At that early hour, there were no visitors but Brode and myself. A couple of patients near the far end of the ward were talking among themselves. They glanced up as we went by, and their eyes followed us as we went behind screens arranged around the bed that held the unknown man.

He lay stiff and still, covered by the sheets up to his neck, and above that by bandages. Only a tuft of his dark blond hair showed near the top of his head. The rest had probably been shaved for surgery, and was now covered with bandages.

Standing beside the bed, I looked down at him. Only his right eye and his nose showed out of the bandaging. The eye stared fixedly at the ceiling. It didn't turn to look at Brode or myself, after one quick glance when we came through the opening in the screens.

I studied that single eye surrounded by bandage-lumps. The white gauze made the eye stand out, gray as slate, and just about as warm looking.

I tried to think of something to say. Finally, I just said, "I hope you're all right soon."

We stood there a moment or two longer. When he still didn't look at us, I turned and went outside the screen and out of the ward. In the corridor, I stood near the policeman sitting there.

Brode followed me out.

"What do you think? Is it him?"

I shrugged.

"It might be the same man. With all those bandages, it's hard to tell."

"Yeah, I was afraid of that."

"It could be the guy," I assured him. "Moonlight is funny. The hair could be the same . . . and it was the right eye that wasn't completely closed."

Brode stood there chewing his lip, staring at me, but not seeing me. Then he nodded.

"All right, good enough. There aren't that many assault cases. This is the same man. Thanks for coming over, Mr.

Brandon. If we need you later on, when some of those bandages come off, we'll get in touch with you."

"Will it be all right if I bring him some cigarettes?"

He had been turning to the policeman as I asked the question. Turning back, he eyed me sharply.

"Do you know that guy? I mean, did you know him before this?"

"No. I just thought I would . . . I mean, none of his family is likely to show up, unless he's from right here in town. Maybe he could use a touch of something . . . something that hasn't got a fist wrapped around it."

For another moment, he kept staring at me. Then he grinned and shrugged.

"Sure, Mr. Brandon, I guess it's all right. Check with the duty nurse about the cigarettes, though. His ribs are taped up, I understand."

"Okay."

I went back down the long corridor past the swift-walking whispering-soled nurses and orderlies.

When I got back outside, the lawn was still there, still uncannily green in that desert sun. I wondered why they bothered.

Walking down the main walk leading through the grass out to the street, I was wondering where I could find the nearest bus, or the nearest beer.

Just short of the street, a big statue of someone stood off to one side. Stopping, I studied it. Its name was on a metal plaque attached to the base. It might have been a doctor who had saved lots of lives, or a money-man who contributed *mucho dinero* to build the place, or it could have been a Mexican bandit.

Continuing, I reached the sidewalk.

Someone called my name.

Back on the shady side of the statue, a crew-cut head with a bronze face beneath it was aiming another holler my way.

Staying where I was, I watched Jack Harvey come striding along, his hand outstretched.

"Hey, how you been, Jim?" he smiled. "You've been out of circulation awhile."

I reached my hand out and helped his hand shake it.

"Been earning an honest dollar," I said. "Just to see what it feels like."

"You should keep in touch," he scolded genially. "I've had plenty of work coming in. I could easily throw some of it your way, and I'd never even feel it."

"Doing what? Catching department store help clipping quarters from the change?"

Smiling, he spread his hands.

"Hey, Jim, it's bread and butter. What the hell, in our racket, we can't pick and choose. The big hunt-that-man-down kind of cases you specialize in don't show up every week. You have to eat in between, right?"

"I'm eating."

"Jim, I'd like a little powwow with you," he said seriously. "One of these days, why not give me a call? I can always use a good man like you, maybe for relief work. That way it don't tie you down."

"I'll think about it."

"Fair enough. Jim, I wish I had a minute right now. We could grab a fast bite somewhere. Maybe next time we'll get to kick it around. You've been out of the loop so long now, I'm gonna have some of my people look into it. Maybe you're grabbing too much business away from me for my own good."

He laughed.

Jack had a big good-looking outdoor-face, and one of the friendliest smiles in the state. Unfortunately, his eyes were as warm as the underside of a glacier.

Just to be saying something while we stood there making conversation, I ventured: "I heard you were going to branch out, set up an office out on the coast."

"Wish I could, Jim," he admitted confidentially. "That's where the real green is. Maybe someday, but not just yet. I want to be in real solid, all through this territory, before I try spreading out."

For a moment, he eyed me speculatively.

"I wish I could get you to work into the big-outfit way of operating, Jim. You might be the right man to handle things for me here, while I head up our first branch on the coast, when we open it."

The 'we' slid into the conversation as smooth as a switch-blade, but I knew it was a word even the wind would have a tough time carrying any distance.

I shook my head.

"No, I like it fine this way," I told him. "My elbows feel crowded by all that paperwork you have to do."

He laughed again.

"All right, Jim. We'll leave it at that. I guess you'll never change. Maybe it's a good thing for me you don't want to break into the big-agency dodge. You'd be rough competition."

We both knew he was lying, but his smile seemed a lot more sincere than mine.

When we separated, I wandered down to automobile row, checking out the buys in smashed-up old cars, where the damage is all on the surface: fenders, sides, doors . . . but I kept my eye open for one with its guts still in good shape.

One or two I looked at seemed pretty good, and they were both less than a hundred. Possibles. But for the time being, I let it go, making a note of the lots where each was for sale. Experience had shown me it paid to look a long time for the sort of car I wanted, and could afford.

Two days later, on the afternoon before my midnight-to-eight trick in the shop ended for that week, I went over to the hospital during regular visitors hours, to see how the un-known Punching Bag was doing.

No cop sat outside the ward door.

Some of the bandages had been removed, but most of the injured man's face was still covered.

His eyes picked me up when I went through the opening in the screens that still walled him off from the rest of the ward, but he still didn't say anything. Pretty soon his right eye turned up to the ceiling and stayed that way.

I just sat beside his bed awhile, listening to the gabble of voices of the other visitors in the ward, gazing out the window at the far-stretching sky.

I left a pack of cigarettes, uncertain whether he could smoke yet. I had forgotten to clear it with the ward aide.

All the time I was there, I didn't say a dozen words to him, and he hadn't said one.

After that, I forgot about him. I worked the four-to-twelve for half a week before the boss called me into the office just after five one evening.

"Phone for you."

Right away I thought it was about the man in the hospital.

"Brandon speaking."

It wasn't the police or the hospital. It was Jack Harvey's office.

I was so surprised that he had called as he said he would that I just listened to his offer and, without thinking, said yes.

"Good man," Jack said heartily. "Start next Monday."

While I was hanging up, I wanted to call him back and tell him I'd thought it over and changed my mind.

Then I looked at the boss, sitting there behind his little desk in the crowded office, bent over papers, wearing a dark-straw fedora. Peering out at the shop, I listened to the whine of the saws cutting through the aluminum, to the air guns hissing, to the rubber mallets gingerly pounding glass or screening into frames.

I decided it was time I gave up being poor but honest for awhile and got back into my line of work before I forgot how to do it.

"I have to quit," I told the boss.

He looked up at me, his eyes disgusted.

"When?"

"I can stay through Sunday."

His glance dropped to the mess of papers in front of him. He was too offended by me to look at me anymore.

"I thought you weren't a fly-by-night."

I shrugged.

For a second, I wanted to tell him off. What did he expect? Loyalty? For minimum wage?

I held it in, though. He didn't own the business. He just had to run it. And he was a fairly good guy.

"I'll help break in the new guy," I said gently. "Including tonight, that gives you four days."

"Okay."

He nodded, but he still wouldn't look at me. I was an outcast. I had defiled the altar of the great god Work.

Back at my air gun, I tried to appease the wrath of the god, but I doubt if he could stand to look at me, either.

The phone call and the sudden feeling of shock I had felt when I thought it might be about the man in the hospital started me thinking about him again.

Early Friday afternoon, I paid him another visit. Brode was standing beside the ward bed. His face was angry when he turned at my approach.

"Your friend here seems to think he's going to get all this attention, and then just say thank you and walk out of here, and go on about his business, and not even tell us his name."

He glowered down at the man in the bed, sneering at him.

"He claims he don't remember his name, and nothing else, either. Especially he don't remember who gave him the workout."

Brode made his own eyes round with wonder, adding in a low, mock-portentous voice: "Why, Brandon, do you know what I think? I think he thinks he's going to get us to think he's got amnesia, just like on television." Brode laughed harshly.

I stood across the bed from him and watched Punching Bag.

All the plaster and bandages were off his face and head, now, except for one section that was still taped, high on the right side of his skull. The hair around it had been shaved for treatment, and to allow sticking space for the tapes that held the patch of gauze in place.

His face was wide, his forehead high, and his nose, miraculously, had not been broken, through it all, and was straight and strong-boned.

Generally, he appeared strong and well-built, wide across the cheekbones, with strong jaw muscles, bunched now, so that the lower part of his face appeared almost as wide and solid as it did up by the Indian-looking cheekbones.

His chin still showed wide red areas and might carry scars. The chin showed thrust, but that might simply have been foreshortening, because I was looking down at him, and saw his face from the lower part upward.

"You seem to have healed pretty well," I said to him. "That night, it looked as if your face would never be much more than hamburger."

His eyes continued staring straight upward, fixed on the ceiling, eyes like slate, bleak as a tundra.

Brode and I stood there, watching him. Neither of us said anything for awhile, until I said, "Oh, you're welcome."

That got to him. His lips looked for a moment as if they might have wanted to grin, if they could remember how. His eyelids narrowed perceptibly. You might almost say it amounted to a hearty laugh, I suppose, considering what he'd been put through.

Rolling his head on the pillow, he looked up at me. When the movement brought the taped part of his skull into contact with the pillow, his eyes wavered for a moment. Turning his head back the other way a bit, he still kept his eyes on me as he said, "Thanks."

His voice was deep, gravelly, husky with disuse. He hadn't been using it much lately, certainly not nearly enough to please Sergeant Brode.

Feeling somewhat ashamed for dragging the thanks out of him, I grinned and said quietly: *"Por nada."*

Outside the ward, I said goodbye to Brode, turned, and walked off. Brode's voice followed me quite a way along the corridor.

"Okay, son, this is the way it's gonna be with you," Brode said angrily. "First, you're going into a detention ward. And when you're all healed, you're going into a cell. I'm going to see to it that you stay in it until we find out about you. And if you think I think your fingerprints aren't on file, some-where, you sure must take me for a simple-minded son of a bitch . . ."

Distance kept me from hearing the rest of it.

I wondered what kind of record the fingerprint search would turn up on Punching Bag.

The following Monday, I began working for Jack Harvey's detective agency. The jobs I was sent out on consisted of the usual crud: catching small-change thieves in big department stores, working usually in groups of three, one day operating against the help to catch the ones who were knocking down and short-changing both the customers and the store itself, and then when the three of us were spotted by the rest of the help, we filled in on the shop-lifter detail.

A couple or three days of that were plenty, but I hung on.

When the desk man handing out assignments in Harvey's bullpen gave me one of the shifts on a twenty-four-hour-a-day stakeout, I almost welcomed it. At least it let me catch up on my newspaper reading. On the third day of that, I noticed the item way in back of the local newspaper: Punching Bag had apparently left the hospital the night before, on his own. The story was by-lined by Chuck Macy, a local reporter I

had met once or twice. It said the police expected to appre-
hend him shortly. They usually did.

With Punching Bag, I didn't think they could miss. Nothing in his pockets, nowhere to go, wearing hospital pajamas,
or half-pajamas. I gave him the rest of the day, if the cops
hadn't already turned him up.

That's what I gave him until I recalled those eyes of his,
and the wide set of his clamp of a mouth. Then I wasn't so
sure.

Maybe he did have someplace to go.

After the morning my two quarts of milk and the two hero
sandwiches had vanished from where I had left them in the
sage bushes beside the dirt road, he had had the rest of that
day and at least part of that night. He had used the time, and
probably needed most of it, for traveling, because at the end
of it, when they finally found him in that alley this side of
Florian's, he was stripped of anything that might have identified him. And since it had been police trying to do the identi-
fying, the stripping must have included labels in his clothes,
laundry marks, everything.

I sat in the agency's car and watched the place I was being
paid to watch, but I was thinking about that identification
business. Nothing was right about it.

Okay, granted, he had somehow gotten across town. Brute
energy and a will of iron might accomplish that: he could just
keep himself crawling, or stumbling, or staggering along.

But for fine work? For scissoring labels off clothes, checking
his shirts and pants and shorts and T-shirt for laundry marks?
That I couldn't see him doing, not in the shape he was in.

After my siege of the day was over and I had been relieved
and signed out at the agency, I walked out along the northwest highway to look over this Florian's casino Brode had
told me about.

Naturally, there were no sidewalks. I walked facing oncoming traffic with the falling sun on my left. Trucks and
cars went whooshing by, shaking the world. I walked on
gravel, on sand, on asphalt parking aprons fronting steel-and-

glass hamburger stands and drive-in bank branches and dry cleaners and auto repair shops. I walked along gigantic parking areas longer than a jet-landing strip, damn near, which fronted shopping centers that seemed even bigger than their paved parking fields.

All the way out beside that highway, I was one of the only remaining breed of vanishing Americans: the walking American.

Striding along beside a busy highway has a curious effect. Cars flash past you. Gigantic trucks shake the ground, belching exhaust fumes, while you plod along beside the well-paved highway using anything there is to set foot on, stumbling into ditches when you can't avoid them, feeling the unyielding gravel through the soles of your shoes, the grit getting inside your shoes, having to stop and take them off to empty them, periodically.

The effect is inevitable: you realize how small a man on foot has become. You feel left out, unimportant. There's no longer any place for you in a country where distances to and from a store are too great to be walked, and therefore no sidewalk is required, since no one is likely to use it.

Yet, at the same time that you feel small and resentful, you also want to join them: you want to get a car of your own. Then you won't feel small and insignificant anymore. You'll have become one of them. Good old General Motors and Mrs. Motors and all his Little Brother Motors. Their rights of way were built for them with tax-payer dollars, free and clear. They had it better than the railroads, back in the days of *their* thievery.

Far ahead, I saw a sign: Florian's.

It took me a long time to reach the casino, even after I first saw the distant sign.

I passed a series of motels, half a dozen used car lots, all interspersed among the usual automobile-row sprinkling of small stores and shops that sold or fixed tires, balanced and aligned wheels, replaced mufflers, put in seat-covers, repaired and installed radios, did body and fender work, automatic transmissions resealed, valve and ring jobs, '*from* only this little on some makes of car' (*to* God knows how much on the make of car you've got).

It didn't hit me until the big sign at Florian's was only about an eighth of a mile ahead. Punching Bag had come all this distance on foot, in the shape he was in!

It stopped me in my tracks. Turning, I looked back the distance I had come so far, and I shook my head. He couldn't have moved from where they had dumped him, either, but he damn well must have.

I shrugged. From here on, I would predicate this on the possible. Forget about how much he couldn't have done something. Just try to figure out how had he actually made the journey.

There at the roadside was a row of stores, a block-long string of small shops located in one long brick one-story building. A dirt driveway ran back from the highway beside the end shop, between it and the side loading-yard of a lumber company I had just walked past. Beyond the rear corner of the store I could see a wooden shack of some kind, and nothing beyond that but the sage flats of the desert stretching away for miles.

That had probably been Punching Bag's route, through the sagebrush.

Off to the west, the sun hung just above the jagged line of a far-off range of hills. As I watched it drop out of sight, Florian's nearby sign was lighted. It startled me, the sudden appearance of that crazy chiaroscuro of reds and yellows and greens and blues. But in the middle of it all, no matter what the weird effect of the mixture of all those different colors, out of the moving moil of brilliance you could always read FLORIAN'S.

Okay, Punching Bag had been found by the cops near Florian's. From out in the desert, he could have used that sign of theirs as a mark to head for: it stood higher than all other lights along this stretch of highway.

Which left two questions. How did he cross the Strip, back in town? And where was he finally found?

The Strip part I could forget. He might have staggered right across it at any time, and happened not to get hit by any cars while he crossed. However he had managed it, somehow he had worked his way west of the old town back there, and crossed the desert almost as far as the big casino just ahead.

But what was he trying to reach? Florian's itself?

I walked on along the row of stores contained by the brown brick building. At its northern end, another dirt driveway emerged from behind the store at that end, and again there was a wooden shack barely visible at the back. That could be an alley behind the row of stores. Maybe that was where Punching Bag finally showed up again, in that alley.

Going on, I passed El Rancho Motel until its property ended and a kind of wasteland began. A stretch of desert had been preserved, perhaps to separate the casino from the last cheap motel that was its nearest neighbor. Rather than throwing money away putting in some kind of lawn to do the separating, Florian's owners had used the plants of the desert to create a primitive garden of sorts, if you liked cactus plants and rocks and sage bushes instead of beds of begonias and roses in your gardens.

Close to the roadside, this wasteland had big slabs of limestone, roughly hewn, standing hip-high, buried in the desert deeply enough to keep anyone but the very drunk and unusually determined from accidentally stumbling past them and being pierced in a dozen places by cactus spines.

Beyond the wasteland, the casino itself was large and long, built horizontally. It looked as if the landing decks of two modern aircraft carriers had been laid one atop the other.

Walking on, I could see ahead a wide break in the median, out in the middle of the road. That was to allow customers from the city to be able to turn across the southbound lanes and enter the casino grounds. A traffic light network facilitated matters. Without those traffic lights, Florian's would have been dead.

Idly, I wondered how many people at the Hall of Justice back in town had profited from getting those traffic lights installed, giving easy access to the new casino.

When I reached the break in the median, I stood there gawking up the three-lane-wide entrance to the place.

It looked like a front entrance comparable to some of the better spots on the *Cote d'Azur*, but newer, shinier, and a lot more expensive.

A good deal of money had gone into Florian's. A lot of money was still going in, from the look of some of the cars driving past me.

Still, that's what it was there for: it was a casino. It was there to make money, anybody's money. Which meant snobbery was out. Maybe you needed your Dun & Bradstreet rating checked out to use the rest of Florian's: the hotel, the lounge. But anyone could drop half a week's salary in the casino, or half an hour's salary, too. That's why it was there.

For a moment, I wondered whether I should go in and drop some of my salary.

No, plenty of time for that. I'd been too close to being broke for too long to begin tossing it around. The memory of three months of grind in the aluminum storms and screen shop where I had worked was too recent to be easily forgotten.

Turning, I started back the way I'd come.

I had almost reached the end of the wasteland where El Rancho Motel's property began when I caught a glimpse of Jack Harvey at the wheel of an electric blue convertible coming out from the city.

The sleek blue job went whistling by on the far side of the grassy median. The traffic light a block to the north was in his favor, so Jack had no wait. He made his left across the two lanes on this side of the highway, and disappeared into the entranceway to Florian's palace of delights, and disillusions.

I turned and went on in the last of the sunset light away in the west, but I stopped in front of the entrance to El Rancho Motel.

Its sign said Vacancy. Once, it had been a working neon sign, but most of its tubes were gone, now, and the few remaining ones were broken.

A chill wind blew in from the desert. It was going to be dark soon.

The traffic hissed past behind me, and the wind sighed from the other direction.

Peering into the motel court, I saw only an old gray Chevy sedan parked in front of the rear unit in the far northwest corner. Nothing else was visible in there, nothing moved. Only two of the units had lights on, this early in the evening. The setting sun threw roof shadows most of the way across to the half-row of units with their backs facing the side of the highway to the left of the entrance leading into the U-shaped courtyard. There was a light lit in the office, on the near-right corner of the place, but I could see no one inside.

Beyond the office and the intervening units, the solitary Chevy parked in the far right corner had its left rear fender smashed in smoothly, leaving a deep depression just forward of the taillights, but not far enough forward to affect the left rear wheel in any way. The depression had no jagged edges. It was the sort of car I was looking for: harmlessly beat up where it didn't matter. It probably ran like the work-horses some of those old Chevrolets had been.

I would have to make up my mind and get myself a car, soon. All the walking I was doing lately was wearing me out.

Walking partway through the entrance driveway, I peered into the office. I could just see a man's head above the near end of the counter in there. He appeared to be fast asleep sitting in a desk chair of some kind.

Rather than returning along the highway, I turned and rounded the outside corner of the office and strolled along the motel's north wall, away from the road.

Out near the roadside, the barren stretch was thickly choked with cactus and stunted mesquite trees slightly larger than a garden's hedge, but farther in, the tangle suddenly thinned and low sagebrush began again.

Across the stretch of wasteland, Florian's southern façade bulked its two levels against the darkening night sky. From my vantage point, I could appreciate even more the sheer size of the place. The side I could see was maybe half as long as the front part facing the highway, which made it roughly as big as many a municipal airport's terminal building.

Near the western corner of the top deck, I saw what looked like a man leaning on the parapet. Stopping where I stood, I watched him. Sure enough, outlined against the pale sunset sky, a man leaned there, smoking and enjoying the evening air.

"Good for him," I thought, after watching him a moment, before starting on.

At the far corner of El Rancho Motel, I angled a hundred paces farther out into the desert, where I got a good look at what was farther along, behind the motel. A row of shacks ran southward facing the rear of the row of stores in the single brick building.

That might be the alley where they'd found Punching Bag.

Keeping a hundred feet away from the backs of the row of shacks, I crunched along, trying to see if there were any spaces between any of the shacks big enough to warrant being called alleys, but nothing seemed to qualify. Fences of various kinds rimmed the property each shack stood on. Any alley would have to be the space between the fronts of the block-long row of shacks and the back of the equally long brick building containing all those little shops facing onto the highway.

At the southern end of the row of shanties, I turned in between the lumber yard's loading area and the end shack.

My shoes had picked up some desert sand. When I reached the alley, I couldn't take the discomfort any longer, so I vaulted up and sat on the edge of the loading platform to empty my shoes. When I finished retying the laces, I sat there a moment, staring across the dirt driveway up along the alley. It was wide enough to take a car, if the driver went slow and drove carefully. Otherwise, the car might take down some of the rickety picket fences that were the front bastions of many of the shacks.

In a town like this, Mexicans and Indians would live in shacks like those.

Instead of following the driveway back out to the highway, I hopped down from the edge of the loading yard and headed across it toward the alley.

Might as well give it a close look while I was all the way out here.

I was about to enter the alley when a car turned off the highway and entered the driveway. Its headlights caught me in their beams for a moment. It approached swiftly.

Hurrying across, I got into the alley out of the headlights, but I was less than five paces along when the car turned into the alley behind me, and I was again caught in its headlights.

Stepping over to my right by the brick rear wall of the store-building, I waited to give the car passing room.

Across the alley, beyond a lopsided picket fence, a little old man with a seamed Indian face sat on a porch, smoking a big pipe.

The car swept up beside me and stopped.

A wide-faced man in the passenger seat peered up at me.

"What are you doing back along here?" he asked.

I stared down at his big face and at his right arm draped over the top of the door. His right hand and wrist hung down out of sight, inside the car door.

I didn't have to be told what he was. The kindest label is Security. I had seen too many of them. Known too many of them. Hell, *been* one of them, too many times.

"You!" he said sharply. "I'm talking to you. What's your business back here?"

"Just walking."

"Walk someplace else. Turn around and go back out of here the way you came. You'll find all the walking you want out by the highway."

"You think that's a good place to walk?"

"The best, brother, the best. Get going."

"If it's that good, why don't you try taking a walk out there yourself?"

His eyes glinted in his wide calm face. He sighed, and his thick lips smiled. Shaking his head from side to side, never taking his eyes off my face, he gently murmured: "Okay, brother, you want it that way, you got it that way."

"Hold it, Fats," the man at the wheel said quietly.

Fats kept staring up at me, but when he spoke next, he was talking over his shoulder to the man sitting beside him.

"Hold it, hell, Jeff. This bastard's got no business back here. This is all private property."

"That's what I mean," Jeff said. "He wants to mosey around back here, all we do is notify the local law. They can mop him out."

"No," Fats said. "I don't like his face. I'll do the mopping myself . . ."

"Fats!" Jeff interrupted. "You been told before. You throw your weight around when you don't got to. They don't like that . . ."

"Hell with what they don't like," Fats snarled. "Put a button on it, Jeff. I mean that. You!" he said to me. "On your way, fast. And now. I tell you this only once. Then I get out of this car and you'll . . ."

Leaning down, I squinted past Fats at the man behind the wheel. He had a thin face with a mouth like a badly healed knife-scar.

"You say this is all private property?" I asked him, talking past Fats.

Jeff nodded.

A semi-automatic in Fats' right hand came into sight. His voice was thick as he whipped the gun around to bring it to bear on me.

"Brother, you do your talking to me, not him . . ."

My left hand closed over the top of his forearm. A moment later, my right completed the clamp. Both hands pulled Fats's arm up and out the open car window.

Stepping back along the side of the car, I hauled his arm right along, gun and all. His left hand was doing some fumbling inside the door, trying to get it open, but the way I had hold of him by then, he'd have to tear his right arm out of its shoulder socket to get that door open.

The top of his shoulder crunched up into the upper rear angle of the window-opening. That left his head inside, and his arm and most of his shoulder pinned outside, with his gun hand held against the edge of the roof of the car.

Through the closed window of the rear door on my side, I could see Fats's face twist suddenly, lose its expression of anger, and take on a look of pain.

I socked the finishing touch to him then, hard and quickly. Both my hands slid along his forearm to his wrist, which I twisted until I had his big handgun pointed up at the sky. I didn't want any stray shots going off and sending bullets through the thin walls of three or four of those shanties across the alley, and maybe through some of their occupants, too. They might be as good as dead already, but maybe they didn't know it. I didn't want some slob like Fats breaking the news to them the hard way.

Once I had the muzzle of the gun pointed the way I wanted, all I had to do was twist his wrist a bit more, the way you'd wring out a wet rag.

It took only a second, then he gave in.

"Aaaah!" grated out of his mouth. Slumping, he quit struggling to free his arm.

When his hand let loose of the gun, I caught it before it hit the roof of the sedan and turned him loose.

Going around behind the car, I pulled from the sling under my left arm the revolver the agency had signed out to me, earlier that day. When I came up on the driver's side, I had it cocked, but I held it down by my side, out of sight, against my leg.

"Here," I told Jeff, handing him the big semi-automatic I had just taken away from Fats. "Better give your friend some more lessons in how to be tough. He could use them."

Jeff didn't say anything, but in the night gloom I thought I caught a glimpse of a wry grimace twisting his face.

"Is there a way out of this alley?" I asked Jeff. "I mean, up ahead, the way this car's pointed?"

"Yeah."

"Then why don't you drive on up to it?" I suggested. "Right now I don't want to be in those headlights of yours."

Jeff chuckled.

Stepping back, I watched the big car move carefully along the narrow passageway between the flimsy front-yard fences and the rear brick wall of the building holding the string of stores.

Turning, I walked back to my end of the alley, where I turned and watched until the car reached the other end, where it turned right, out of sight toward the highway.

Walking quickly up the dirt drive to the front of the store at that end, I peered carefully around the corner just in time to see their sedan edge out into the stream of traffic, headed southward past me, toward the Strip, whose distant glow was already filling the sky off to the southeast.

I lost sight of their car a moment after it entered the swift-flowing stream of traffic, but I went on standing there, remaining in shadows, there at the corner.

When they hadn't returned in ten minutes, I went back to the alley and walked the length of it.

The old man was still sitting on his low-roofed porch. I could see the faint glow of his pipe.

No one else was visible along the alley. At the other end, I turned right and went back out to the highway, where I walked along beside it toward the distant Strip until a cab slowed questioningly.

Signalling him, I got in.

"Just to where I can catch a bus," I told him.

His shoulders told me what he thought of me. I couldn't think of any way I could do the same to him, so I didn't bother trying.

Three

Next day, the assignment desk sent me out on the stake-out job again, but I was only on it an hour or so when another operative relieved me.

"They've got another assignment for you."

He took my place in the car. Fifteen minutes later, I was getting into another car with another, younger gumshoe.

"Where we headed?" I asked him. "They tell you?"

"Out to that new place, Florian's. The big boss will tell us what to do. He's out there himself."

Okay, Florian's was just another job. I had seen Jack Harvey . . . the big boss . . . out at Florian's the night before. Drumming up business, presumably.

For a moment, I found myself wondering if I could get my job back, at the aluminum storm and screen shop. Then I grinned at myself. If I needed to, it was there, waiting. Or another job, just like it. I still didn't have enough scratch stashed even to rent myself a desk and start out on my own again.

My co-worker had obviously been out at Florian's before. He didn't stop at the front entrance, but gave a high sign to the uniformed parking guard and drove past him, around to a good-sized parking area, where he got a ticket from another uniformed man and headed over to a side entrance.

Inside, we went up a short flight of carpeted stairs. A gray corridor took us a short distance toward the front of the building, where another door let us into the rear end of the entrance lobby.

Five or six showgirls in brief costumes swept past us. All those long legs were dazzling. A couple of them giggled at the two of us standing there, gawking at them, as they went by. The last one, a tiny thing, gave me a big smile just before they all disappeared through a doorway behind the lounge.

My guide grinned at me.

"Looks like you've got a little friend, there," he observed.

"I couldn't afford to buy breakfast for her."

"There's Mr. Harvey," he said, pointing.

We strolled toward Jack Harvey, who excused himself to the man he was talking to and came to meet us.

"Good. Fast work, boys. Tom, you've been here before. Go around to chuck-a-luck. Tell Angelo you're here to relieve for awhile. He knows about it."

Tom nodded and went off, moving silently on the deep carpet.

Jack grinned at me.

"How do you like the layout here, Jim? Wish I had points in this place."

"You'd likely need a paid-up plot in a cemetery, to go along with it."

He glanced at me oddly, then looked quickly away, with a shrug.

"Oh, these boys aren't so bad," he said. "Anyway, the reason you're out here is to relieve some of their regular men. There's a big shipment of cash, coming or going, I'm not sure which. They need their regular guys to handle it, so that leaves a personnel gap or two to fill. Come on."

I followed him up four steps, into and through a glass-walled cocktail lounge, which overlooked the big front room of the casino.

Harvey nodded toward a small elevator, just beyond the bar and to the left.

"Take that to the third floor. Tell them you want Mr. Wyatt's office."

I got into the elevator with the young uniformed guy who ran it. Harvey smiled at him and told him: "He's one of my men."

The elevator operator flashed teeth in a smile, and ran me up to the third floor.

"To your left, sir."

The carpet up here was even thicker than the one in the casino downstairs. I bounced along on it until a man in a dazzling sport jacket seemed to step right out of the corridor wall in front of me.

"Mr. Wyatt's office," I told him. "I'm from the Harvey agency."

"That's right," he smiled.

He was as big as I was and probably in better shape. His smile was certainly a lot nicer than mine ever was.

He held his hands out, palms up, flipping his fingers upward.

"Just lift your arms a little," he said genially.

For a moment, I hovered there. Then I thought, Hell, it was Harvey's gig. His other men went through this sort of routine as a matter of course, every time they were sent out here to help.

I held my arms well out from my sides. A moment later, the Agency gun was locked in a drawer in a built-in desk at the back of a shallow niche in the corridor wall. The desk could have been genuine fake Chippendale.

Smiles went over the rest of me as if he still expected to find other weaponry. When he didn't, he handed me a little ticket.

"For your hardware," he explained. "When you're leaving."

"I even get a hatcheck," I laughed. "And without leaving a hat."

"That's right," he said, still smiling. "Down this corridor straight ahead to the end, then turn right. Mr. Wyatt's office is the second door on your left."

I knocked on the appropriate door. A moment later, I found myself standing in an outer office, facing a plate-glass barrier beyond which sat a blonde receptionist whose face cost more to cover each day than my whole body cost in a year.

"Oh, yes, the relief man," she said. "You stay out there. Sit or stand, whichever suits you, except when someone comes in or out. Then you stand."

"That's all?"

"That's all. I'll handle any questions. If I'm gone and someone comes in, just ask them to wait."

I started my day's work seated in an easy chair, over near the wall, where I could just glimpse the blonde's forehead, whenever she leaned forward a bit.

Time passed. Not much time. My glance strayed over toward the plate-glass wall. A round-faced man was standing beyond it, watching me. His mouth was moving, but I couldn't hear a thing he said. I realized that the plate-glass was sound proof. The blonde could talk through it when she wanted to by flipping a switch. I remembered her voice had sounded slightly odd, earlier.

The round-faced man noticed me watching him watching me. He said something to the girl. Her voice came out to me: "This is Mr. Wyatt . . ."

His voice broke in on hers.

"You're from Jack Harvey's Agency?"

I rose and went over.

"Yes."

He stared at me through the glass. He may have noticed there was no Sir after the *yes* I had given him.

After a moment of using those dark muddy eyes of his on me, he spoke again.

"What's your name?"

I told him.

"You know what you're here to do?"

"Your secretary told me."

"Fine."

The sound went off. He turned half away and his lips began speaking soundlessly again to the girl.

Turning, I went back and sat down again. Lighting a cigarette, I glanced over toward the plate-glass again. Wyatt's eyes slid away from me. A moment later, all of him slid soundlessly out of sight into the inner office.

I wondered if the soundproof glass was bulletproof, too. It probably was. Why be half-safe?

Sometime afterward, two men came in.

I stood up.

The slimmer of the two, a young man with a carefully tended pencil mustache, gave me a quick glance and ignored me from then on. The older man didn't look in my direction, simply went on with what he had been saying.

"How long has she been like that, down there?"

His voice was crisp and clear, but he sounded weary. He looked tired around the eyes, tired all through.

Mustache shrugged.

"Maybe half yesterday and all last night."

"Has she lost much, Ted?"

Ted made a face.

"Brock, you know the way Jan can be. She has so much credit on tap, she could probably buy half this place, if she wanted to."

Over the sound system, the blonde's voice materialized.

"Good morning, Mr. Townsend. Hello, Mr. Fenton."

The older man smiled, a nice smile. You almost didn't notice how much effort it took for him to bring it up.

"Hello, there. If I may see Mr. Wyatt . . ."

"Of course, sir. Please have a seat. I'll tell Mr. Wyatt you're here."

Ted went on speaking in his confidential tone.

"Brock, I don't want to go near her when she's like that. You know what she thinks of me . . ."

For the first time, Brock Townsend glanced in my direction. His mouth tightened. Turning away slightly, he muttered something to Fenton.

"He just works here," Ted said, his voice lower now.

"All the same, I don't like her name being . . ."

The blonde's voice broke in.

"Will you come in, gentlemen? Mr. Wyatt will see you now."

The door in the plate-glass wall clicked and swung inward. After the two men went through it, the door swung shut, soundlessly. I watched them pass the receptionist's desk and disappear.

For a time, it was quiet again, and I could sit down. But not for as long as I would have liked.

The outside corridor door opened again. A young woman in an evening gown, with a length of mink thrown casually over one shoulder, came through the doorway and leaned against the wall beside it. Beyond her for a moment, I glimpsed the smiling face of the sport-jacket type who had frisked me on my way in. He winked at the receptionist, glanced blankly at me, shut the door behind the woman, and was gone.

I stood up.

The newcomer leaned against the wall with her eyes closed. One end of her mink dragged on the floor.

Her hair was light brown, and, although she wasn't a raving beauty, she had a strong pretty-looking face, even drawn and tired-looking, as it appeared right then.

"I don't understand," she murmured to no one, without opening her eyes. "A credit check? On me?"

Her head was tilted back against the wall. Her eyes remained shut while she thought about it.

Presently the voice of the receptionist brought her eyes open.

"Won't you come in, Miss Thornton?"

After blinking at the receptionist behind the thick glass for a moment, she pushed herself away from the wall.

"Oh, yes, of course."

The mink slipped from her shoulder and settled soundlessly on the floor around her feet.

Stopping, she stared down at it for a moment, then her gaze wandered around the outer office. She seemed startled to see me standing there, off to one side.

Going over, I picked up the fur. She was either too drunk or too tired after her night at the tables to be able to pick it up herself, without possibly landing on her face on the floor beside the mink.

I held it out to her.

"I didn't see you standing there," she said. "You surprised me."

I handed her the mink. She draped it over her arm, doubled.

The door in the plexiglass wall opened with its click. She made no move toward it, but stood looking at me with a curiously hard look about her eyes. After a moment, she shook her head

"You're not very beautiful, are you?" she asked.

I laughed.

"Not very."

"Miss Thornton?" the receptionist's voice said tentatively.

The automatic door stood wide open, waiting for her.

Laughing softly, breathily, she turned and went through it.

I went back to my sofa-sitting.

Time passed. No one else came or went. Once I saw the one with the mustache, Ted Fenton, talking to Wyatt beyond the glass barrier wall. He glanced in my direction once or twice, but I didn't stare at him. I stared straight ahead at the blank wall opposite where I sat.

Eventually, the receptionist's voice came through the speaker.

"Mr. Brandon? You can go now. Report to Mr. Harvey downstairs."

In the corridor, I retrieved my Agency gun from the smiler.

"Do you want the ticket back?" I asked him.

"Not important," the smiler said. Even when he wasn't smiling, he looked as if he was.

"I thought if I could keep it, maybe I could have it stuffed."

Handing the ticket over, I went down in the elevator, found Jack Harvey bucking a blackjack game. He must have been doing all right, because he told me: "Knock off for the day, Jim. I'll clock you out, back at the Agency."

"I can go back on the stakeout job," I suggested. "It isn't even noon yet."

"Forget it," he said cheerfully. "Take the afternoon off. Here, want some chips? Try your luck."

I grinned and shook my head.

"I have no luck. Thanks for the time off, though."

I left Florian's by the front entrance and strolled down to the highway.

So I had the afternoon off and no way of getting back to town.

I started slogging it.

A gila monster slipped sluggishly off a rock beside the road. He disappeared with a swift slither into the patch of tangled shrub and cactus and sage between Florian's and El Rancho Motel.

The motel courtyard was as deserted as ever. Dust swirled with the wind in the restricted space. Not even the old gray Chevy sedan with the crumpled-in left rear fender stood parked in the far corner of the U-shaped courtyard.

That reminded me of my hunt for a car of some kind. Automobile Row was not far ahead. When I reached it, I began a little shopping.

In the third yard I canvassed, I found something that would do well enough: ninety-five dollars for a twelve-year-old Ford sedan. It was light and trim, and rotten with rust here and there, where you could see it. Ignoring the unsightly rust, I went over the heap carefully, especially under the hood and back beneath the transmission.

The motor sounded like a tough little bugger, good for perhaps twenty or thirty thousand more miles. The rust only looked bad, but it didn't slow down the machinery any.

I put something down on it. They said they'd handle the registration and plates. I could pick it up later that afternoon.

I walked on into town.

Four

A fter I ate lunch, I caught the bus along the Strip. A quarter mile short of the end of the line, I got off and started up my street. The houses in there cut the impact of the wind some. Up high, cottonwoods thrashed in the wind.

After the pavement ended, I walked on along the dirt path in the lea of the adobe wall fronting the street to where Sergeant Brode sat waiting in an unmarked car beside another plainclothes detective.

As I came strolling up, Brode got out, grinning, but his eyes didn't grin along with his mouth.

"That's some wind you got out here," he observed.

For a moment, I studied him and his partner curiously, until I figured out why they were there.

"Oh, I see."

"You see something?"

"Why don't you both come in and visit awhile? I think there's a little Irish sloshing around in the bottom of a bottle, somewhere upstairs."

"This is my partner, Callahan," Brode said, tilting his head toward the one in the car. "He might like some of that Irish, except we're on duty. Regulations say . . ."

Nodding to Callahan as he climbed out from behind the wheel, I led the way to my corner door, beyond where they were parked, and on inside and upstairs.

Entering my rooms at the top of the landing, Brode took off his hat, again saying: "That is quite a wind."

He wasn't just talking to make conversation. He was really impressed.

"You don't know how rough a wind like that is," he elaborated, "until you get indoors, and you're out of it. Then you kind of miss it."

"Like a hammer on the head," Callahan put in.

46

"Yeah, kinda," Brode agreed, absently. Idly, he poked around the room and peered into the john, opened the door of the closet the rest of the way it wasn't already slightly open, and studied the clothes that were hanging and dumped in there. "This all the closet space you've got?"

"That's it," I said. "You forgot to look under the bed."

Now his grin was real.

"Habit."

"I gather you can't find Punching Bag." I said it instead of asking it.

"Punching Bag? Oh, yeah. We call him Assault, on account of he was assaulted."

"Assault was a racehorse."

"Hell, I'll call the bastard Pain-in-the-ass until we get our mitts on him again. Then we can start calling him mud."

"He's sure making us work like a horse," Callahan interjected solemnly.

Brode and I both looked at him, and when there was nothing more from him, I turned back to Brode again.

"Nothing from Washington? No record from his prints?"

Brode shook his head.

"Not yet. They'll have something on him, I'm sure of it. He was too quiet. There's too much metal in that lad, even if he was as weak as a kitten. I don't like that much iron in a guy like him. And I don't like finding out you work for Jack Harvey as one of his private dicks. You didn't tell me you had a license."

"You didn't ask. Anyway, what's the beef with Harvey? He's still this side of the line, isn't he?"

"Just barely, like most private dicks. What I don't like is you kidding me along into thinking you're just a hard-working citizen helping a stranger who got mugged. Now I find you're a gumshoe. And you're mixed up with that crowd out at Florian's."

"You work fast, finding out all that about me. What's the matter with Florian's?"

"Florian's is just another one of those places where the dough is made too easy and slick to suit me."

"You're living in the wrong state," I pointed out. "So I had an assignment out there this morning, working for Harvey's Agency. I put in a few hours of work. That's all Florian's is to me."

Brode's eyes were level, cold, and unfriendly on me, all of a sudden.

"That's where Assault seemed to be headed when he was picked up."

"Sergeant," I said slowly, "if Assault wanted to get to Florian's, he would have gotten all the way there. He crawled or stumbled what? three, four miles from this southeast end of town, all the way out there to the northwest, and you want me to believe he finally passed out?"

When he made no reply, I shook my head.

"No. Like you said, there's too much iron in him. He had something to do. He did it. Then he passed out."

Silence filled the room like an invisible gas. They both just stared at me.

Finally, Brode spoke.

"I hope to God you're straight, Brandon. If I find out you aren't, I'll . . ."

I waved that aside impatiently.

"What about the clothes you found him wearing? That bothers me. There should've been some laundry marks, something your forensics people could pick up, to localize him, pin him down, find out about his neighborhood. We've all got a neighborhood, you know . . ."

Brode glanced archly over at Callahan.

"He's sure enough a detective, all right."

Callahan grinned.

"What's that supposed to mean?" I asked, irritated.

"All the clothes he wore were brand new," Brode said. "Khaki shirt, sun-tan slacks, cheap two-buck genuine Indian moccasins manufactured in Hoboken, New Jersey."

"He wasn't wearing any of that when he was dumped out there in the brush," I objected.

"That's right," Brode admitted. "Apparently he bought them so that's what he'd be wearing when he was found. No underwear, no jacket, just a shirt, pants, and moccasins. Nothing at all in the pockets."

"Did you find where he bought them?"

Brode nodded.

"Of course. No lead from there, though. A little Army-Navy surplus shop so close to wino row you couldn't tell the difference, even by the smell. The proprietor of the store is used to dealing with all kinds of slobs, in all gradients of busted-up condition. Our boy was just a bit more banged-up than usual. The storekeeper had himself a quick cash sale and thought no more about it . . . until we found him, and he identified the clothes."

Impatiently, Brode stopped talking and went over to look out the window at my waist-high, adobe walled terrace-for-one. Turning back, he went on.

"I tell you true, Brandon," he growled. "I don't like what I smell about that guy. I think he's got it in his head there's people he's going to see. I've had that feeling about him all along, since I first laid eyes on him in the hospital. Now he blows out of there, and I still have that same feeling, worse than ever."

"Well, I'm not in on it," I assured him. "I don't know as much about that guy as you do."

"Okay," he said. "I'll settle for that. For now. But don't hold out on me. You're one of the few people who could recognize him. If you catch a glimpse of him, get in touch with me, and quick."

I nodded.

After glowering at me a moment, Brode turned and went out onto the landing and down the stairs to the street door. Callahan didn't look at me, simply followed Brode out, leaving the door of my room wide open behind him.

Standing on the landing, I made sure they shut the outside door, and then I went back inside again.

The closet door had swung open a bit. I pushed it shut absently, but a moment later it swung back out again a few inches. The catch didn't catch right.

For awhile, I stood by the window, staring over the edge of the adobe wall of my narrow terrace at the sea of sage bushes stretching away eastward to the edge of the world.

In the closet, I dug out my .38 Police Special and gave it a cleaning. It hefted better than the gun the Agency signed out to me, whenever the job of the day required one. Or maybe I was just used to this one.

After spreading a thin layer of oil back on the weapon, I wrapped it in cloth and gave the shoulder-holster a going-over with linseed oil until the leather was pliable again.

Stuffing the handgun, cloth and all, into the holster, I sat holding it in my lap, staring down at it.

It took me awhile to figure out where I could keep it so it was out of sight but easy and quick to get at.

A nail stuck out a little from the back of the bureau, over against the wall. I had to keep hammering it in and it kept working its way back out, although probably I didn't do it often enough. It was kind of like the closet door would never stay shut. I'm not much of a householder, when the furniture isn't mine . . . and it was never mine.

Shifting the bureau away from the wall a bit, I felt for the protruding nail. Still there. Hanging the gun-heavy shoulder sling on the nail, I waited to see if it would take the weight. When it did, I worked the bureau back in, closer to the wall again, until there was just enough space left between the back of the bureau and the wall for my hand to reach in there.

When all that was taken care of, I got a cigarette going, wondering why I was going to all the trouble with the gun.

Maybe I knew why, or sensed why, even then.

❈ ❈ ❈

There were no more stands at Florian's, but the grubby business of nosing into other people's shabby lives continued.

I even picked up an occasional job on my own. The Agency didn't like that sort of thing, but the hell with them. I was with Jack Harvey's outfit only until I raised enough of a stake to go back into business for myself. I owed them nothing but time, like any other job. Employers can never see it that way. They think they buy everything you had and were, with their weekly paycheck, but all anyone ever bought from me was time.

Looking back, I suppose I was just waiting, doing my stints in stores or alleys or behind the wheels of parked cars or inside stuffy little apartments late at night, waiting for two people to begin making out, so the husband or the wife of one of them could break in on them and heave both into court so the divorce wouldn't involve any kind of split of property, or not so much of a split.

Maybe I wasn't exactly waiting, but I had that expectant feeling. I'd had it ever since the night I found Assault tumbled beside the dirt road, out there in the sage flats, the cuts on his face already caked with dried blood, the ones on his body seeping patches of blood through his T-shirt to his outside shirt. A feeling half of dread, half of expectation, of waiting for the other shoe to drop.

Almost a week passed after Brode's visit. Sometimes I would call Jack Harvey's Agency to check myself out after a day's work. Sometimes I'd stop at the office downtown. If I didn't need their weapon for the following day's assignment, I'd turn it in. The day I made the final payment on the car, I left the Agency gun with the dispatcher, snagged someone's newspaper and headed home.

It was still daylight, and still plenty hot. The showplaces along the Strip flipped by on either side as I drove the Ford down the length of it. Half a mile short of my turnoff, I heard sirens, decided I couldn't make my street before they came up behind me, and pulled over to the side of the roadway.

It turned out to be the fire chief's car shooting past.

Far ahead, out in the desert to the south, there was a gray column of smoke spiraling into the sky.

It was starting early. Brushfire season usually waited until late July or early August.

Traffic on the Strip started up again.

After making the turn into my street near the southwestern end of the Strip, before it starts its swing to due west, I stopped halfway along the block to get a look through a clear space between two of the houses on the south side of the street.

The smoke down there was still pretty much the same.

Driving on to the near end of the adobe-walled building where I roomed, I parked and went in the front way to pay the landlord my week's rent. When I came back out, the Ford was still idling. At first, she had done some stalling, but a little fiddling, and a fractional turn on the screw that fed idling gas, and that solved the problem.

I had already done some work on the rust patches that showed, painting them over with red lead, then over that with regular paint. I did that so I could use my own car on the job, and make extra money for the car, too. But you can't tail anyone in a car that has too many distinguishing features, like scabs of rust as big as your fist or as long as a chorus cutie's legs. Or even as short as the legs of that tiny little knockout who'd given me the angel-smile that time.

As I got back into the Ford and drove the length of the adobe wall to my end of the old place, the sun was half out of sight.

I didn't bother turning the car around, just parked in front of my corner entrance and got out. After hooking the car keys under the dashboard for secrecy and convenience, I slammed the door shut, and only then noticed a dark green sedan backed into the sage, beyond the end of the dirt part of the street. Even with some lingering sunlight, I almost missed spotting it, standing in the shadow of a little willow that grew in the yard of the last house across the street.

Making sure I didn't do any staring, I turned and went inside, closing and locking the street door behind me, thinking: "As if this door and its ten-penny lock are going to stop anyone from coming in here if they want to."

I took the steps two at a time.

This had to be one of the nights the Agency wanted their goddamn cap pistol turned in!

When I opened the door of my room, I thought I had it made. I even relaxed for a moment. Perhaps that wasn't too bad a move, although I made it without knowing it *was* a move.

After making certain the door was locked behind me, I started across the room to get the .38 from where it hung from the nail behind the bureau. Then I felt it, and stopped moving.

I stiffened. I wanted to keep moving and try to reach the gun, but I made myself move easily, no special rush, trying to figure out what was wrong. And what I had sensed, I now saw: halfway out of the closet, Jeff stood there with a little automatic in his hand. The thing seemed to have an enormous muzzle at the business end of it.

Jeff had been savvy enough to let the closet door do whatever it usually did. It had swung open a couple of inches. Since it was usually like that, I hadn't noticed.

"Relax, Brandon," Jeff said quietly.

I nodded and stood there.

"I'm relaxed."

"Somebody wants to see you."

"Of course somebody wants to see me."

"Smiles is coming up. Move away from that door. Leave enough room for him to get in here."

Footsteps climbed the stairs. Easing off to one side of the door, I told Jeff: "I'm not wearing anything. The Agency had me turn in their gun at the end of the day."

"We'll check anyway."

"Jeff, would I lie to you?" I asked, pained. "After all we've been through together?"

Jeff's scar-stitch of a mouth wrinkled a bit. It might have been a very small grin.

"We'll check anyway," he said again.

The steps reached the landing, and the doorknob rattled.

"Jeff?" a voice called.

"One sec," Jeff replied. To me: "Unlock it, then move away from it again."

Opening the door, I got out of the way.

The big hard-as-nails-looking young man who had re-lieved me of the Agency's pistol out at Florian's stepped into the room on light feet, closing the door soundlessly behind him. Smiles. And sure enough, he was grinning.

"Frisk him," Jeff said.

"Here we go again," I said, lifting my arms a little out from both sides.

Smiles laughed. He went over me with practiced thor-oughness.

"Clean."

"Let's shove," Jeff said. "You first, Smiles. Then you, Brandon. Then me."

And that's the way we went: Smiles, then myself, then Jeff, down the stairs, out into the early evening dusk, the air still hot and soft, hardly any wind, then across the dirt road, and into their big car. In the front seat, Smiles and myself. Behind us, Jeff.

You could barely hear the motor, but I could feel the smooth surge of power under all that velvet. Even on the dirt stretch, before we reached the paved part of my street, we rode smoothly.

Peering past Smiles' profile behind the wheel, I could see the far-off blossom of flame out in the desert to the south.

"Like that fire, do you?" Smiles grinned.

I shrugged.

"It's a little early in the season for brushfires."

Smiles gave a short laugh.

"Brushfires."

In back, Jeff growled: "Smiles, cut the talk."

Smiles still looked as if he was almost grinning, but I could see his jaw muscles tighten.

He stopped at the Strip for traffic. We waited while cars and SUVs and trucks tore past in a steady stream. Then, in a gap in traffic, Smiles jumped the car out into it, whipped it across to the far side, snapped into that lane just in front of a zooming sport car, and headed south out of town, accelerating rapidly.

A moment later, the sport car racketed past us, the guy at the wheel yelling something. Smiles just grinned affably and waved at him. The sport job took off and quickly grew smaller ahead of us.

I checked our speedometer. We were doing close to eighty. And the other guy was leaving us as if we were standing still.

Behind us, the last of the lights along the Strip fled and were gone, and we were out under the first dim stars.

Far off to the half left, the fire in the desert still glowed dull orange. When the highway completed its swing half to the right, we stayed with it, following the long curve all the way in its third of a turn until we were pointed due west.

Now the distant fire was at our side once more, nearer, but not much nearer. I still couldn't gauge how far away it was, or what was burning.

We stopped for the light at the intersection where, if we made a right turn, we'd end up at Florian's, if a left, we'd reach Mexico, eventually. We did neither, just crossed and went straight ahead.

Gradually the fire fell behind to our left rear, and I faced forward again.

Presently Smiles slowed, turned right abruptly onto a paved side road, and picked up speed again.

The sage flats flowed by, clear in the headlights, a blur on either side. Bugs whizzed and whirled in the lights. Occasionally one of them splattered against the windshield.

Off in the brush, every now and then you could glimpse lights from an isolated home. Then they would fall behind, and everything would be dark again, except for the head-lights and the high huge stars.

Our car slowed again as we approached another lit-up building, back from the road about a quarter mile. Smiles turned left into its entrance drive, scattering gravel until he slowed on nearing the place.

It was a ranch built on a rise, its rambling outlines bulky against the star-studded western sky and the pale afterglow of the fallen sun.

Swinging the car around a circular drive in front of the place, Smiles left the car facing back the way we'd come.

Opening his door, he got out.

"Slide over to this side, Brandon," he told me. Now he was holding a pistol, too.

He stood well clear, as I shifted under the steering wheel and got out on the driver's side.

"Jeff will shut the car doors," Smiles said. "Move. I'm right behind you."

Crossing gravel, I went along a flagstone path up toward the house.

Smiles pushed a button beside a big wooden door. Four-tone chimes sounded distantly inside.

Turning, I gazed across the desert at the wide glow of the lights the Strip threw up into the eastern sky.

Along the paved road, the headlights of a passing car went by, then I couldn't see them anymore, only the beams they threw ahead of them.

Jeff climbed toward us up the sloping flagstone walk.

When the door behind me opened, I turned. Smiles twitched his handgun and followed me inside.

The squat wide-bodied man who admitted us wore a suit that looked too tight for him but really wasn't. Anything he wore would look as if he was stuffed into it.

I followed the short man up more flagstone steps to a land-ing. He pointed to the right, up still more steps. I climbed, with Smiles beside me and to my right, and Jeff coming along behind both of us.

The man who'd admitted us exchanged a few quiet words with Jeff. I couldn't hear any of them.

At the top of those stairs, I found myself entering a big fieldstone-walled room with very modern furniture and a big desk over on the right near a set of wall-wide sliding glass doors, which opened onto a terrace. A cigarette glowed out there against the darkness.

Behind the desk stood Les Wyatt, his eyes watching me out of his round face. He was putting a cup and saucer down onto the desk beside a gleaming silver coffee service.

Wyatt went around the far end of the desk as I crossed the room toward it.

All around the room, animal heads stuck out of the stone walls. Big Mexican serapes hung here and there along the walls, too.

Wyatt went outside onto the terrace, where he spoke to a tall figure gazing off into the night. Coming inside again, he went back behind the desk and sat down.

"Come on over here, Brandon," he ordered, waving a hand. "Let's have a look at you."

"Yes, that's right," I said, crossing the rest of what was undoubtedly a real Persian rug to my side of the desk. "I heard somebody wanted to see me. I dropped everything and came right over. I'm a man who likes to be seen by people who want to see me."

He nodded, but the words might not have been said, for all the response they got from him. He watched me with that curious remote look their eyes sometimes have, a look that tells you they've long ago gotten used to making that final move which settles forever whether anyone gives them trouble. They would be patient with you. They might even try to make a deal with you. But they always had the ultimate solution, and they would use it, if they had to. Only if they had to, true, but they would use it.

Underneath a moose head in a distant corner of the room, a door opened. Jack Harvey came through it with a drink in his hand. He nodded to me

I glanced back at Wyatt. He looked as if he hadn't taken his eyes off me for a second.

"How's that friend of yours?" he asked. "The one that was laid up in the hospital?"

"Friend of mine?"

"Sure. Mugged by some young hoodlums, wasn't he?"

"Maybe they weren't so young."

"I hear he jumped the hospital before they could bill him for the repair work they did on him." He laughed heartily. "Good for him. I like a guy like that. Screw those doctors, and the damn hospitals, too. Them and their health plans! I wouldn't let them operate on a bug, most of them. All they're after is the buck."

"Not like you and me," I said. "We just work for the love of the work itself."

"Hell, you know what I mean, Brandon. I get some change across the tables. You do your private peeping. But those butchers! They take it right out of people, like literally right out of their hides. You don't have any dough, you don't get operated on, even if you die without it. If they do operate, some crumb does it that you wouldn't let near a bug, unless you really hated the bug. Why, right now, just for an example, one of my employees is banged up pretty bad. Concussion. A lousy hi-jack job. You think I'd send him to one of those hospitals? The hell I would! Any X-rays, we got our own connection, the best equipment, the best MD's, the best of everything, all around. Costs more, you say? Sure, but in the long run, it pays. Keeps the help happy."

"And healthy," I added. "And no police reports."

'That's right," he chuckled. "Where'd that friend of yours go off to? The one that jumped the hospital bill?"

"I have no idea. That friend of mine, I don't even know his name."

"I think you do."

Nobody spoke for a moment. To my left, out of the corner of my eye, I was aware of movements Jack Harvey made, but Wyatt was playing deadlock-eyes with me, and I hated to break up the game.

Jack started to say something, but Wyatt's right hand lifted an inch from the desktop and sliced the air. Harvey stopped whatever it was he'd begun to say.

"I think you do know his name," Wyatt said slowly. "And I think you know where he is, right now."

"You're thinking wrong. I don't."

"Uh-uh!" He shook his head positively. "Either you know, or you can find out. You can feed the cops any kind of crappy story you want, but me, don't try it with me, Brandon. I'll bend you out of sight like nothing."

Turning, I glanced at Harvey. He was watching me. He raised his drink and took a pull at it.

"Where's the guy at?" Wyatt asked.

"I don't know."

He stared at me for a moment, then pulled open a desk drawer, reached down into it, and tossed a packet of money across the desk. It plopped on the side nearest me, and slid almost to the edge of the desktop before it stopped.

"You find that guy," Wyatt ordered. "That's half your retainer. When you turn him up, you get the same again. Any expenses it takes, I'll pay, no problem."

His round face, with those muddy Mediterranean eyes, was glistening with sweat, all in a moment.

"And, Brandon, you find that guy quick or you're through around here."

Taking a deep breath, I looked past him through the wide wall of glass doors behind him. The man out there wasn't smoking anymore. He stood leaning on the terrace railing, his back to me, outlined against the distant glow of light from the Strip.

I told Wyatt: "No."

His face became congested with blood. His mouth twisted. He looked as if he was going to come lunging across the desk at me. In case he did, I shifted my feet, to be ready.

He didn't move. He got hold of himself, holding on hard, he was that angry. Swiveling his head, he barked at Jack Harvey.

"I thought you said this bastard had some smarts."

"Jim, do what he wants," Harvey said quietly. "Take the job. It's just an assignment. The retainer's all yours. I'll detach you from my outfit for this special job. You can find that guy, easy."

"Maybe I can find him," I replied, but I kept my eyes on Wyatt. "I just don't cotton to the way this job was handed to me. How much money is this?"

"Count it," Wyatt snapped.

Picking up the package, I riffled through the bills. All hundreds. Twenty five of them. I tossed the package back onto the desk.

"It's too much."

Wyatt stared, then threw his head back and laughed, a harsh guttural laugh.

"Too much!" he yelped. "Now I've heard everything!"

"That's right," I replied. "Too much. And I don't like the conditions of the job, either."

"Keep it up, peeper," Wyatt growled. "Tell me what you don't like about the conditions."

His lips compressed. Tiny red veins showed around his eyeballs.

"If someone wants me to find somebody, I'll hire on and *try* to find him. I guarantee nothing. You pay regular day rates, like anyone else. And I'll do as good a job of hunting as I can."

"Damn your day rates," Wyatt snarled. "I'm willing to pay twenty, fifty times your lousy day rate . . ."

"That's what I mean," I snarled back. "You're not hiring me to do a job. You're *telling* me: find this guy. Not *try* to find him, but *find* him, or else. I don't work like that."

"Listen, you son of a bitch," Wyatt whispered in a voice that seemed to fill the room, "you're gonna be lucky if you work at all, from now on. You aint gonna be around to work, if you don't do like I . . ."

"That's what I mean," I interrupted. "What did he do to you?"

Wyatt blinked and straightened. The anger flowed out of him. Everyone else in the room seemed to be holding their breaths.

"Where did he hit you?" I asked. "How hard?"

Wyatt's fury just seemed to back into him, leaving those muddy eyes of his staring out of the round face at me.

"What did you just say?"

"You heard what I just said. He must've hit you where you live, to get you this steamed."

One of them moved behind me.

Smiles's voice said: "I told you this creep was in on it."

Turning, I looked at Smiles. He was almost on top of me. His eyes were slits, but he still looked as if he was smiling. He swung the pistol he held. The barrel slashed across my left cheekbone. The room turned a tumblesault, crashed away, and wasn't there anymore, for a long moment.

Five

I could hear their feet doing soft muffled dances on the thick rug all around where I fell, but I couldn't see anything except a white-hot ball of pain.

Filmy ragged crimson curtains began to close in on me from both sides. I thought those curtains were going to shut completely and smother the searing light that brought the pain.

They almost did shut. Both curtains hung there, letting the last of the blinding light get through to the me inside me. Then, after a long wait, the curtains began to part. The pain came back, more and more, until I couldn't see the crimson curtains at all, anymore. They were drawn off too far to the left and to the right.

Now, nothing in the world remained but the burning light and the waves of pain I could feel turning my stomach over, inside me.

Suddenly, I could see again. The burning light really was a light: it shone down on me from the ceiling.

I tried turning my head, to get the light out of my eyes. I was on my back, on the rug. Rolling over onto my face, I tried to get up.

Hands beneath my arms and shoulders lifted me.

"Get away," I muttered thickly.

They didn't. They held on, Jeff on my left, and Jack Harvey on my right, both of them supporting me.

Trying to shove them away, I ended up pushing myself backward, out of their gripping hands. I still couldn't stand by myself, though. My legs gave. If I hadn't tilted back against the edge of the desk, I would have landed on the rug again.

I kept trying to breathe, to end this dizziness that kept me floundering.

Jeff stepped forward again, and with his left hand, he kept me propped, half standing, half sitting on the edge of the desk.

My head hung down. My chin rested almost on my chest. From beneath my eyebrows, I watched the semi-automatic in Jeff's right hand. If I could get squared away to him so my left hand was near enough to make a grab for that gun-hand of his . . .

Lurching to my left, I tried sliding along the edge of the desktop, but Jeff had been around too long for that to work. He sidestepped right along with me, keeping his free hand shoved against my chest to hold me upright, but not taking any chances with the hand holding his gun. He'd been around a long time, and not because he took foolish chances.

I had to let it go.

Gradually, my sight cleared. Tears no longer filled my eyes, making the room in front of me swim, and making me desperate by filling my eyes up again each time I wiped them free of tears.

My left cheekbone throbbed with an angry pounding throb that made my head ache.

Finally someone said something that made sense.

"Get a chair over here."

A moment later, Jack Harvey and Jeff lowered me into a chair they had dragged around in front of the desk. After a minute, I looked around.

Wyatt was out on the terrace, talking with the man out there.

Closing my eyes, I endured the pound, pound, pounding of my own blood beating through where Smiles had belted me with his gun barrel. I wondered if the skin over the cheekbone was laid open. Gingerly, I probed with my fingertips, but I couldn't tell, so I took the exploring fingertips away.

Wyatt came back inside and sat behind his desk again.

"Send Little Flores up here," he told someone. "And keep that grinning fool downstairs."

He looked at me.

"Smiles is an all right guy," he explained, "but right now he's kind of worried."

He stared at me across the desk, his muddy eyes showing nothing.

"Brandon, I don't like this rough stuff," he complained, "but maybe it had to happen. The boys aren't happy about that guy you found beat up in the desert. My advice is, you better take the job I offered you. Find that bastard. I mean it. I won't have to say a word to some of these boys of mine, if you don't find him. All I'll have to do is turn you over to Smiles and another guy. They have damn good reasons for wanting that guy from the hospital found."

"I'll bet they have," I managed to croak.

"Does that mean you won't?" he asked, after waiting a beat.

"That's what it means."

Shrugging, he turned away.

"Okay, that's that."

Rising, he went around the window end of his desk and stood at the near corner of it.

"Jeff, you keep an eye on Smiles," he instructed. "We want this jerk alive. We need information from him. I still think he was in on that little job, yesterday. If he wasn't such a dope, I'd be sure of it. Make sure they leave him alive."

Jeff nodded and came over to me.

"Take him to that place up by the lake," Wyatt added. "You know the one. Maybe some of that treatment will soften him up . . ."

"Les!"

The man on the terrace was calling, and his voice sounded urgent.

Wyatt hurried out there.

I could hear snatches of conversation.

"You don't think he'd try coming here? Brock, the son of a bitch must be nuts . . ."

Finally, I knew who was out there, Brock Townsend. When he had called out, I hadn't been sure, although the sound of the voice had rung a faint momentary bell.

Standing beside my chair, Jeff waited, watching me and the two silhouettes, out on the terrace. Beyond Jeff, I saw the short man who had admitted us to the house earlier, Little Flores. Somewhere in the room behind me, Jack Harvey moved around restlessly.

Out of the night beyond the terrace, the sound of an approaching car could be heard, coming fast.

"Jeff, you better get downstairs," Wyatt called in. "Make sure Smiles doesn't . . ."

Jeff nodded and turned toward the door.

"Keep your eye on this one," he told Little Flores.

The squat man nodded.

Outside, the car was quite close now. The wheels made harsh scraping noises when it turned in a circle at the foot of the flagstone-stepped path, which led up to the front door. There was a sudden rattling of sprayed gravel thrown violently against the front of the house as the vehicle turned, then a loud thump, and finally the screech of gears as the motor was gunned savagely.

Someone down there shouted. Smiles. There was a sharp crack, another.

On the terrace, Wyatt was leaning over the railing, shouting down to Smiles. He came running back inside, pulled open one of the desk drawers and hurried back out carrying a snub-nosed revolver.

Jack Harvey went out with him.

I checked Flores. He was watching me, paying no attention to the uproar going on outside, nor to the shots still being fired below.

The three men were silhouetted against the far-off glow of light from the distant Strip. There was a flash: Wyatt was firing his revolver.

The sound of the car was getting farther away, and then I couldn't hear it anymore.

Townsend said something I couldn't make out.

Wyatt yelled down: "What's going on? What happened?"

"He's stopped," Jack Harvey's voice reported.

"How do you know he's stopped?" Wyatt snapped. "He's got no lights on . . ."

I saw one of the terrace doors star before I heard the distant report of the shot and heard the whoosh of the bullet, the smack of it against the wall behind me, high up, near the ceiling. Plaster rattled softly on the carpeted floor.

From the corner of my eye, I saw Flores flick his head toward the hole in the glass door, then back to me. He was a tough man to distract, when he was told to watch someone.

Downstairs, in front of the house, a fusillade of shots was fired, quickly, one after another. Then a heavier handgun joined in, but slower, the shots spaced, fired deliberately. That would be Jeff, trying impossible shooting at that range with any kind of handgun.

Out on the terrace, Wyatt crouched down slightly. So did Jack Harvey.

"He's using a rifle on us," Wyatt murmured. His voice was soft, astonished.

Beside him, Townsend called over his shoulder.

"Turn off those lights in there."

Just then, the glass door in front of me starred again, lower than before. Flakes of glass rattled onto the desktop.

Sliding down in my chair, I watched Flores glide swiftly along the wall past the door to the landing, to where the light switches were.

A moment later, the room was dark. I eased out of my chair onto the floor. I couldn't see a thing, but neither could Flores, I hoped.

Keeping the big easy chair between him and myself, I wormed on my hands and knees around the inner end of the desk just in time for the third rifle bullet to hit the glass terrace wall, lower than ever, almost at floor level. There was a rush of air as the slug punched through the plexiglass.

I twisted flat while particles of glass showered down all around me. I could smell the dust in the rug.

Whoever was using that rifle was getting his shots off faster. I listened, trying to time the intervals between shots. It could either be a bolt action or a lever action weapon.

But no more shots struck the glass. Now the rifleman seemed to be aiming at Smiles and Jeff down below, replying to their fire, perhaps sighting on their muzzle flashes.

I didn't hear any more shots from Jeff's heavy caliber gun, but Smiles was still blasting away down there. I wondered if Smiles was going to live through this night. I hoped he did. I still owed him for that crack across the face he'd given me.

Suddenly, Wyatt was shouting.

"Get after him, you guys. He's moving. Take the car. Get that son of a bitch."

A moment later, I heard the car I'd been brought in start up and move out.

I was just getting up off my face, wondering if I could make it to that far door in the corner of the room Jack Harvey had entered by.

"Light that room, Flores," Wyatt called in from the terrace, "before Harvey's shamus tries to powder on us."

That killed it. I managed to stand up and get around the corner of the desk to the chair I'd been sitting in before the lights came on.

Seeing me approximately where I ought to be, Flores slid the gun he held back under his jacket. He stayed close to the wall, though. I wished I were nearer the wall, too, in case any more of those rifle bullets came smashing in here.

Instead, I had to sit back down in the easy chair, well down in it, just as Wyatt and Jack Harvey came back inside.

Wyatt stared down at me for a long moment.

"All right, Jack" he finally said, "drive Brandon back to town. I still don't like it. I still think he's in this, somewhere along the line, but maybe you're right. That crazy out there could have blown Brandon's brains out as well as any of ours, so maybe the two of them aren't in this together. Get him out of here. I might want to see him again, so keep tabs on him, understand? Keep your eye on him, or we'll find you, instead."

Jack nodded.

All through it, Jack had been nodding his head, not saying a word, himself tall and rangy, looking down a good half a foot at the little round-faced man telling him what to do.

When Jack was sure Wyatt wasn't going to tell him anything more, he glanced at me and said, "Come on, let's go."

I followed him out of the room and down the flagstone steps and out the front door. Behind us, the lights on the ground floor were still lit. They had never turned them off.

When I was about to pull the front door shut behind me, I spotted something sprawled on the lowest of the wide flagstone steps. Instead of closing the door, I opened it wider and stepped to one side, so more light from inside would shine through.

Even with the extra illumination, I still couldn't make out what it was down there, although I suspected.

Halfway down the front steps, Harvey hesitated and looked back up at me, before going down the rest of the way, where he leaned over it.

"Which one of them?" I called.

"Of who?" he asked. He didn't look up. He got out a pencil flash and began using it.

"Smiles or Jeff?"

"Neither. It's some other guy. I've seen him around, but I don't know his name."

Shutting the door behind me, I went down and joined him at the foot of the steps. One look at what lay there and I knew who it was.

"Jeff called him Fats."

"What are you two looking at?" Wyatt shouted from above.

He was standing at the terrace railing beside Brock Townsend.

"One of your people," Jack replied.

After a moment, Wyatt called: "All right. "We'll handle it. Get going."

I followed Jack Harvey along the perimeter of the traffic circle in front of the house to a branch gravel drive that ran along the north side of the house, back toward what were probably garages. We didn't go that far. Harvey's car was parked halfway along the side of the house.

He got behind the wheel of his electric-blue convertible. When I slid in beside him and closed the door on my side, he was sticking the ignition key in, muttering, "The bastard didn't even ask if Fats was dead."

"Was he?"

He turned the starter.

"Of course."

The motor kicked over. For a second or two, he raced it savagely, then he kicked the brake off and we moved forward, went around the front corner of the house, into and across the circular driveway and, faster now, down the private road to the paved secondary road.

Instead of turning right and going south to the big highway . . . the way Jeff and Smiles had driven me out there . . . Jack turned left and headed northward.

Far off to the right, I could just make out the lit-up Florian's sign. Even farther in the same direction, the general glow of the entire Strip filled the sky softly, a long stretch of it along the eastern sky, but still looking small, swallowed up in the immensity of the desert night.

"They won't be bothered too much when you turn up dead, either," I told him.

Taking his eyes off the road ahead, he glared at me.

"That's a hell of a thing to say."

"What do you expect me to say? Thank you? You're in with those bastards up to your tonsils, and you just dragged me in, too."

"I'm just doing a job for them," he muttered. "I've been just doing a job all along."

"On me."

"All right, on you. They hired me. I'm for hire. So are you. Don't give me any of this . . ."

"Better not tell me don't give you anything," I growled. "Not right now, not after that pistol-whipping I had to take back there. I'm not exactly in a mood for . . ."

"What could I do, Jim? You know what they're like . . ."

"Yeah, you're right," I agreed. "I know what they're like. Apparently better than you. That's why I steer clear of them. I hope you live long enough to learn to do the same . . . but I'm beginning to doubt it."

"Jim," he said patiently, "you talked to Wyatt back there as if he was dirt . . ."

"He is dirt. They're all dirt."

He rolled his eyes up to the sky.

"Jim, I thought you were on. I thought you had gotten some sense by now . . ."

"Oh, turn it off, Jack. We've got different ways of looking at things, you and me. You're gonna keep an eye on me for Wyatt, are you? He may want to see me again, and when he wants you to, you're going to turn me up, are you? Well, Jack boy, from here on, I'm packing a gun, all the time. My gun. Not yours. And if your Mr. Wyatt or any of his friends wants to see me, he's going to have to come to me, not the other way around. And if he tries to deal with me in any cute way, he's going to have to be damn fast and very lucky."

"Don't worry, he will be. Any guys he sends will be experts."

"Fats was an expert, too."

He didn't say anything.

"Okay," I began, when the silence between us had gone on long enough. "Now you'd better start telling me what this is all about. Wyatt hired you to keep me under your thumb by giving me a job. Why?"

"You're getting kind of raunchy, aren't you, Jim?"

I turned to face him. There was a small smile on his lips. His eyes were squinted a bit against the glow from the dashboard lights.

"Telling me I'd *better* start telling you . . ."

I hit him with the edge of my left hand, high on his near cheekbone. His head snapped away from the blow, and he yelled something.

"Give that to Smiles," I told him, "next time you see him."

The car swerved on the two-lane blacktop. Jack almost lost control of it. I braced my right foot against the tilted part of the floorboards, beneath the dashboard. My left elbow I hooked over the seatback behind him, and got my left hand on Jack's near shoulder, sliding it toward his neck.

He pulled his foot off the accelerator and jammed it down onto the brake pedal, fighting the steering wheel, trying to keep his car from rocketing off the road out into the brush.

I slid my left hand down across his chest and beneath his jacket, under his left arm.

By then, Jack had the car under control again, slowing it enough so he could release the steering wheel with his right hand. He swung his upper arm down on top of my left forearm, hard, then grabbed for the gun under his left armpit, twisting his body away from me just as my fingertips brushed against the handgrip.

So I had to settle for a fistful of the soft part of his right shoulder, grabbing it with my left hand and squeezing.

He groaned.

I squeezed harder.

He thrashed around some, but he still needed his left hand on the steering wheel, and the way I had him, he couldn't do anything with his right. He squirmed, trying to bring the car to a complete stop.

Now my left hand could reach under his gun arm. My hand gripped the weapon and pulled it clear of the clip holster.

Relaxed now, I sat back while he finally brought the car to a stop, cursing steadily, massaging his right shoulder muscle gently with his left hand.

I gave him a few minutes to recover from the sore muscle. Then I told him to get started talking.

"I want to hear all of it. By now, I know some of it, but I want you to tell me, just to make sure I'm looking at the same picture you are."

Taking his hand down from gently kneading his shoulder muscle, Jack Harvey stared at the gun I had taken from him. When he raised his eyes, his lips twisted, and his cold eyes were thoughtful.

"Jim," he said slowly, "after this little stunt, you aren't gonna be around this town long. There isn't that much business here. In our line of work, you need every friend you can get. Well, you just lost hope of getting any crumbs I'll ever toss your way again. Mister, you're going to starve, and I won't even have to lift a finger to see that it happens. It'll happen all by itself."

"Let me worry about that," I replied. "Get on with your story. Or are you in so thick with them you don't dare tell me anything?"

Facing forward, he put a cigarette in his mouth, and used the dash lighter to get it started.

"Don't wear out that bit about me being 'in' with anyone. I'm in with me. Those people are just customers, like anyone else. Touchier, maybe, but still just customers."

He glanced across at me.

"Okay if I drive while I fill you in?"

"Drive away."

He started the car moving again, but kept his speed in the forties and fifties. I noticed he used only his left hand on the steering wheel. The grinding I had given his ropy right shoulder muscle made him favor it. His right hand and forearm lay carefully in his lap.

"Someone held up their skimmed-off-the-top shipment, early yesterday. That was the result of it, back there. Fats was missing."

"He isn't missing now," I pointed out.

Jack chuckled.

"There were three of them in the car," he continued. "I don't know who Wyatt was more sore at: whoever did the hijacking, or his own strongarm men who let it get done to them.

"As near as I can make out, from the little they told me . . . which wasn't much . . . the cash run was about their usual amount, nothing out of the ordinary, twelve to fifteen G. You filled in at Florian's a week or so ago, remember? Well, you were there to replace one of the men for the same kind of cash run as yesterday's, except these three dudes stopped at a gas station south of town. They go that way once in every two or three trips to make sure no one gets used to a pattern. So much for alternate routes, huh? They still got skunked.

"Anyway, one of them had to use the can. The others got gas while they were waiting. Used a credit card. The gas station attendant later found the one in the john out cold, after the heist was all over. He didn't see anything else.

"So he gave them their gas, processed the credit card, they stayed parked at the pump a few more minutes until the one using the latrine came back, and then they drove off. That's all the attendant saw. Except pretty soon, he hears noises in the back, goes around there, and finds the jerk in the men's room, still half out of it, but coming back up for air.

"The gas station guy calls the cops, before the casualty was fully awake. Wyatt doesn't like that, now. It brought the cops in on part of it. Wyatt's boy got on the phone real quick and filled Wyatt in on all he knew about what went down. That guy is okay. Just a headache. But he doesn't really know a thing. Says he just heard someone come into the men's room behind him, and then, curtains. Scratch one of the three. Two to go.

"Fats, the one we saw back there on the front steps, he was the wheel man. Scratch two. For information, anyway. No way of knowing what or who he saw, not anymore."

"What about the third guy?" I asked.

"He's the one they got some kind of story out of, Wyatt did. They don't think that one gave the police very much. His skull may have been fractured. At the gas station, he was in the back seat with the money, leaning forward, talking to Fats. Says he heard footsteps approaching behind him, thought it was the one who used the john, until he saw Fats look past him at whoever it was and go for his gun. And then Fats stopped. He froze. Note that. Fats froze."

"It's duly noted," I assured him. "Go on."

"Before the one in the back seat could turn his head, it gets bashed. Their doctor says it could have been done by a gun butt. The one in the men's room had his iron lifted."

Putting out his cigarette in the dash ashtray, Jack Harvey drove on through the desert night for awhile without speaking.

Then he went on.

"The guy in the car was unconscious for some time. Doesn't know how long. When he came partly out of it, he was on the floor of the back seat area, his wrists were tied behind him, his gun was gone, and the car motor was stopped. The only thing he knew was that he was no longer at the gas station where he'd been slugged.

"Outside, near the car somewhere, he could hear Fats being worked on. Over and over, whoever did the working was asking Fats the same questions. 'Who were the others? Who gave the orders?' Something like that.

"Understand, this guy's skull was probably fractured. Says he kept blacking out and coming to, and like that. After quite a lot of it, Fats cracked. 'Me and Smiles and a creep named Ted Fenton.' He thought that was the name. He also admitted Wyatt was the one who told them to pull the rough-house. Just a favor for a friend. Then the fractured skull guy told Wyatt there was one last question: 'Why?' And he said Fats answered: 'For fooling around with this friend's girl.'"

Jack Harvey glanced across at me.

"That's about all Wyatt got out of him before he passed out again," Jack added.

I thought about it.

"The dough's gone?" I asked.

"Oh, sure. Twelve to thirteen grand, cold cash, in handy-size bills. Nice, huh?"

"Nice isn't a word I would have used," I murmured absently. "Where did they find the guy with the skull fracture?"

"Near the burning car, out in the desert."

"Was that what was burning down there?"

"Yeah. The hijacker set fire to it, with the slugged one still on the floor in back."

I whistled.

"How'd he get out of the car?"

Harvey shrugged.

"He got out, somehow. Opened the door himself, crawled out and off a ways, into the brush. This was after he heard another car drive away."

I stared out at the night while the passing wind roared by.

"No wonder Wyatt was sore."

"Yeah," Jack laughed. "Be glad you're still in one piece. For awhile, anyway."

I let that one pass.

"What happened next?"

"That was pretty much it. The cops didn't get there till early afternoon. An ambulance brought the one with the skull trouble back into town, but the first casualty . . . the one in the gas station . . . he'd already clued Wyatt in, so they managed to get their own doctor and maybe a lawyer into the hospital, to help keep their second lad from telling the police any more than he absolutely had to, until they had time to decide what was going on, and who ought to handle it, the law or themselves."

"Running skim money would pretty much guarantee the law would be kept out, I'd think."

Jack chuckled and nodded.

"Wyatt wasn't sure it wasn't some mob stuff, maybe a probe, someone checking for soft spots out here, in case things might be getting ripe for someone to move in. They have so little of that kind of crap out here, they can't remember how they used to handle it."

I couldn't help chuckling at that.

"Then again," Harvey went on, "if it turned out to be just a one-shot hijacking, fine, then they'd let the cops help. They never expected it to turn out to be something like this. Now they don't want cops in on it at all."

"How can they keep them out? Twelve thousand is a lot of nickels, even to an outfit as big as Florian's"

"What twelve thousand?" Harvey grinned. "There's no twelve grand. A guy slipped and fell in a gas station men's room and knocked himself cold. His friend got careless or clumsy with the car's dashboard lighter while he was driving along a dirt road out in the desert, and the car caught fire. And damned if *he* didn't knock himself cold, too, getting out of the burning car."

Jack threw his head back and laughed with delight.

"Hell, Jim, you know how it goes with those guys. Nobody knows nothing. They were all born the day before yesterday. That white stuff around their mouths is their mothers' milk. They just haven't had a chance to wipe it off yet."

"And Fats? Or what's left of him, back there on the front steps of that ranch?"

Jack shrugged.

"Who's Fats? There wasn't any Fats. They'll work out whatever story they need. If they want all this kept quiet . . . and I think they do . . . they'll go find this guy, or guys, themselves."

"Or try to make me find him."

He didn't say anything to that.

I thought about Jack's version of the story. It figured. Or it was close enough, anyway.

He slowed and turned right for a few miles, and slowed again on reaching the highway Florian's was on, except this time to the south. I thought he was going to turn down that way, but he didn't, just crossed the intersection and went straight ahead toward the reservoir area.

"Who was the friend Wyatt did the favor for?"

"No idea. They're always doing favors for people."

"What's the story on the one out on the terrace tonight?"

"Name's Townsend. Brock Townsend. Big operator. Many dollars, well spread out. He's into pictures, TV, real estate. Plenty of other areas, from what I've heard around. All legitimate. A piece of Florian's, I'd suspect. A big piece. Owns a million acre spread, off to the north, beyond the mountains north of the reservoir."

"Legitimate, huh?"

Harvey shrugged.

"Once upon a time, maybe not so legit, but a very smart citizen."

"Well, he can tell Wyatt to stand up straight," I observed. "And Wyatt doesn't even get restive when he does."

"Perhaps they're old school chums," Jack chuckled. "Choate? Or Andover, maybe?"

"More like Dannemora Prep," I grunted. "Maybe he was the friend Wyatt had his boys pound hell out of that guy for, the one I found in the brush, awhile back."

"Could be," Harvey said carelessly. "On that, your guess is as good as mine, Jim."

"And you came into all this where?"

"Wyatt quietly wanted to know anything I might hear about some guy who was dropped in the desert."

"No name on the guy?"

"None that they told me."

"And you heard I was the one who found him there, is that it? Then when he finally let himself get found again and taken to the hospital . . ."

"That's when I made the contact with you." He flicked a quick glance at me. "Hell, Jim, I just rolled with it. I signed you on at my Agency because that's the easiest way to keep tabs on you."

"And you can even charge my salary to Wyatt as an expense."

"Hey, I never thought of that. Maybe I'll do it, too. Even pennies and nickels add up in this business we're in."

He shot a malicious glance across at me, slowed as we approached the reservoir highway, across from a little roadside state park, which picnickers could use in the daytime.

After making a full stop, he turned right and headed toward the distant glow of lights from the city, off to the south.

Far ahead, away to the right, the Florian's sign was in constant movement, with its various colors switching around in every direction.

I wondered if Wyatt's *friend* was there at Florian's tonight. Or was he still back where I had been, just awhile ago? I wondered if the friend's girl friend would turn out to be the cool tired number I had encountered with her mink stole, in Wyatt's outer office.

I hoped she wasn't.

Six

"So you bring it to me," Detective Sergeant Brode muttered. "At my home. At this hour."

I sat on the top step of his three-steps-up front patio. A squat wide-fronded palm tree fought a losing struggle for survival in the middle of his front yard, and the struggle had turned the palm tree ugly.

"Why don't you shoot that tree?" I asked him. "Put it out of its misery. Why make the damn thing suffer? It doesn't belong in this climate."

"It was there when I bought this house," he said, out of the shadows where he sat in an aluminum folding chair. "My wife likes it, too. Why couldn't you wait till morning?"

I hesitated.

"Who says I'm still going to be around in the morning?"

"You thinking of leaving town?"

"No."

"Then why . . . Oh! I read you. It's that bad?"

"I don't know. It might be. All I can say for sure is this: if you find me some night with six through the pump, try not to get the case dropped in the suicide file."

He chuckled in the darkness.

"I'll try." Then he sighed. "Brandon, I sleep here at home any and every chance I get, because I never know when I'm going to get home to sleep in my own bed again. Sometimes it's days, and it feels like weeks. I'm a cop, on call twenty-six hours a day, thirty on Sundays."

"That's why I came to you," I reminded him, "because you're a cop. You want me to go tell a fireman?"

"Good! That's the way. Give me a chuckle with your wise-cracks. I don't need TV sitcoms. I've got you."

"I told you what Jack Harvey told me," I pointed out, "in addition to what I've seen tonight, to wit, one slightly dead man, who's a bit low on the local hotshot totem pole. So far as I'm concerned, our boy Assault is starting to live up to the name you pinned on him, and with a vengeance."

"Yeah, it could be him."

"Any word on him yet from the Feds? Prints? DNA?"

"Nothing yet. Takes time."

"Can't you get anything from Army or Navy records? Everyone's been in one or the other. Or the Marines?"

Impatiently, Brode replied: "I've checked his prints wherever regulations permit me to. There's nothing come back on him yet."

"Did you get any photographs of him, while he was in the hospital?"

"Unofficially. A day or two before he checked himself out."

"That's something, anyway."

"Except his face didn't photograph too well. Even you and me . . . and we've both seen him several times . . . even we couldn't make a positive I. D. from those snapshots. The lens picked up every lump they put on his face, but it couldn't seem to get what he looked like. I was going to give it a second try, but he took off before I could get the camera team available again."

"Great!"

"Well, hell, Brandon, I run my tail off every day. That case was only one of plenty of other things I still had to get around to. I knew I ought to do it, but I just couldn't get to it in time. How'd I know he was gonna pull a powder?"

"Okay, sorry. You're right. Now what?"

"I've already called in what you told me, just now. They'll send a car out there. Wyatt'll tell them that you and Jack Harvey were mistaken. It was just one of his friends who fell down drunk. They'll probably produce the friend, too. And he'll be drunk, too."

"Probably."

I squinted up the street.

"That looks like a nice car parked up the street, there."

Brode turned his head, outlined by dim light from inside his house.

"Okay," he said. "I'll be your straight man. Which car, and where up the street?"

"The one up at the corner. The car that's been there ever since I got here, the one that's going to leave when I leave. And I'll bet cash money on that."

Brode just grunted.

"I'll bet you something else, too." I added. "Jack Harvey will be calling in, or he has already called in, to report on Fats. And you'll find Fats out there at Wyatt's ranch, right where he was dropped."

"Excuse me," Brode said, rising. "I think I'll go inside now and lie down on the floor in the cellar. You stay as long as you feel like."

Laughing, I stood and went down to the sidewalk to my new used Ford.

There wasn't much light, back at the corner, where the car I had spotted was parked.

I didn't try any fancy stuff, just drove to the nearest corner, turned left and headed for the Strip. When I turned south along it, they were right behind me. They didn't get too close, but they followed me home, stopping half a block short of my rooming house.

Before going to see Brode, I had stopped off at the room and picked up my Police Special. Now, as I climbed out of the car, I held it in my hand, cocked and ready.

No pineapples exploded. No sub-machineguns spat fire and metal at me. I simply unlocked the ground-floor door, went inside, swung the door shut behind me, made certain the lock caught, and went on up the stairs to my room.

When I opened the door, I banged it back against the wall, in case anyone was behind it. No one was. No one was inside the closet. Even the can was unoccupied.

I let the hammer down on the .38, but I didn't turn on any lights. Keeping low, I crawled out onto the adobe-walled balcony. From there, I could see their car, the lights off now, parked on the other side of the dead-end street, pointed back toward the Strip a block and a half to the west.

Someone inside the car was smoking: there was an occasional glow with each inhalation.

There on the terrace, I squatted until my legs ached.

Finally, groaning, I crept back inside. My legs were stiff from the prolonged crouch.

Hell with it! I went to bed. But I took the .38 to bed with me, and kept it there beside me on the mattress, all through the night.

It was still there in the morning.

I shaved, dressed, ate, and went downstairs and outside. Their car was no longer there. Mine was. I started to get in, but I stopped and stepped away from it.

Sweat burst out on my forehead. I cursed myself. I didn't curse them. I cursed myself. They had me on the run already. They had me scared shitless, and they hadn't done a thing.

Grabbing the door handle, I almost yanked the car door open to prove I wasn't going to let them buffalo me, but I stopped myself from opening the car door.

Don't be scared, I told myself. Just be careful.

If they wanted me dead, and I helped them by being foolish, I would only be playing their game.

Play your own game, I advised myself irritably. Stay alive. Survive.

Carefully, I checked the exhaust pipe, peered underneath the car, up and down, both sides. Gingerly, I raised the hood. When it didn't go up in a sheet of flame, I looked the motor over, checking for wires that didn't belong there, especially ones that might be attached to the ignition system. Nothing.

Opening the door on the passenger side, I crawled across the front seat and examined the inside of the door on the driver's side. Nothing that might go off when I opened the door from outside.

Next, I checked the gear stick, all the way down the steering post.

And finally, I felt carefully beneath all the pedals.

No bombs or grenades were waiting to go off.

And for all my care and caution, when I inserted the ignition key, I still held my breath.

That's how I felt for the rest of the morning.

I had a doctor look at my left cheek.

"No break in the skin," he assured me. "It should be okay."

He swabbed it with something, taped a patch of gauze over it, and I left, giving some money to his receptionist.

With no more job to go to, I hired desk space down a side street from the Strip, near where I lived. A phone answering service went with it. Two hundred a month, cash in advance.

The desk was one of ten others in the big room. Small businessmen were doing everything conceivable, from selling insurance to selling girls, that last being done by a man I recognized, who had twice been arrested but not yet convicted for pimping. He had obviously gotten effective help in the legal area, because he had himself a desk here, and he was back in business.

I put an ad in the paper: James Brandon, Investigations, and the phone number. It would be in time for the next morning's edition.

Today, I sat there awhile, looking over the rest of the desk renters, then ignoring them.

My desk was off in a corner, the furthest one from the entrance door. To my right was a window, which faced onto an alley.

Around noon, I went out and around to the back of the building to check out the alley.

A tall man could stand on tiptoe in the alley and see in through the window near my desk, which was over a little to the left, in the corner of the room. I decided that when I got back from lunch, I would swing the desk around a bit so I would always be able to see out that window.

Walking back from lunch along a narrow side street, a car swept in toward the curb, just ahead. I had my hand half inside my suit coat, when I recognized Brode's grinning face looking back at me.

"Easy there, Wild Bill," he called.

I went over and leaned down beside him on the passenger side. Callahan was at the wheel.

"You win that bet," he said. "They both reported it, first Jack Harvey, then Wyatt."

I was looking at his face, but I was thinking, trying to line it up, to figure my way through whatever they might be up to.

"So what comes next?"

With a chuckle, Brode said, "Wyatt claimed Fats didn't work for him anymore. Wyatt said that when he discovered Fats had a record, he had to fire him. Didn't want convicted criminals on his payroll. See you." He started to laugh. When the car swept away, he was still laughing.

I went on back to my new office.

Late in the afternoon, when I ran into Brode again, he wasn't so tickled. He was coming out of a store. At sight of me, he blinked.

"Who's following who?" he asked.

Then he tilted his head, and I went with him along the street to where the stores ended and a few residences began.

He broke down a stick of chewing gum in his mouth before he said anything.

"Something for you, maybe. New faces have begun drifting into town. We made a few of them and hauled them in, fast, told them to shove along out of here, today. They shoved. But there are others coming. Looks like maybe something is building here."

"It could be," I agreed. "They're like vultures. When they think they smell a rotting corpse, they start to hover."

"They're crazy," Brode said, shaking his head in disgust. "In this state, people like Wyatt run legitimate businesses. No takeovers are possible. Ownership is recorded, each owner is licensed. Any newcomer buying in has to pass the licensing commission."

I shrugged.

"Maybe they're just tourists passing through and slowing down in case there's some quick action."

"It's possible," he conceded. "But it looks too coincidental. I mean, so soon after yesterday's little job out in the desert. I'm beginning to think there might be a bunch of ignoramuses who think they've got territory here they have a chance of taking over. That means, the desert thing might not be our boy Assault, after all. Oh, by the way, they traced his prints. His name's Benjamin Crane."

"That's a step forward, anyway," I said. "Any record?"

"Not yet. The Army turned over his military history. Served in Nam. Nothing outstanding, no medals or anything. But he was one of the volunteers who went into the tunnels to root out the Viet Cong."

I whistled, impressed. "But nothing outstanding."

Brode chuckled.

"I take it you're not working for Jack Harvey anymore." He said it rather than asked it.

"That's right. I hung out my own shingle. I want to see how it swings in the wind while what little dough I've got lasts."

"Good luck with it," he said, starting back toward the stores.

"I'll need it," I called after him.

I took a couple of steps toward where I'd parked my own car, but I thought of something, turned, and called after Brode again.

"Hey, wait a minute."

He stopped and waited until I caught up to him.

"Couple of things I meant to ask you. Are you assigned to that business out in the desert yesterday?"

Chewing his gum ruminatively, he shook his head.

"No, that case is for the big boys: Sheriffs, Deppitties, the Chief, even one of the Inspectors. I get to read some of the reports, though."

"How about Fats? Did you take a look at his remains?"

He nodded.

"Did you notice his wrists? Was he tied?"

"Oh, sure, wrists and ankles both." He watched me with his strangely mild blue eyes. "What are you getting at?"

"Sloshing something around in my head."

"I think I know what's bugging you. That's one of the reasons this may be the start of some gang stuff. No man could have pulled off that heist alone. The gas station is miles away from anything else. We know at least one guy got into the car, after clobbering the second man in the back seat. My guess is, he had help dealing with Fats after they both took care of the first one in the men's room of that filling station. Out in the desert, we know what happened, from the guy whose brains are still scrambled, but who was partly conscious part of the time out there . . . we know from him at least one hijacker was working Fats over, putting questions to him the hard way. And I really mean the hard way: you should see the shape Fats ended up in. I think he would have died from the working-over he was given, even if they didn't put a bullet through his face, out at Wyatt's ranch last night.

"Anyway, they burn Wyatt's car, the one they got at the gas station. They drive away, taking Fats with them. Where'd this second car come from? Could one man have left it there in the desert? Me, I don't think so. It supposes too much. There was no way anyone could know that the gravy car Fats and his two buddies were driving was going to stop at that particular filling station. They had to be followed to it, in a car. The only other way is ridiculous: it has a guy leaving his own heap out in the middle of the desert, walking a roundabout series of old dirt tracks to get out to the highway, to a gas station the Florian's cash car never stopped at before."

Brode shook his head.

"No, I can't buy that. There had to be two of them. There was no other way for their getaway car to get out there in the desert to take them away, after they put the torch to Florian's car out there."

He stopped talking and stared at me, waiting.

"It makes sense," I had to admit.

"Couldn't have happened any other way," he insisted. "Now, this doesn't rule out this Crane fella. He might have a friend in this area, someone who'd help him. But that would change my thinking about him being hot for their heads, the people who gave him that punching out."

Shrugging, he stared into the distance.

"It isn't usual anymore," he added, almost as an after-thought, "but in the old days, out in this country, they handled things their own way. But if you saw what Fats looked like in the morgue, you'd change any sentimental notions you might have about your friend Ben Crane. It makes him no better than Wyatt and Fats and any others who gave him the working over he got. And if Crane is wearing their stripes, you and I better forget the picture we had of him: of a guy who tried to put in some sack time with somebody's girl, and suddenly found himself getting the bejesus pounded out of him by people who knew what they were doing from long practice."

"And then some," I said. "Okay, I see what you mean. If it was Ben Crane and a pal, he might be a hood himself, and they just haven't turned up any arrests on him yet. If it wasn't him who did the job on Fats, I suppose the only other possibility is some of those outside people you mentioned."

"Right. In which case, the more of themselves they knock off, the better. Just so they don't dirty the sidewalk with a lot of mobster blood. It ain't neat."

"Not to mention innocent-bystander blood," I pointed out. "Okay, Sarge, thanks."

I started off.

He went the other way.

For awhile, I sat inside my car, thinking over what he had told me.

I should go home, I thought. I'd had a brutally hard day sitting around my new place of business.

But instead of doing the sensible thing and going home, I drove past my street and on out of town, to the gas station where yesterday's hijacking took place, or where it started.

It was on the left side of the highway that led down to Mexico. Pretty isolated. I swung across the road and parked in front of the gas station, so I could look it over.

Two sets of pumps stood in front of a good-sized white building, with the small corner office on the right-hand end, and the shop on the left taking up three-fifths of the available inside space. Back in the gloom, a car was up on the hydraulic lift, but no one was working on it. The attendant was busy feeding gasoline into the rear end of a big Hollywood job.

Ahead of me, the highway stretched off southward, narrowing in perspective in the sea of sage bushes spread out on each side of it. The wind was coming from the west, as usual, riffling the tops of the bushes. As far as I could see along the road ahead, there was no house, no other gas station, nothing.

Chalk up some points for Sergeant Brode's theory.

The customer getting gas finally took off. I drove over to the pumps and had the attendant fill my tank and check the oil and water. While he was at it, I asked where the men's room was.

"Around on the side," he told me. "Second door. But you need a key. It's hanging on the inside of the office door."

Finding the key, I used it. No one was in the men's room, conscious or otherwise. This was one of the station's dull days.

Outside once again, I stood on the narrow concrete sidewalk that ran along the side of the building. Two cars were pulled up, facing the side of the building. A bald patch of the desert had been worn free of sage bushes by long use, but fifteen or twenty feet away, the desert began again.

The car farthest from the highway was ready for the junkyard. The other probably belonged to the attendant.

Going around front again, I paid for the gas and oil he'd put into the Ford, but when I tried to talk to him about yesterday's excitement, it turned out he wasn't there when it all took place.

"I take the evening shift," he said. "Youngster has the daytime. You a cop?"

"Private," I told him. "A friend on the force was telling me about it."

He nodded. He was a big, slow-moving man, and he would always be sunburned or wind-burned, or both. I wished he had been the one on duty, the day before, at the crucial time. He struck me as the kind of man who would notice a good deal more than you would think.

We eyed each other for a moment. On impulse, I dug out my credentials and showed him my P. I. license.

He hardly gave it a glance.

"Come on inside," he said. "I get enough of this wind when I have to, without standing out in it when I don't have to."

We went into the office. He left the door open, but the corner was so situated that none of the wind reached us, once we were past the office doorway.

"The key," he said.

I still held it in my hand.

"Sorry. I forgot." I hung it on its nail.

He grinned.

"I didn't mean that the way it sounded, but it's just as well you leave it here. I've got a spare somewhere, but I'd never be able to find it, with all the stuff lying around. The key just started up again. After yesterday, I mean. Before that, anyone could get into the john without a key." Almost as an after-thought, he added: "I was the one who had to clean up in there."

"There wasn't any blood, was there?"

He shook his head.

"No, but the injured man threw up a little, while he was regaining consciousness. He wasn't feeling any too good, for awhile, after taking that crack on the skull. Can't blame him none."

"I understand that whoever did it burned the car, out in the desert, later in the afternoon."

"That's right. You could see the smoke going up in a column, a mile or so back of here. We did a lot of business. People just kept stopping to watch the excitement. Some of them bought gas just because they were handy to it. I could have used extra help, for awhile there."

"I saw the smoke from this end of town," I said. "I thought it was an early-season brushfire."

"Nah," he scoffed. "Too soon for brushfires. Don't wish any brushfires on me, not this early in the season. We have enough trouble with those later on, every summer. No way to help it. One of these days, this whole place will burn real bad, if the owner don't keep the brush cleared, out back. If those tanks ever go, huh!" He chuckled. "Forget about it."

"Something you said," I put in. "About the burning car. You said it was only a mile back in the desert from here. I gathered from the police story it was seven or eight miles away."

"Well, maybe a bit more than a mile," he said carefully. "Nowheres near seven miles. Call it a mile-and-a-half, at the most two. Distances can be tricky in this country."

"Are the police aware it was that close to here?"

"They must," he said, with a shrug. "They were all over the area. Even the fire chief was down here."

"Show me, will you?"

"I don't know if we can pick it out from here," he said. "The fire was put out before I came on, around four o'clock. I think they even took what was left of the burned car away, too. Quite a lot of dust roiled up out there, for awhile. Now it's all settled and quiet."

"But there might be a blackened patch we could see," I suggested.

"Might be able to see something," he admitted.

We went outside, and I followed him around to the south side of the building, back along the narrow sidewalk to where the junk pile was parked at the rear end of the walkway.

Standing at the rear edge of the sidewalk, he squinted across the sage-covered desert. The late afternoon wind was picking up. Clumps of sagebrush tossed under the steady pouring force of the wind.

"No," he decided, after trying to pick out the location of the fire. "Can't make out anything. The brush itself helps hide it. There would have to be a pretty big patch of burn-off out there, before you could pick it out of all that."

He swept his arm around at the immense plain stretching away to a horizon so distant that it seemed to blend imperceptibly with a low dim violet jagged line of a mountain range far beyond the horizon.

"Okay if I climb up onto this relic?" I asked, pointing at the old car.

"Good idea."

We both climbed up onto the wreck's hood, but after staring for quite awhile, I realized it was still no use. We could see nothing out there, no trace of the fire of the afternoon before.

"Anyway," he said, climbing down from the old car, "she was burning about there."

He pointed. I sighted along his arm. There was nothing out there to use as a landmark, so I was no better off than if he hadn't shown me the approximate location of the burn site.

"Okay, thanks."

Back in the office, I asked: "Can you show me on a map how I can get in there?"

"Why not? I know those old traces as well as anyone, I reckon. I even had to help the police yesterday afternoon, when I first got here."

Taking a road map down from a rack of them, he opened it up.

"Here, I'll draw it on a regular road map. The tracks don't show on road maps. They're mostly only old dirt roads. Hardly anyone uses them, anymore."

With his drawn map as a guide, I drove almost three miles farther along the southbound highway before turning into a little dirt road winding off through the brush. The track it connected with was right where he said it would be, but I probably would have missed it on the first pass if he hadn't given exact mileage to guide on: 1.9 speedometer miles from the highway turnoff.

The track went meandering through the sage flats for half a mile before it brought me to a crossroad of sorts. Following his drawn-in directions on the road map, I turned left and went a couple of miles north along that until I came to the area I was seeking.

The late-afternoon sun was taking on a red-gold tinge, but it wasn't enough to soften the black ugliness of the place where the car had been set afire.

The entire area was black with soot. Quite far out in all directions, some of the bushes were scorched on the stems and branches of their sides nearest where the car had burned. Closer in, clumps of sage were gone completely: only black, smoke-smudged roots showed, sticking up out of the ground.

As the station attendant had said, they had hauled the burned-out car away, which left not much else to look at. A year from now, perhaps less, the desert would have even the scorched patch wiped clean and completely grown over again.

Clambering up onto the hood of my own car, I couldn't help grinning at what I saw.

"All the smart cop-work," I murmured aloud in the silence. "All the high-powered brass."

Because there, no more than a mile away, off to the west, was the back of the gas station building.

And, of course, everything fell into place.

I knew the hi-jacking could have been pulled off by one man. And if Ben Crane could crawl for miles through the desert after the beating he had taken, those weeks ago, he could certainly get through this stretch of sagebrush and pick up his own car from where he had left it at the paved highway, when he began his spur-of-the-moment hijack play, at that gas station.

I was satisfied it could have been done, but I decided to check it out.

Taking an old red waste-cloth from the trunk of my car, I tied it as tightly as I could to the top of the Ford's radio antenna, then I pushed the antenna as high as it would go. Noting the time, I started walking through the brush toward the distant gas station.

Every so often, I stopped and looked back, to make certain that I could still see my improvised red beacon. I didn't want to lose track of the Ford and have to spend the oncoming night wandering back and forth, out there, trying to locate the car it was tied to.

It was all right, though. When I was halfway to the gas station, I could still see the little red flag, so I walked the rest of the way without worrying about it anymore.

Fifty feet or so from the back of the gas station, I checked my time. I had walked it in twenty minutes. From there, I could still just make out the barest glimpse of dull red. The car beneath it was completely out of sight in the sea of sage, but the red cloth was still visible.

Good enough.

Before starting the return journey, I checked my time again, because I intended to make the return trip at a trot.

It was a long way to jog, and getting buffeted by the rising evening wind from the left rear quarter didn't help any. But finally the red cloth was just ahead, whipping straight out in the wind.

Taking out my watch, I burst through the breast-high sage into the burned-clear patch and stopped, panting from the run.

Twelve minutes.

And something told me Ben Crane could certainly have run it in less. If he was the one who had pulled the hi-jacking in the first place.

I didn't understand what the voice said. The sound of any-one's voice out there was shock enough. Even as I jolted into motion, I was thinking gratefully: "For once I'm ready, up on my feet and prime for anything and anyone."

Even the watch was in my left hand: the right hand was free.

I drove it under my coat, turning in a balanced spin at the same time. The gun was out and cocked. The muscles of my jaw and face were as tight and taut as the tendons in my right hand and wrist.

I was not about to be a pushover again for another Jeff/Smiles combination.

The woman's eyes stared at me, round with astonishment and horror. She reached out one hand toward me in a push-ing motion, while she gasped, "What is it?"

For one long eternal second, she was lined up in the sights.

Somehow, I held the shot. The sudden tension slackened inside me. My muscles loosened. I straightened from the shooting crouch I had fallen into naturally, from habit and training going back a long ways.

Easing the hammer down, I slid the .38 Special back into its socket under my left arm. The palm of my right hand was slick with sweat. Taking out a handkerchief, I first wiped my quivering mouth with it, pressing it, still folded, against my lips until they stopped jumping. Then I wiped the palms of both hands, before putting the handkerchief carefully away.

Then I walked over to her across the patch of blackened desert.

It was the young woman I had seen in Florian's, the one with the mink stole, in Wyatt's outer office.

"I'm sorry," I told her. "You surprised me. I wasn't ex-pecting anyone to be out here."

Her laughter was nervous. Her voice had a breathless catch in it.

"I surprised you!" she cried. "You came running out of those bushes so suddenly, I didn't know what to think."

She glanced toward where I had emerged into the clearing.

"Is anyone chasing you? I can leave, if there's going to be any . . ."

"No one is chasing me," I assured her. "I'm practicing for my debut on TV tonight, for the next Olympics tryout."

Her brown eyes snapped suspiciously.

"Are you kidding me?" she asked, almost in a threatening tone.

I nodded.

"Yes. Are you one of those women who don't like to be kidded?"

"By someone I know and like, I don't mind. But I don't know you, and I think I don't like you, either."

"That's been known to happen before, too."

Turning, she walked around my car, headed for her own, a short distance beyond mine. Glancing back at me over her shoulder, she stopped walking, turned, and watched me for a moment, frowning.

"Where have I seen you?"

She still looked irritated, but her eyes were curious now, too.

"In Florian's," I told her. "I picked up your mink."

After a moment, she smiled.

"Oh, yes, now I remember. I was a bit squiffed."

Strolling around the back end of my car until I was reasonably close to her, but not too near to start her on her way again, I ventured to disagree.

"You looked more exhausted than anything."

"No," she said positively. "I was squiffed, no doubt of it."

"No one gets squiffed anymore. It's gone out. It isn't done nowadays, it simply isn't."

"I do," she insisted. "I get squiffed. And quite often, too." Gazing off at the evening sky in the west, she added: "Too often, I suppose."

After thinking about that a moment more, she shrugged and was with me once again.

"What was that fast-draw gun business there? If for any reason you can't tell me, please don't, of course. But . . . I'm curious."

The wind tossed her long brown hair, held it in a rippling stream behind her head. She turned her head slightly to face directly into the wind, but her eyes remained on mine.

"And what happened to your face?" she asked, examining me closely. "You know, with a face like yours, you really ought to be more careful."

I couldn't help grinning. Maybe that was what she'd been trying for. I touched the bandage taped across my left cheekbone. It felt a bit swollen.

"Why don't we sit in my car?" she suggested. "While you decide just how much you dare tell me."

Her eyes were closed almost to slits, perhaps squinted against the wind, but maybe she was simply trying to keep me from seeing the glint of amusement in them.

She strode across the rough ground so strongly that I was surprised to notice that she wasn't wearing flats on her feet. Her high-heeled shoes interfered in no way with her long, free-swinging walk.

I slid into the passenger seat beside her.

"Leave your window open," she advised. "I'll close this one. That should keep the wind out of here, and we'll still get enough air. God, how I hate that wind! No, I don't, either. Oh, hell, I do and I don't."

"That dashboard of yours," I observed, "looks good enough to eat."

She laughed.

"Have a bite."

"Later. It'll spoil my supper, eating betwixt meals."

"Betwixt," she murmured, holding out cigarettes toward me.

I shook my head and took out one of mine.

"What's your name, gunslinger?" she asked, after lighting up.

"Jim Brandon. What's yours?"

"Make it Jan. Now, why the gunplay, back there? I think I have a right to know. I have a shivery feeling I'm lucky I'm still breathing."

"You're too right," I agreed. "Gave me a turn, too."

"A turn, yet!" She laughed, throwing her head back and giving the laugh full throttle.

"What are you doing out here?" I asked. "A spot this isolated . . ."

She shrugged.

"Nothing better to do, I suppose. I wanted to see where all that smoke came from, yesterday. Besides, someone sort of told me not to. Not exactly told me, but . . ."

"And you're a girl who doesn't like being told what not to do," I finished for her.

In response, her smile was quick and her eyes seemed to dance.

"Right. There's only been one man who might have told me what to do and what not to do. But he didn't stay around long enough to do it."

She gazed straight ahead through the windshield, but I didn't think she was engrossed by the spectacle of the wind tossing clouds of desert dust up into the air. Gradually, her features softened. When she finally turned back to me, it was as if she had forgotten that I was there.

Her eyes were touched with pain. She seemed almost bewildered. Whoever she had been remembering had gotten through to her, and apparently she was unable to get him out.

"Sorry," she said, laughing lightly, embarrassed. "Day dreaming . . ."

"This guy who told you, or asked you, not to come out here: did he say why?"

She shook her head.

"No special reason. Just that the police might still be going over the crime scene out here, and they wouldn't want sightseers hanging around."

"No other reason?"

She shook her head, then turned and looked at me closely.

"No other reason." She continued to watch me a moment before saying: "You sound as if you know who told me . . ."

"Brock Townsend?"

"Hey, wait a damn minute!" she cried, sitting up straight behind the steering wheel. "I want a little more of this, Mister Jim Brandon. Just how could you know that? Neither Brock nor I have tried to keep our little games a big cute secret, but we haven't had any skywriting done about them, either. Not that I'm aware."

"Relax, Miss . . . Relax, Miss Jan . . ."

"You can leave off the Miss part, Brandon. We're not back on the old plantation. And you haven't answered my question, either. I want that question answered, because if I don't get an answer that I like, I have an idea you just might get the same question put to you by some of Brock's friends."

"I already have."

"What?"

"A couple of good old Brock's friends already asked me a few questions. Where do you think I collected this welt on my face?"

"Good for them," she said through clenched teeth. "And if I'm not happy with the answer I get, that's just a sample of what you'll get. Give, cowboy. How does a sleazy little man like you know anything about Brock Townsend and me . . . unless you've been doing some snooping. And, so help me, if you *have* been snooping, I'll see that you . . ."

She stopped talking. Her hands gripped the steering wheel so hard, the knuckles were white.

I spoke slowly and carefully.

"The day I handed you that mink at Florian's, the one you forgot to pick off the floor, I had been sitting and standing right where you saw me, for most of that morning. A few minutes before Smiles poured you through the doorway, two men came along and talked to each other. The older one called the younger one Ted, and the receptionist called the older one Mr. Townsend. Shortly afterward, Ted called him Brock. Now, Brock seemed worried about a young woman named Jan, who had stayed up overnight, gambling. Ted didn't seem worried at all, but he tried to ease the other man's mind. The receptionist let them go on inside. A few minutes later, you showed, dropped your mink, got it back, and also went on inside"

Before going on, I watched the darkness deepen outside.

"It doesn't take a towering genius to figure out the cast members in those scenes. I am a man of reasonable perspicacity. I took one, and added it to another one, and came up with the sum of two. Would you really call that a case of snooping, Missy Jan, Ma'am?"

Slowly, she settled back against the seatback's upholstery. She didn't seem to like my explanation to be so simple.

"That's how you know?"

"I don't know anything," I insisted. "But I can do a bit of guessing."

Her upper teeth gnawed gently on her lower lip. Her eyes had that venomous look any woman can give you, for any reason at all. Or for no reason at all.

Gradually, the look left her eyes, but not as if she wanted it to.

"Sorry," she said abruptly. "I guess I'm a little on edge."

Without a beat, she whirled on me again.

"The way you pulled that gun on me, awhile ago, it's no wonder I'm . . ."

"That's right," I interrupted. "It's my fault again."

"Well, isn't it?" she snapped.

"All right, goddamn it, it is," I shouted.

"All right, then," she said, her voice mild and gentle and sweet.

Her face wore a look of satisfaction. She wouldn't quite permit her lips to wear the smile they wanted to, but she couldn't keep them from hinting at it.

She had gotten my goat. All was well. She had won all the chips she wanted to win.

I watched the almost smug expression on her face.

"You really didn't have to put me through all that," I chided her. "You already knew you could handle me without half trying."

"Through all what?" she asked, without looking up from the meaningless fussing her hands were busy performing. "I have no idea what you're talking about."

"Of course you don't."

I let it go.

"All right, Jan, so your loving man was behaving the way loving men always act, telling you what to keep away from, where not to go. And, naturally, you had to go precisely there."

Indifferently, she gazed out the window on her side of the car.

"Naturally," she murmured.

I watched as her face lost the pleased look and became empty of expression.

"And you're right," she said presently. "About what the lover man always gets around to doing. I suppose I should have left him long ago, before it got to him this badly. But he has been . . . very good to me. I hate to . . ."

She let the sentence die without even attempting to finish it.

I tried not to yawn, but apparently part of it got out.

She glanced across at me, stiffening.

"If I'm boring you with my problems, please let me know," she drawled icily.

I shrugged.

"All women bore all men with their problems. It's one of the penalties women exact of men, in exchange for their less boring qualities and capabilities."

"Is that so? Well, if you'll be kind enough to get the hell out of my car, I'll see to it that you are bored no more."

Opening the passenger door, I got out.

She started the motor and raced it. I could hardly hear her parting words over the racket the motor made.

"Nice to have seen you, Mr. Brandon . . . although not to have would have been nicer still."

She started off fast. Her tires slashed at the ground.

I had to jump back quickly to escape the choking swirl of dust they raised.

In a few minutes, the wind cleared the dust away in a fleeing cloud, but by then I could no longer see her car, only the trail of dust its wheels had churned up, going rapidly farther away across the early evening desert.

Seven

When I got back to town, I tried to reach Sergeant Brode. He was out. I left my new office phone number, and asked to have him call me, when he had a chance.

Supper came off the hot plate, after which I bought a newspaper, before going back to the office.

Only one of the other desk-renters was there that late, which explained why the place was still open. He was bent over insurance policies spread out on the desk in front of him. When I went in, he glanced up, nodded politely, and went on with what he was doing.

In my rear corner, I remembered I hadn't turned my desk so I could easily see out the alley window. Swinging it around, I sat behind it and it was the way I wanted it.

The place was silent except for the occasional rustle of one of the insurance policies. I switched on my desk lamp. That made two lights in the office, mine and the insurance guy's.

During the day, with all the other renters there, the office was a quiet bedlam. Now it was silent. I could hear the far-off blast of an auto horn from the Strip, half a block away, but it was muted by walls and distance, and it seemed to come from another, more strenuous world.

I wished I had a drink. Maybe I ought to get a bottle and keep it in one of the desk drawers, like the private dicks in movies. Who knows, it might even be good for business. Atmosphere. Give the clients confidence. Maybe they don't trust a P. I. who stays sober, most of the time: they felt they weren't getting as arduous service as they were paying for.

Checking the desk's drawers, I found it hadn't been designed with the special bottle needs of private detectives as a main consideration. There was no deep-drawer to keep a bottle in. Perhaps if I got going again, and began making money, I could get a desk with a drawer deep enough to hold my bottle of booze. It always takes money to make money.

For awhile, I browsed in the local newspaper. There were still a dozen lines on the hi-jacking, but nothing new on it. The only other item that caught and held my attention had Chuck Macy's byline, and told about a shooting victim who had been found in the desert, early the previous afternoon.

For a moment as I read that, I could feel my pulse quicken from sluggish to slightly activated. Sitting straighter, I read it through carefully. The victim turned out to be a small-time hoodlum they had identified as Mindy Kemp. And he hadn't been shot with a rifle, which may have left Ben Crane out of this one, at least.

When I thought that, about the rifle, I had to grin at myself. By now, this Crane fellow not only had twelve or thirteen grand for financing his revenge spree, but at least three handguns he had gotten from Fats and the other two hoods he had buffaloed, out at the filling station south of town. More than enough firepower to shoot Mindy Kemp.

Up front, the insurance man was preparing to leave. Before turning off his desk lamp, he turned and called: "Good night."

I wished him good night and watched him leave. I used the phone, but they told me Brode hadn't yet returned to headquarters. I left my number again.

After going through the rest of the paper, I dropped it in the waste basket beside my desk.

A man was standing on the other side of the desk, watching me.

I caught my breath.

When I could get words out, I said, "Good evening. I didn't hear you come in."

He may have nodded. The desk light didn't illuminate his face, just distorted it a bit. He wore a yellow-checked jacket over a soiled electric-blue shirt, which he hadn't buttoned. I could see his torso, completely hairless but brown from much sun.

"Your name Brandon?"

"That's right."

"Mr. Mercator wants to see you."

"That's fine. Now that you know where I am, you can tell Mr. Mercator where he can find me. He can use any map of the area."

"Mr. Mercator wants you to come with me. Now."

"Tell Mr. Mercator I can't come with you. Now. Tell Mr. Mercator I'm waiting for a vital phone call from my associates in Istanbul."

His brown right hand disappeared somewhere inside his shirt and a blade clicked into sight.

"No," he said seriously. "Mr. Mercator wants you to come now. He wants to see you."

Raising my eyes from the switchblade, I studied the sections of his face that were partially revealed by light shining upward from my desktop, and reflected downward from the ceiling. I used my right hand to slowly scratch my chest through my shirt.

"Tell Mr. Mercator I'll be delighted to see him, here, now, tonight."

"Mr. Mercator wants . . ."

"Oh, hell," I growled. "Listen, go tell Mr. Mercator to come here himself. When you tell him I am unable to leave my office, he will understand and he will then decide to come here himself."

He stared down at me. His hair seemed to be combed in that careful way young men wore it lately. It looked sloppy and quite dirty, but whenever you saw one of them taking infinite pains combing it and arranging it, and it still turned out looking a mess, you wondered if perhaps your own values of neatness weren't somewhat out of whack.

"Mr. Mercator . . ."

"It's all right," I told him gently. "Mr. Mercator is nearby. This is a small city. He will understand. Go tell him to come here, and I will be delighted to see him. It is all right. I will wait here for another half-hour, at least. I wouldn't want to miss meeting Mr. Mercator."

Out of the caves of his eyes, he stared from beneath thick eyebrows below the prow of his forelock.

It took awhile, but finally he seemed to make up his mind . . . what there was of it . . . and turned to walk silently toward the front of the office. He wore dark sneakers and no socks. The skin of his heel tendons wore parallel dirt lines.

Once he was out of the light of my desk lamp, I couldn't see him, and I could never hear him at all.

I gave him a minute before I went to the front of the office and turned on a couple of desk-lights near the entrance door. I wanted no more switchblade morons geniing before me out of the darkness.

Shortly afterward, Brode called.

"Our boy Ben Crane could have done that hi-jacking by himself after all," I said, and I told him why.

He thought about it a minute.

"Okay," he said, "I'll keep that in mind. Chances are, though, I won't be able to use your theory. The higher-ups are convinced it's mob work. Different types have been oozing into town all day. Some of them are nesting out at Florian's, so I guess Wyatt sent for those. But a few just disappeared. We're alerted to keep picking them up, whenever we spot them."

"The name Mercator mean anything to you?"

He was quiet awhile.

"I seem to hear a small tinkle in my brain-pan, but I can't fix wherever it's coming from."

"All right, maybe a tinkle is good enough for a start," I said. "Check into the name, if you get a chance. He might be one of the ones who disappeared."

"Will do. And about our boy, Ben Crane, I'll try to slip what you told me through to someone . . . but you know the way they are, upstairs."

"Yes, I know."

I was just hanging up when I had my second visitor.

This one I saw coming through the door, the brown-and-white shoes, beige slacks, maroon silk shirt, sky-blue silk scarf, and a beautifully tailored jacket that may have been anything between blue- and purple-colored in a daylight sun, but which only confused my optic nerves in the lights of that office.

I was looking at Ted Fenton's tiny pencil-thin mustache, at the almost offensively healthy appearance of his skin, and at his only slightly disdainful china-blue eyes.

"I don't believe this," he marveled.

He stood across the desk with his hands on his hips and examined me.

"What can I do for you?" I asked politely.

"You really are a private detective, then?"

"That's what the license says."

He shook his head in mock wonderment.

"And you do your highly confidential work out of this sort of place?"

His hand fluttered around. Every stick of furniture in the joint seemed to shrink and age slightly, as if they were suddenly ashamed of being the mass-produced junk they had been intended to be from the beginning.

"I sure enough do," I said. "And I think you've got the wrong address. You go outside and turn left, up to the corner. There, you turn either way, and the first place you come to with lights too high for you to spit over, that's where you go in. Go right up on stage . . . they all have stages . . . and start right in with your cute little act. You'll kill them. I sense you've got it, that certain something that only comes along every so often."

"Oh, it has a ready wit," he chortled. "Leaden, but ready."

Weary of it, I sighed.

"Look, Teddy Boy, it's been one of those days, like. State your business and go, or vice versa."

"I'd certainly prefer to go," he said primly.

Shrugging, he checked the steel chair standing at one end of my desk, took a handkerchief from the breast pocket of his jacket and flipped it at the dust he apparently discovered there. I caught a whiff of something when he pulled out the handkerchief. It might have been Brut.

"Is that Chanel I smell?"

He stopped in the act of seating himself and glared at me. His eyes were mean as only blue eyes can get. His mouth pinched in a tad at the corners, but those opaque eyes still stared right at me.

When he spoke, he said tightly: "Don't let whatever you think you see here fool you, Brandon. In my time, and in a place or two, I have watched some people squirm for a good deal less than . . ."

I held up a hand.

"Please, it's late. What do you want?"

His eyes were still frosted, but he seemed to be working on himself. In a moment, his teeth flashed in a smile, white in the tanned field of his face.

"Not a thing. I want nothing for myself."

I stood up.

"Fine. Then we can both go. Thanks for dropping by."

"But Brock Townsend wants some protection," he hurriedly added. "And for some incredible reason, he thinks you can provide it for him."

"Protection?" That surprised me. "From what?"

He chuckled.

"That's what I was wondering. But . . ." He shrugged elaborately. "He wants you. So I came to get you for him."

"Just like that."

He looked puzzled.

"What's that supposed to mean?"

"You waltz in here, snap your fingers, and I'm supposed to go hurrying out, trundling along in your wake, like a poodle you just bought and paid for." I stood staring down at him. "Not this time, Teddy Boy."

"Cut out the Teddy Boy bit," he snapped.

"Shove off."

"Are you for hire or not?"

"I take clients, but not this way."

Waving a hand impatiently, he persisted.

"Are you in business or not? Just tell me, yes or no. If it's no, I can go back and tell him that. It wasn't my idea at all. To me, getting you is getting less than nothing."

He busied himself, ranging his glance around the office, shaking his head in disdain.

"A private snoop with an office that might as well be on the corner of Hollywood and Vine."

Ignoring that, I said: "I'm in business, all right. The client comes and tells me what he wants. He doesn't send his secretary, or his man Friday, or whatever you are to Brock Townsend. If he wants to see me, he'll have to come around himself. He . . . especially he . . . will have to do his own job of selling, this time."

Slowly, Fenton rose. Although he was quick and lithe, he seemed to unfold. He was tall. His eyes were almost level with mine. He peered at me quizzically.

After a moment, he murmured, "That's interesting, that 'especially he' part. Why?"

I didn't bother answering.

After waiting a moment, he smiled and turned away.

"Stay out of dark alleys, Brandon. You never know."

"I do my best work in dark alleys."

He laughed.

"I don't doubt it."

Fenton glided the dark length of the office into the lighted area near the entrance doorway. Then he was gone.

I wondered what protection Brock Townsend thought he could get by hiring me.

Turning off all the lights on my way out, I made sure the door was securely locked behind me before I descended the three corridor steps to the street door.

Outside, I glanced toward the glare of lights along the Strip, half a block away, but I couldn't see anyone who might have been friend Fenton.

My car was parked the other way.

I shouldn't have looked toward the lights. Before my eyes got used to the darkness, I had walked almost to the end of my building, where a vague figure leaned against a tall slim palm bole.

For a second, I thought it might be Fenton, but dismissed that possibility. Then I heard the whisper of footsteps coming rapidly behind me from the alley beside my building.

Spinning around on my left foot, I braced the right foot behind me. His arms were spread wide, reaching for a body-grab.

I didn't put too much into the left, just laced it out, fast. It jolted him. I felt teeth under the center knuckle, so I pulled the punch to keep from getting any unnecessary knuckle cuts.

He was hurt, but his forward momentum forced him to keep coming.

The left hadn't done much more than cut in fast and slow him. He lunged clumsily, trying to straighten up, already turning toward me again, one hand pawing against my chest.

I brought the right around, and I put weight and muscle into it. It crunched into the side of his skull.

He hit the sidewalk, moaning. For a moment, I felt a touch of panic. You can kill a man, hitting him in the side of the skull, if you hit too high, and too hard.

Then I remembered the other one, who had been leaning against the palm tree farther along. I stepped quickly away from the one on the sidewalk and pulled the gun.

Sure enough, there he came. The lights on the Strip were behind me, now. They glinted on the blade in his right hand.

I held the gun out, so he could see it.

"Don't do it," I warned him. "Mr. Mercator wouldn't like that."

Whether it was seeing the gun or because he was alone now, I don't know. But he slowed and stopped moving, and just stood there, panting, looking from me to the one down on the sidewalk, and back to me again.

"Put the knife down," I ordered.

"Mr. Mercator wants . . ."

"First, put the knife down," I told him impatiently.

I felt as if I was caught in some kind of pointless rehearsal for a thirty-year-old vaudeville skit involving a character named Mr. Mercator, who never appeared, but everyone talked about him until after awhile it got to be funny. I hadn't reached the laugh-out-loud stage yet, but I suppose I could get there, if it kept up much longer.

"Put it down on the sidewalk."

After a moment, he stooped and laid the knife carefully on the sidewalk at his feet.

"Now go help your friend."

Going over, he bent above the one on the sidewalk.

"Hey, Chavez, you okay, man?"

Keeping an eye on the two of them, I eased over and put the heel of one foot on the blade of the switch-knife and yanked up on the handle. The blade snapped off, close to the hilt.

Its owner saw what I'd done.

"Hey, you broke my knife."

"It was an accident. I'll get you another one."

"That was a good knife," he said mournfully. He seemed genuinely bothered.

I kept an eye out, up toward the Strip. Now would be a terrific time for a squad car to show. Naturally, none did.

I watched as he helped Chavez sit up. Chavez held one hand against the side of his head above the ear, and the other in front of his face. He didn't moan or make any sound after that first groan, when he went down. Now, he staggered to his feet, shaking his pal's helping hand off. They both stood there staring at me.

I wondered whether I should bother turning them in.

"Have you two got a car?"

Chavez just stood there, staring at me.

The other one said, "Yuh."

"Let's go see Mr. Mercator."

It took a moment for it to get through to them. Then the knife-swinger nudged Chavez with an elbow, and they walked past me.

I kept the gun in my hand as I followed them down the street past my car to an old Plymouth, parked near the corner.

"Get in front," I told them. "Both of you."

Chavez slid behind the wheel and started the motor. It sounded wheezy. Switch-Blade sat beside him. I got in back.

They stayed away from the Strip, once they got across it, working their way through the darker side streets until they reached the highway that went northwest past Florian's. They turned onto that and drove out almost as far as El Rancho Motel, then cut left on the dirt driveway beside the lumberyard and ducked into the alley behind the row of stores.

I didn't have time to see if the old man was still smoking, back in the darkness of his porch.

They drove almost to the far end of the alley before stopping in front of a shack, two short of the end of the row.

It was as black as a faro dealer's heart when Chavez cut the lights.

"Leave the lights on," I told him.

"It'll drain the battery," he growled, in a guttural voice.

"Turn the lights on."

Petulantly, he pulled out the light switch and threw open the door beside him.

"Don't get out."

Swinging his head around, he glared at me, his teeth showing in his broad Indian face, his lips drawn back in a silent snarl.

"I get out first, then you."

We did it that way. I watched carefully as both of them climbed out.

"Now, where's Mr. Mercator?"

"In there," Switchblade said, jerking a thumb over his shoulder at a broken-down shanty that had what looked like opaque paper instead of glass in two lighted windows fronting the alley.

"Go on in," I instructed. "You first, then Chavez, then me."

I didn't want Chavez too far from me. The other one didn't seem especially dangerous, for all his knife act, but Chavez seemed cut from different cactus.

We picked our way across a tiny front yard, which was littered with empty tin cans. The bonehead leading the way was almost to the front door when we heard sirens coming out along the highway from the city. The wailing rose as it came nearer, reached a high sustained pitch as it passed the brick stores separating us from the highway, and went howling north toward Florian's. By the time the siren sound dropped lower, more of them were screaming out from the city after it.

All three of us stood where we were, listening.

Switchblade turned his head and looked at me over Chavez's shoulder. I didn't say or do anything, just listened to the siren racket. It sounded like a regular flock of them, but I suppose it could have been only two or three making that much noise.

They went howling past, sounding as if they were right there in the alley with us, although the highway was easily almost an average city block away.

Finally I told Switchblade: "Go on inside."

Stepping onto the wooden front porch, he opened the door. Light poured out on him and Chavez. We stepped forward into the glare of light. The room we entered was brightly lit. A door in the opposite wall stood wide open.

Following the two of them across the first room, I kept a little to one side, trying to stay out of the dimmer light from the second room. I didn't want to find myself entering a roomful of rough specimens.

A quick glance through the open doorway showed me only a man seated at a big wooden table, over to the right. I didn't notice the girl until I went through the doorway and stepped quickly over to the left to lean my back against the wall.

I still held the .38 down at my side. It seemed a sensible precaution.

The man sitting at the table noted the gun I held, then glanced at Chavez and Switchblade.

He didn't smile. Very seriously, he said, "Thank you for coming, Mr. Brandon."

"After awhile it seemed the easiest thing to do," I said. "You're Mercator?"

He nodded slightly.

To Switchblade, he said, "Bernard, you and Chavez wait in the other room."

To the girl, he added: "You go with them, Roberta."

She was sitting on a porcelain-top kitchen table across the room from Mercator. She paid no attention to him, instead taking me in with her lively eyes. She smiled.

"Hey, Daddy-O, you're kinda cute. I mean, underneath all those bumps and cuts and welts and things."

It took me a moment to recognize her. She was the tiny one at the end of the line of Florian's chorus girls I had seen the day I worked out there, or the half-day. She was the one who had smiled at me.

"You're not so bad yourself," I told her.

Her face was young. Her smile was pert and mischievous. Her eyes twinkled pale blue through the squinched-up flesh around them, whenever she smiled.

She wore a blue-gray sweater, tight as a drum skin over a marvelous pair of breasts. Her skirt was short and too tight, and showed off her legs five or six inches above round knees. Her feet wore black-patent-leather high-heeled pumps. She wore no stockings, and no hat on her ear-length silver-yellow hair.

The skin on the insides of her thighs was very white and smooth-looking.

While I was taking in the unexpected vision of loveliness in that squalid room, I found myself wondering once again how a little thing like her could get work at Florian's, along with the usual long-legged types they always hired.

"Bobbie," said Mercator quietly, "go along with your boy friend. Mr. Brandon and I have business to discuss."

"Say, Brandon," she asked, "have you got an extra dose or two?"

Sharply, Mercator ordered, "Stop that, Roberta."

She ignored him, keeping her eyes on mine. When I didn't answer right away, she made a jabbing motion at the upper part of her left arm with her right hand.

"You know," she explained. "Just a little kickee-o. I'm on horse, or I was, before I got to this tanktown. Now . . ."

She flashed an irritated glance in Mercator's direction.

"Now anything will have to do, Brandon-Daddy."

Her eyes crinkled. The left eye winked at me.

"I'll screw for you," she wheedled, smiling impishly.

She said it so artlessly, that somehow I wasn't repelled by the notion. I couldn't keep from smiling.

"Sorry, Roberta," I told her. "I haven't got a thing with me."

Lightly, she sprang down from the table.

"Oh, Daddy-dear, that's the very end. Not nothing? Honest Injun?"

I shook my head. She was such a tiny little thing, but a knockout. I couldn't take my eyes off her.

"Not even nothing, I'm afraid."

She shrugged.

"Okay, poppa-mia. I still think you're cute, even if you do the square thing."

Coming over to me, she reached up and caressed my cheek with the palm of her hand, and flashed her brilliant joyous youngster's smile at me. Turning, she went through the doorway into the front room of the shack, leaving the connecting door open behind her.

I could hear her husky happy voice talking excitedly to Chavez and Bernard out there.

It seemed a waste.

"Mr. Brandon, you must pardon Roberta," said Mercator. "She is like a lot of these young people, essentially good, but much too wild. I believe it's something called kicks."

Rising, he crossed the room to close the door she had left open, then returned to seat himself again behind his table.

"Please have a seat, Mr. Brandon. I'd like to talk to you."

"I'll stand," I said. "Thanks, though. What did you want to talk about?"

His face was swarthy and wide, the nose and jaw strong looking and prominent. He wore a conservative brown pin-striped business suit, which he hadn't bought at a discount store. He also hadn't bought it recently.

Mercator puzzled me. The two punks he had sent for me didn't seem to be in his league at all. Except for a barely noticeable wilting of the collar of his shirt, he had every appearance of a prosperous man in complete control of a money-earning enterprise.

"I should like you to secure certain information for me," he said slowly. "I will, of course, pay your customary fee."

"One fifty a day and expenses," I told him, to see what he'd do with it.

His lips pursed. Nodding, he took a thin leather wallet from an inside pocket, and opened it in front of him, there at the table. It looked like a limp book that stayed open without spine enough to snap it shut.

Drawing out some bills, he put them on the corner of the table nearest where I stood.

"Will a hundred dollars be all right as a retainer?"

"First, I'll have to know what kind of information you wish me to secure for you."

"Naturally."

Returning the wallet to where he had gotten it, he leaned back in his chair.

"If you're wondering about . . ."

His head tilted toward the door to the front room.

". . . my associates, and my use of this place, I want to assure you that I'm not ordinarily this Spartan. Mr. Chavez lives here, and he has very kindly allowed Bernard and his girl and myself to lodge here, off and on, and to use it as a meeting-place, such as this between you and myself. Strictly temporary, until a certain condition of tension . . . I might even say of danger, which we have encountered in this city . . . has been given sufficient time to disperse itself. Or until I can discover the source of the danger, in which case, I may be able to disperse it myself."

He chose his words with such care, that I couldn't bring myself to tell him he hadn't told me a thing so far.

So I just asked: "Danger?"

"Did you notice a certain article in today's newspaper?" he asked, watching me closely. "About a man who was found shot to death, out in the desert?"

"Yes, I read it. I can't recall his name."

"Mindy Kemp was his name," Mercator said. "I sent him down here, a sort of reconnaissance. Recently I heard that there might be possibilities in this town. I thought I would come by and look into them."

"What sort of possibilities?"

Mercator studied me, with his dark eyes surrounded by a field of finely-lined skin that had seen a lot of desert, over a period of years.

"That," he replied softly, "is part of the information I would like you to secure for me."

I shook my head.

"Mr. Mercator, I'd like to oblige. Believe me, if there was any reasonable way I could earn that bill, I would do it. But I would be less than honest with you if I didn't tell you, up front, that you're whistling into the wind about moving in on anything down here. It just can't be done. Not the way I think you're thinking of trying it."

His eyes continued to examine me. His face was without expression, the lines of it strong, effortlessly aggressive, a credit of a man to whatever grandsire had slithered off a Middle-Eastern wharf into the hold of an America-bound fig-freighter.

"My thanks to you, Mr. Brandon," he said, "for being so frank and open with me. But I will be the one to judge whether I can do what I mean to do. What I need here is a pair of eyes and an intelligent mind, someone familiar with this city, a man who has contacts, here and there. Above all, someone who can find out for me why Mindy Kemp was murdered, and by whom, and if the same fate is intended for me. As you can readily see . . ."

Again, he tilted his head toward the front room of the shack without taking his eyes off me.

". . . the pairs of eyes presently available to me are not also balanced with suitable intelligences, not for this sort of problem."

Or any other sort, I couldn't help thinking.

I shrugged.

"About the Kemp killing, I'll ask around. About solving it, finding out who did it, all I can say is, I'll tap a cop or two that I know, and try to see what they've got on it. Whatever I get from them, I'll pass along to you. More than that, I can't guarantee."

"I cannot ask for more than that, Mr. Brandon, and also, if you could keep a nose to that wind you think I'm whistling into, a finger on the pulse of this community, as it were, the part of it that counts, I would appreciate that. For the next day or two, I need intelligence, in the military sense. I have got to know the . . . ah . . . how the enemy is deploying his forces, what shift of alliances are being made, if any. A man from around here, like yourself, may be much better for that purpose than Kemp would have been, had he lived."

"On that part, again, no guarantee," I told him. "But I will keep an ear to the ground, and pass along whatever I come up with. Is there a phone number I can reach you at?"

"Yes, there will be. I will call you at your office when I have it. If necessary, perhaps I can send one of my . . ."

He chuckled.

". . . my available force to see you."

"Better send the girl," I said. "Chavez hates my guts. Bernard is too dumb to get a message right, a talking message, I mean. I take it we won't be sending anything in writing?"

"No, of course not."

He watched me thoughtfully for a moment before nodding.

"Perhaps you're right. Although her work as a dancer at Florian's doesn't always leave Roberta available, she is, as you say, at least able to remember anything you tell her, and is able to relay the sense of it to me."

I told him the office phone number and that I had no phone at home. He jotted the number in a neat little book, rose from his chair, and came around the table, picking up the money and bringing it over to me. I took it, wrote him a receipt on a page of my spiral-wire notebook, tore the page out and gave it to him. We shook hands.

"I'll have you driven home," he offered.

"Thanks, no," I said. "I can get a cab up at Florian's."

Nodding agreeably, he said, "You can go out the way you came in, then. The alley gives access to the highway at either end, but turning to the left will take you closer to Florian's than going the other way would."

"Thank you. I'm familiar with this area," I assured him.

Going into the front room, I closed the connecting door behind me.

On a mattress over by the left wall, Chavez was banging Roberta. The mattress lay on the floor. Chavez had left his shirt on. Roberta had simply lifted her skirt.

Her legs looked white as milk against his Indian-brown flanks. He wore an expression more purposeful than pleasurable.

Roberta opened her dreaming eyes, saw me and smiled her sudden bright smile, but her eyes remained misted, waiting.

"Hi, Daddy-O Brandon," she whispered. Her voice sounded as thick as cream, without its earlier crackling impish lilt. "See what you're . . . missing?"

"I do, indeed," I leered. "Looks good."

"It's lovely," she sighed.

Her eyes closed. She winced, and shifted her hips a bit on the mattress. Chavez's next stroke was apparently on course once more, and she relaxed.

I crossed to the front door.

Her boyfriend Bernard sat on a cardboard box across from the busy mattress. He was watching them with disinterested eyes, his shoulder blades tilted back against the plank wall. His right ankle rested atop his left knee, and at the end of his limp hand, dangling down from where its wrist lay on the bent right knee, a burning cigarette sent a tiny wisp of gray smoke straight upward in the airless room.

Maybe he'd had his share already.

Eight

Outside, I picked my way carefully across the shack's littered front yard, making a racket by kicking all the tin cans in reach of my feet. In the utter darkness, I swung back some sort of gate and stepped into the alley where I had first run into Fats and Jeff at the far end.

Now I turned the other way, toward Florian's, wondering what all the excitement had been about, when the sirens went howling past, out on the highway. I headed that way.

Feeling tired, I didn't hurry. Maybe my day was done, and I could soon find a cab, get home, and grab some shuteye.

At the end of the alley, thinking of Roberta and her white, white thighs, I turned up toward the highway along the dirt driveway skirting the northern end of the row of brick stores.

Out at the edge of the highway, there was little traffic in either direction, but there was quite a crowd up near Florian's entrance drive. I was too far away to be able to see much, but I stood awhile, waiting for a cab. None passed, so I finally gave up waiting for one, and walked toward the crowd.

I might as well see what was happening, too.

For the first time, I saw some of the tenants of El Rancho Motel. Several of them were gathered by the little corner office, talking to the manager and gaping up the road at the action in front of Florian's. From where they stood, there wasn't much to see, except the crowd and the cars, and the nearest roof-corner of the main casino's top deck, just this side of the towering hotel beyond it. The rest was concealed by the stretch of brush and cactus, which extended twenty or thirty feet in from the roadside.

I strolled on past the motel.

Almost all the car traffic had stopped, up near the casino entranceway. People inside the cars were staring up the entrance drive toward the casino. Once in awhile, one of the cars would ease slowly past a uniformed cop who was trying to keep the crossover through the median clear.

Reluctantly, the cars he shooed on would drive a short distance, then park beside the stretch of wild brush and cactus. A string of about ten cars were parked in a line. Some of their occupants got out and craned their necks, still trying to see what was going on back there.

The uniformed cop noticed my approach and waved me along.

"No standing on this side of the highway, mister," he told me. "You want to hang around, do it across the road."

"What happened? Somebody break the bank?"

"You'll see it in the papers, what happened. Just move along."

Crossing to the median, I paused and looked back. The cop was watching me. He waved me on. Continuing to the far side of the highway, I stood between two of the cars stopped at the roadside over there, and from that vantage point I could see up the entrance drive to Florian's floodlit front façade.

Except for an ambulance parked near the canopied casino entrance, there wasn't a thing else to see.

Some uniformed police emerged from the casino and disappeared around the building, out of sight.

For another minute or so, I stood there, watching, until I thought the hell with it and went back across the road to the median.

The vigilant cop saw me and yelled something. I shook my head and pointed down the road, toward town. He watched me suspiciously. He didn't want me to know any more about what was going on than he did.

Moving fast, a squad car came down the driveway, sweeping me with its headlights when it made the turn onto the highway and headed south. When it went by, I had to retreat back onto the median grass. Then I tried again, and finally got across to the west side of the highway.

Behind me, tires squealed. Turning along the side of the road away from the entrance drive, I kept walking. Ahead, the squad car had come to a stop, then it began backing up. Someone was leaning out a side window on the passenger side.

When the squad car came grinding to a halt beside me, I saw that the man leaning out was Brode.

"Get in here, Brandon," he called brusquely.

The back door of the car swung open. Sliding in beside a uniformed cop, I pulled the door shut behind me. The car started forward again, picking up speed so fast that the tires squealed again.

Beside the driver, Brode turned in his seat.

"What are you doing out here?"

He didn't so much ask it as bark it.

"Heard the sirens. I thought I'd see what the excitement was about."

He stared at me a moment longer than he should have.

As we approached the city proper, the one at the wheel kept his attention on the road ahead. Beside me on the back seat, his partner kept his eyes straight ahead, too.

Facing forward once more, Brode spoke softly into the two-way radio. I heard my name mentioned amid the squawking of the box, but I couldn't make out any of the rest of it.

When Brode was through with the radio, he faced me once more.

"They sent someone out to where you live. You weren't there. Where've you been?"

"Why? What happened?"

"I asked you where you've been," he snapped. His eyes were narrow and his mouth was clamped tight shut.

"What's the matter with you?" I asked, astonished.

The cop beside me stirred, but stopped himself from turning toward me and went back to gazing out his window.

"Never mind what's the matter with me," Brode said evenly. "Where the hell've you been?"

"Wait a minute," I said. "Is this a pinch?"

"It could be, Brandon," he admitted, after a moment's pause. "It's up to you."

"I've been in my office all evening."

"Can you prove that?"

I thought back and nodded.

"Yes. Strangely enough, I can."

"Good. You may have to."

Without another word, he faced forward again and we rode on into town in silence.

The squad car slowed for the Strip, turned onto it briefly, then swung off it again, and we were parking outside the Hall of Justice.

"Come with me," Brode ordered.

I followed him into the police entrance, around at the side of the building. We passed a uniformed sergeant on duty at the desk, and went along a hallway. Brode held the door of an office open and waited until I passed through. Following me in, he shut the door behind him and told me, "Have a seat. Someone will be back for you."

He went out through another door in the room.

A policeman seated at a desk in the little office pointed with a pencil. I sat in the chair he pointed at. He went back to whatever he was doing.

Ten minutes of staring at a desk, a busy policeman, four drab walls with dreary green filing cabinets shoved against most of their lower halves can become rather boring. I had to wait slightly longer than ten minutes before the side door opened and a detective beckoned me into the next room.

When I reached him, he held out his hand.

"Gun," he said. "Sergeant Brode said you packed one."

I handed over the revolver.

"License."

Taking out my wallet, I worked the pistol permit out of its clear plastic envelope and handed that over, too.

"On your way out," he said, "see the desk sergeant outside for both of these."

I nodded.

Pointing across the room behind him with a thumb, he said, "Through that door, go left down the hall to the big door at the end."

I went through the door with him right behind me. I expected him to stay right behind me, but he remained in the doorway, watching until I opened the big door at the far end of the short corridor. As I turned to shut the door behind me, I glanced back in time to glimpse the last of him, as he swung his door shut.

Turning, I found myself in a large office with a rug on the floor. Five men were seated at a desk that didn't need an Executive sign on it. Four of the men faced the desk, behind which sat a large man with a white mustache and a ruddy outdoorsman's complexion.

Two of the seated men facing the desk wore uniforms of the State Highway Patrol, the third was plainclothes, and the fourth was Brode.

"Mr. Brandon?" asked the man behind the desk.

I nodded.

"Please take this seat," he said, pointing to an empty chair directly across the desk from him. "We have some questions to ask you."

I took the seat.

"I'm Sheriff Carroll," he said. Nodding to the two men in uniform, he went on: "This is Inspector McKenzie and Captain Lake of the Highway Patrol, my Chief Assistant Deputy Dillon, and you know Sergeant Brode."

For the first time, I noticed a fifth man, leaning against the wall, off to one side, beyond where Brode sat.

Taking the seat facing the Sheriff, I asked: "Don't I get introduced to him, too?"

I jerked a thumb toward the standee.

The Sheriff's eyes narrowed slightly.

He was a man who could smile in a right enough fashion to get as many votes as he needed to go on getting himself elected Sheriff. He was also a long-time law-enforcement public servant who knew pretty much anything he needed to know about modern crime-solving methods. And he knew people. He knew how to handle them. He handled me by sticking with the business at hand.

"I understand you can account for your whereabouts this evening."

"Yes. Why should I have to?"

"Go ahead and account for yourself," he said. "You'll understand the why afterward."

He was still keeping himself focused on the business at hand, but his pale gray eyes had turned an icy shade paler gray. His thick competent jowls seemed to bulge out a bit more than they had, on both sides of his wide clamp of a mouth.

I accounted for myself, using the insurance man in the front end of my office, and Ted Fenton for the rest of it. I left out the part about Mr. Mercator and his helpers.

For a moment or two after I finished, Sheriff Carroll gave some thought to what I had told him. His almost colorless gray eyes kept boring into mine. I hoped I was drilling mine into his half as well, but I doubt if I was.

"The insurance man part is all right," he decided. "We can check with him. But who is this Fenton? What did he want?"

"He wanted me to go with him to see somebody who might want to hire me. I didn't like Fenton, or his proposition. I told him to send the potential client to me. Then I'd listen."

"And . . .?"

"And he went away."

"What time was that?"

I shrugged, and glanced over at Brode.

"A short time after I spoke with Sergeant Brode on the phone. Whenever that was. Seven? Seven thirty?"

The Sheriff looked at Brode.

"What time was that phone conversation, Sergeant?"

"A little after seven," Brode said. "That doesn't leave him off the . . ."

The Sheriff held up his left hand, the palm toward Brode, and swung his head back to face me.

After a moment, he said, "Mr. Brandon, I am inclined to accept your story. We'll check into it later, but I think you're in the clear . . ."

"Clear of what?"

I felt the eyes of all of them staring at me. I had no choice but to hold onto my patience. They had their little games, and naturally they liked to play them. I was not accustomed to watching that much police brass playing the game all at once, but it could have been worse: they might have brought the Governor along to play.

"Tonight," the Sheriff said slowly, "Leslie Wyatt was shot to death out at Florian's casino."

It took a beat or two for me to take it in. Then I began getting angry.

"So right away quick you think, 'Let's see if Jim Brandon has got himself an alibi.'"

Ponderously, the Sheriff shook his head from side to side.

"Not only Jim Brandon. Anyone walking around within fifty miles of this town we don't like the look of. Within thirty-six hours, there have been three homicides in this jurisdiction. We mean to find out about them. And we're going to find out, too."

"So why me?"

"Sergeant Brode finally got someone to listen to him," Sheriff Carroll said, "about the possible connection of some of these recent homicides with a certain unidentified victim of an assault, some weeks ago."

The man leaning against the wall went around behind the desk and murmured into the Sheriff's ear. Carroll nodded.

"Apparently there has been an identification," the Sheriff corrected himself. "Fingerprints from the military seem to link one Benjamin Crane with the assault victim."

"And you think he did these recent killings?" I asked.

"We don't think anything, Mr. Brandon. We're including this fellow Crane in our list of people we'd like to question.

There are plenty of other people we intend to bring in on this, more than I like. But we want you here, in custody, to supplement Sergeant Brode's possible identification of that assault victim, Crane . . . if he gets caught in our net."

For a drawn-out period, he stared across at me before continuing.

"As I understand it, there are about five people we can use to make the identification: yourself, Sergeant Brode, the doctor who handled his case at the hospital, and one, perhaps two, nurses who worked the ward he was on. We can't drag the doctor or the nurses into the station house to look at lineups for the next twenty-four or thirty-six hours, but . . ."

"Ah!" I said, finally catching on. "But you *can* drag me in for that long, or for as much longer as you might happen to feel like."

The Sheriff's eyes twinkled slightly.

"Well, Mr. Brandon, you are by way of being an unofficial officer of the court, licensed by the State. Naturally, you wish to do everything you can to cooperate with your local law enforcement agencies, don't you?"

The son of a bitch had me beaten.

I nodded. Slowly. Five times.

"Sheriff," I said, "you put it so much better than I could ever hope to. And you are absolutely correct. Of course I want to cooperate with my local law enforcement agencies. I always do."

"I am most gratified to hear that, Mr. Brandon," Carroll said. "Inspector McKenzie will be in charge of the lineups. You will take your instructions from him."

The Sheriff and I both glanced over at Inspector McKenzie, who didn't look either happy or unhappy. He really didn't look anything but imposing in that uniform of his.

I assumed he was one of those who hadn't listened early enough to Brode's idea that Ben Crane, not gangs of intruders or local gamblers, had been responsible for killing Fats and hi-jacking the cash car from Florian's casino.

Swinging his gaze from McKenzie back to me, the Sheriff wound it up.

"The desk sergeant will have your weapon and pistol permit. He will tell you where to keep yourself in readiness, until the Inspector wants you."

That ended my part of the interview.

Getting up, I glanced at Brode, and went out to get my stuff from the desk sergeant. He turned it over and told me to park myself in a little room, just the other side of the squad room. He would let me know when I was needed.

Nine

I didn't have to stay there for thirty-six hours. I wasn't even needed for twenty-four hours. They made me go home after only nineteen hours of it.

They went out onto the highways, in amongst the hedges. They probably tore some of them away from banquets, or from lunch counters, anyway. Maybe some had been inspecting farms, or trying out new wives, when they got the call.

Others they got from gutters, or from alleys, or from whatever they're calling Bush-villes these days. Some were undoubtedly yanked out of whorehouses, whilst the majority had certainly been pried away from some game of chance or one-armed bandit around the town or its environs.

They even brought in an old prospector who hadn't quite managed to get back into the hills fast enough. He kept worrying aloud about his burro, wanting to know why they didn't let him bring the beast indoors with him. I kind of wanted to see the burro myself. It would have been a change, after all those long lines of sleazy humanity I had to check out.

There were the weak, the average, and the strong; the clean, the middling, the dirty, and the abysmally filthy. They came past me in lots of six or eight, or sometimes in batches of ten. They could have been crooks or God-fearing zealots who just happened to forget to shave that morning, and maybe left their auto registration papers in the other suit, or the other car.

They came in an endless stream, angry or irritable or frightened or patient or giggling foolishly. But they came.

And they kept coming.

After looking over more than twenty lineups, I began to get the feeling that the entire population of the state was being herded in slow grumbling masses, waiting until they could file in through the back door of the Hall of Justice so I could take a look at each and every one of them.

I didn't get much sleep. I couldn't. After awhile, I told Inspector McKenzie that I had reached a point where I wouldn't
recognize my landlady, I was so bleary-eyed.

He sent out for some coffee. I drank it, and went on looking them over.

Night ended. Around mid-morning, I was no longer the
only one stuck with the detail. The hospital doctor spent
awhile there. Early on in the afternoon, Brode joined me. He
was hot and sweaty and tired. A bit later, we saw a stocky
woman seated nearby whom I recognized as one of the
nurses from the hospital.

Presently, Brode had to leave. The doctor had already
gone. Awhile later, the nurse went out, too. But McKenzie
kept me there until the bitter end.

The bunches of hapless humanity were taking longer to
collect. Or perhaps the rest of the people roundabout had
gone into hiding until I collapsed or went blind or just died
of boredom from too much coffee and bad sandwiches and
worse cigarettes.

The final group consisted of only three people: a teen-age
kid in black leather jacket and cowboy boots; a ranch hand
who just might have been one of the guys I was trying to pick
out of the lineups, except his top teeth stuck out almost an
inch farther than they should have; and a thin little man who
liked the taste of wooden matches and was a numbers collec-
tor who apparently had the best fade-joint of anyone else in
town to have kept clear of the dragnet as long as he had.

After I negatived those three, I still had to hang around for
another half-hour.

Finally, they turned me loose, just before five in the afternoon. Inspector McKenzie instructed the desk sergeant to
have me call in every two hours on the hour until he told me
to stop, in case they could find any more people to drag up
and across the platform.

Out on the Strip, I stepped back down from the bus I had
almost boarded. I had forgotten my car was parked near my
new office.

Whatever the bus driver yelled at me, I couldn't hear: my ears buzzed for sleep.

After floundering up and down the side streets near the office, I finally located the Ford and bumped my head sliding behind the steering wheel. Twice on the drive home, I nearly racked up. I couldn't seem to hear properly, and my eyelids kept falling down over my eyeballs.

After parking beside the isolated entrance to my furnished room, I think I left the car keys in the ignition. Going up the flight of stairs inside, I fell only once.

Somehow, I made it into the bathroom, dashed cold water onto my face, then washed myself thoroughly, from the waist up. I could have used a shower. I could have used a shave, too, but both would have to wait until after sleep.

I stared at my eyes in the bathroom cabinet's mirror. Tiny pink veins spoked outward from the eyeballs. They looked like pale pink lightning bolts. I was even seeing double. I closed my eyes, squeezed them tight shut, then opened them. Still seeing double . . . except one of the faces in the mirror was smiling.

A small pin-prick of pain hit my upper arm, near the shoulder.

Automatically, I reached around to rub it. My fingertips came in contact with the needle coming out.

Starting to turn, I never quite made it. Whatever they shot into me either worked real fast, or lack of sleep gave their shot a booster shot.

A wave of warmth engulfed me. Grabbing for the edge of the sink, I held on with both hands, but it was no use. The torrent of warmth pouring down on my face pushed me down until I was staring into the bowl of the sink with my jaw hooked over the edge.

For a long moment, my chin caught and held on the smooth wet edge of the sink. Then my head tilted slowly upward until the weight of all that warm water pouring down onto my forehead just pressed so hard that my chin slipped off the sink-edge and I fell backward and downward beneath the foaming swirling warmth of the inundation.

For a time, bright colored lights skyrocketed all around. Then everything stopped. For a long, lazy interval, I floated on the comfortable foam. Then, even that stopped.

Ten

"Hey, Brandon, you up yet?"

"Yes. Be right out."

I put the breakfast dishes inside the disposal unit and started for the front door of the cottage. Halfway there, I paused, puzzled.

How had anyone known to call me Brandon, and why had I answered to the name? And answered as if I knew who called?

"Hurry up, will you?"

"Coming."

I opened the front door. A tall handsome man with a dapper-looking mustache leaned against the porch railing.

"It's about time," he smiled.

"Do I know you?"

Stepping away from the railing, he studied me, shaking his head.

"Every day we go through this routine, and every day I tell you my name's Larry Belton."

Then I remembered.

"Yes, that's right. Belton. Your name was right on the tip of my tongue, but . . . I just couldn't seem to come up with it."

He nodded patiently.

"That's the way it is every day. I hear you made another effort to walk out of here."

"Another?" I couldn't remember a thing.

"Last night. Two of the zoo-keepers found you trying to pick your way around the big rocks, down below, at the edge of the lake. Fourth time. You never quit, do you?"

"Quit what? I don't even recall . . ."

Belton grinned.

133

"I guess that's the funniest part," he observed thought-fully. "You really don't recall any of it yet . . . but you keep reverting to type."

"What type?"

Belton shrugged cheerfully.

"Whatever type you really are . . . or were, before all the hypos and pills and therapy and questions."

He buttoned his light-brown sports coat.

"Come on, Brandon. Let's go down to the commissary. I'll buy you a cup of coffee."

I followed him down hewn log steps and along a gravel path. Other cottages like mine were scattered among the trees, but no cottage was too close to any other. Each was partially sheltered by bushes and carefully tended hedges.

Ahead was a bigger building on a sloping lawn. From this high, only the red tiles of its roof were visible until we descended the slope along the gently curving path and approached it, when the remainder of the building appeared, tan-walled in a Spanish style.

"What is this place?" I asked.

Belton chuckled and shook his head.

"Again? Practically every day we go over the same ground, Brandon. When is Hancock going to cut down on your pills enough so you'll be able to remember things?"

I had to agree with him.

"You're right, Larry. I do seem pretty forgetful. How did you know my name was Brandon?"

"They told me, when they brought you up here to dry out."

"Dry out? Was I hung up on something?"

"Who knows? Most of the people old Townsend-the-pa-tron-of-the-arts lets in here seem to need withdrawal time a lot more than they need peace and enough quiet to get some of their work done. You seem to be in quite a unique with-drawal category, although you sure don't seem like any kind of artist I ever saw."

We climbed steps and went out of the morning sun into a shaded roofed-over terrace that ran along the front side of the commissary. A few people sat or stood in the cool shadows, alone or in small groups. Some were bearded and wore colorful hippie garb. Others wore denims. Still others were in suburban shirts and slacks.

More people were inside the commissary than out front, but they were just as mixed a bag as the ones outside.

Belton paid for our coffees and led the way past a candy and cigarette counter to a south wall made entirely of glass. We sat at a table in the sun with a view of the far side of the canyon, which was still in shadow.

"Who's this Townsend you mentioned?" I asked.

Resigned by now, Belton smiled.

"All right, we'll do it all again, just as if I didn't tell you yesterday and the day before and every day for the last half of last week, too. Brockton Townsend, Philanthropist. His family made their start-up money generations ago. His grandfather formed what turned into Intertex. Brock periodically bleeds from the wallet, trying to buy the world's forgiveness for being rich . . . but he makes certain never to bleed too much. Not that he could. There's too many bucks stuffed into that wallet of his for any one man to give away, no matter how hard he tried."

"And he runs this place?"

"He pays for it, so I suppose you could say he runs it. Sometimes I wonder if he even remembers that he set up this artists colony to house homeless artists."

"Is that what it's for?" I looked around, thinking about it. "It's a nice place to do art work, is it?"

"How should I know?" Belton laughed. "I'm no artist."

"Then how come you're here?"

"I'm here because I *qualify* as an artist. I have exactly the correct prep school background, went to the best art school, and I have a technique that would make a troglodyte salivate. Andrea Del Sarto lives! Therefore, every so often I become eligible to come out here and spend six months or a year working on what we can call a sort of Brockton Townsend Fellowship."

"What do you do when you aren't eligible to stay here?" I asked, fascinated.

"Then I'm pretty sure to be jungled up in some *other* posh little artists' nest, much like this one. The same in purpose, at least. None of them are quite as large-scale as this place."

A tall, powerfully-built young man in slacks and T-shirt came gliding across the vast room and stopped beside our table.

Belton glanced at his wristwatch.

"Here he is again," he murmured. "Good old Gilbert."

"Time for your appointment with the Counselor, Mr. Brandon."

I looked up at his wide smiling face, but I couldn't think what to say.

Seeing me hesitate, Belton said: "Go on along, Jim. You have an appointment every morning, same time. Doctor . . . I mean, Counselor Hancock thinks you'll soon be able to buckle down and do some of your best work." To Gilbert, he murmured: "He still doesn't remember."

Nodding, Gilbert reached down and took my arm. Pulling me gently to my feet, he smiled.

"Come along, Mr. Brandon. You don't want to be late, do you?"

Pulling my arm free, I stood there beside him, puzzled, looking up into his hard, smiling, pale-blue eyes.

"Oh, I'm so sorry, Mr. Brandon," the attendant chuckled. "I keep forgetting you don't like me to take your arm when we're going anywhere. All right, you just come along with me, okay? Just like we do every day."

"All right."

"See you later," Belton called.

I followed Gilbert out of the commissary, down the gentle slope past tennis courts and a swimming pool to a single-story structure, which was simply a smaller version of the commissary building we had just left.

Inside, Gilbert ushered me into an office where a distinguished-looking gray-haired man sat behind a desk.

"You can wait outside, Gilbert," he said.

"Orders are still the same, Mr. Hancock," replied Gilbert. "I'm to stay in here whenever Brandon is here."

He sat me in a chair facing the desk.

"The man is harmless," Hancock said impatiently. "There's no danger at all."

"He made it down as far as the lakeside again last night."

"Again?" Hancock watched me curiously. "Amazing how much the unconscious retains."

"I think there was someone else down there with him," Gilbert said, "but I couldn't find anyone but him. Somebody had to show him how to get down there without breaking his damn fool neck."

Hancock nodded, opening a folder in front of him.

"How's the memory today, Mr. Brandon? Anything coming back?"

I shook my head.

"Your memory is apparently going to require longer to return to its normal condition than is usually the case with the tranquilizer dosage we administered."

Glancing up, he chuckled.

"We are all of us more or less the causes of our own discomfiture, aren't we, Mr. Brandon?"

I smiled slightly, but I didn't say anything, because I didn't know what he was saying.

"You remember nothing yet?" Hancock persisted.

I shook my head.

"Mr. Brandon, will you please tell me that you remember nothing? Don't just shake your head in response to my questions."

"I remember nothing."

Hancock wryly smiled, glancing at Gilbert, somewhere behind me.

"Just like a parrot," Hancock said. "An agreeable parrot."

Gilbert laughed, quietly. The small sound seemed to irritate Hancock, but he kept his attention on the file in front of him.

Turning my head, I saw that Gilbert sat on a chair in a corner.

"You don't remember coming here to the Colony?" Hancock asked.

"No."

"Do you recall yet what happened before you came here, what you did to one of the men giving you your initial medication?"

I shook my head, then remembered I should speak my replies.

"No."

"You don't remember hurting the man seriously?"

"No, I don't remember. I'm sorry I hurt him."

Hancock nodded, watching me with intelligent, sympathetic eyes from beneath bushy gray eyebrows.

"I believe you really are sorry, Mr. Brandon." After studying the file another moment, he closed it. "All right. Yours may only be a temporary condition. We've had late recoveries before, but seldom this late. It may be caused partly by the head injury you sustained during that . . . during the time you were first administered medication. Still, the doctor who attended you claims there was no severe injury. The laceration caused by the blow to your head has long since healed."

He smiled.

"All right, time heals, too. We'll just have to give you a bit more time. How do you feel today, Mr. Brandon? Are you happy?"

After thinking a moment, I shrugged.

"I don't know."

"I'm sorry. I should have asked, are you comfortable? Is your cottage satisfactory?"

"Yes, it's satisfactory."

"Do you suppose you will be producing any work soon?"

"I don't know."

"You're a painter, aren't you, Mr. Brandon?"

"I don't know. Am I a painter?"

"Perhaps you're a sculptor. Your hands look as if they have done their share of the hard work of a sculptor, rather than the more delicate tasks of painters."

He waited, watching me. When I couldn't think of anything to say, he went on.

"Do you wish you could get to work once more, Mr. Brandon? To feel your hands holding hammer and chisel, to twist pliers and cut metal with a small acetylene torch again?"

I thought a moment. He seemed so curious that I told him: "I suppose so."

Hancock laughed.

"That will be all, Mr. Brandon. I'll put you down for another appointment, same time tomorrow. The assistant counselor here will bring you your new medication at bed check." He inclined his head toward Gilbert and rose behind his desk.

I stood, too.

"See you tomorrow, Mr. Brandon. Don't over-exert yourself. You haven't made a complete recovery yet, you know."

"I won't over-exert myself," I assured him.

Chuckling, Gilbert led me outside, and back up to the commissary, where a dark-haired young woman was coming down the steps from the terrace.

"Good morning, gentlemen," she said cheerily, smiling at us.

"Morning, Miss Barclay," replied Gilbert. When I said nothing, he told me: "Say good morning to the lady, Brandon."

"Good morning, lady."

Grinning at Gilbert, she said to me: "See you at the pool this afternoon, Mr. Brandon. Remember, you promised you would pose for me today."

I glanced at Gilbert. He nodded. So I called after Miss Barclay as she walked away along the path: "All right, Miss Barclay."

Placing a hand in the middle of my back, Gilbert shoved me roughly toward the steps leading up to the commissary terrace.

"Go on inside, dumb head," he growled. "It's time for lunch."

When I recovered and straightened, I turned and looked up at Gilbert. Seeing me look at him, he came over and once more shoved me toward the steps, using both hands this time.

"Go on inside, you son of a bitch," he ordered quietly. "I think you're pulling a fake routine, you know that? But don't try the little kid bit with me. I saw you in action, remember? When they first brought you here. Get going."

The second time Gilbert shoved me, I tripped on the bottom step. Sitting there on the third step up, I watched him walk off, uncertain what to do. I wanted to do what Gilbert told me to do: go on up the steps and inside the commissary. But I also wanted to do something else . . . except I couldn't think what it was.

Rising, I watched Gilbert's wide T-shirted back disappear around the nearest corner of the commissary building. After another moment of hesitation, I climbed the porch steps and went on inside.

I didn't have time to get confused about my next move. Across the flagstone lobby, Belton waved at me.

"Lunchtime, Brandon. We're having steak. Hurry up."

"All right," I said, following him into the dining area.

After lunch, we all took a dip in the pool. Miss Barclay came over to where Belton and I were lying at poolside, drying in the sun.

"All right if I sketch you now, Mr. Brandon?"

She held up her sketchpad. It was almost as big as an open newspaper.

"Okay."

I rolled over on my back. I liked Miss Barclay.

She opened the pad.

"I only want to do your hands and arms," she said.

I held out my arms.

Noticing that, she laughed.

"No," she said. "Stay the way you were, just now. Don't pose. Simply settle back and allow your left arm to just lie there."

Lying down again, I raised my head and looked down at my left arm. Long, ropy muscles wrapped around the heavy arm bones. A thick rectangular wrist. A long bony hand.

I wondered why she would want to sketch any of it.

"That's the way," she said encouragingly. "Simply relax. You're just right, exactly as you are."

I turned my head. Through a notch in the nearby bare yellow hills, I could see flat blue water stretching away to more bare yellow hills on the far side, miles away.

I could hear the scraping sound as Miss Barclay drew the sketch on her pad. Once I felt a faint urge to get up and look at the picture, but after a minute I forgot and drifted off into sleep.

In the middle of half-asleep, she helped me put on my shirt and draped my trousers over my legs.

"Too much of that sun isn't good for anyone, Jim Brandon," Miss Barclay murmured from beside me.

Insects buzzed and clicked nearby. A cool wind blew up from the water. I could hear people plunging into the pool. It sounded a long way off.

Larry Belton's voice woke me.

"Excellent, Barclay," he was saying. "You've captured something there. Jackson Pollock's ghost would drool at the way you've gotten that arm."

"Stop critiquing me, Larry," she laughed.

"Come on, both of you," Larry called, from farther away. "Let's get started. We'll miss the dancing . . ."

"Oh, is that today?"

I could hear sounds of her packing up her sketchpad and drawing materials. Opening my eyes, I rolled over.

Belton was partway up the slope, calling to us over his shoulder.

"A short walk will do both of you a world of good. Get up, Jim. The Dryads of Diana the Huntress await."

Stumbling to my feet, I struggled into my pants and followed them up past the commissary to a grove of trees higher up.

It had gotten cooler as the afternoon advanced, but as long as we stayed in the sun, it remained warm. I felt too warm. I wished I had left my shirt off, until we went in among the trees to a grassy bowl. Then it was cool, and I was glad I had the shirt on.

Seated between the two of them, I watched the other people scattered around the dip in the ridge-side.

"Here they come!" Belton said.

"Oh, don't they look lovely!" Miss Barclay cried.

Six young women came out of the trees from the direction of the parking area behind the commissary and began to dance in a slow relaxing way. They moved gracefully, trailing long wispy gauze-like scarves behind and around their bodies as they pirouetted down there in the center of the grass-grown cup they were using as a theater.

Most of the dancers were tall and willowy. The one on the end of the flowing line was short, but she was easily as graceful as the others. Once, she came close to us and swept by where we sat, and she smiled down at me as she passed.

"Daddy-O!" she cried in delight.

Belton turned his head and grinned.

"Looks like you've got a friend."

"Isn't she adorable!" Miss Barclay cried.

"Where do you know her from, Brandon, you old devil?"

"Larry, don't," Miss Barclay cautioned.

"You're right," he agreed. "I keep forgetting: he can't remember yet."

"He might have met her at the casino," Miss Barclay speculated.

"Makes sense." Belton nodded. "These girls probably work there in the main room. Florian's is very big on kulchuh."

"Although something tells me this dance of the Dry-ads wouldn't go over too well at Florian's, not even in the lounge."

Belton laughed.

"And sure as hell not in the main room, except maybe as backup to somebody's act."

"Ah, they've finished. Too bad it's so short," Miss Barclay said sadly. "It really is so lovely."

We watched the line of young women stream up the gentle slope of the glade and disappear in among the grove of trees surrounding it. The tiny girl went last, and, just as she disappeared from sight, she turned her head and smiled at me, and waved her hand goodbye, too.

Belton shook his head in admiration.

"Whatever it is, Jim-boy, you've certainly got your share of it."

He started off after them.

"Where are you going?" Miss Barclay called.

"Find out who she is," he replied. "Be right back."

Miss Barclay shook her head.

"The busy, busy man," she murmured.

Most of the other people in the audience were drifting away, back down the way we had come, toward the commissary.

Gently, a bell tinkled in the distance.

"Supper time," Miss Barclay sighed. "Well, James, it has been a hectic afternoon, hasn't it?"

"It sure has, Miss Barclay."

I helped her collect her sketchpad and the boxes of pencils and nylon tipped pens that went with it, and we joined the others headed down the path.

Belton caught up to us partway there, in the open again. Even that late, the sun still felt warm.

"Her name's Bobbie," he gasped, as he turned and walked along with us.

"Are they putting on another show this evening?" Miss Barclay asked.

Belton shook his head.

"No. They were taking off in a station wagon, when I caught up to them in the parking area. They're headed back down to the casino. That's where they work. This is an extra gig, I guess."

"They are good," said Miss Barclay. "So graceful!"

I went back to my cottage and got out of my clothes and the bathing trunks. After taking a quick shower, I joined the rest for supper.

Afterward, there was a lecture in a hall to one side of the front room of the commissary.

When I woke from my evening after-supper nap, Belton was there to accompany me over to the amphitheater, where everyone sang songs. When Belton nudged me, I joined in on the simpler songs, but mostly I just sat and listened, and watched the sun push the shadow-line higher up the barren yellow hills on the far side of the vast stretch of blue water far below.

At dusk, a heavy hand fell on my shoulder. It was Gilbert.

"Time for your medication and lights out, Mr. Brandon," he said heartily.

"See you in the morning, Jim," Belton said. "I'm going to stay awhile longer."

"All right," I said. "See you in the morning."

"Don't do any more sleepwalking," he laughed. "Gilbert gets annoyed when you sleepwalk, don't you, Gilbert?"

"Not annoyed, really, Mr. Belton," Gilbert smiled. "I just can't figure out how Mr. Brandon manages to pick that lock on the front door of his cottage every night. Nobody can pick a good lock like that in their sleep."

I stood there beside Gilbert, looking up at him, waiting until we were supposed to leave. His lazy eyes gazed down at me.

"Sometimes," he said, "I think maybe Mr. Brandon is putting on a little bit of an act, with his sleepwalking routine. Are you, Mr. Brandon?"

"I don't remember sleepwalking," I told him, frowning as I tried to remember.

With a laugh, Belton returned his attention to the singing, calling out: "Sounds like sleepwalking to me."

Gilbert and I climbed up out of the amphitheater and went along the path to my cottage. The sound of the many singing voices became softer, the more distance we put between ourselves and the singers.

Inside my cottage, Gilbert handed me a pill.

"Here's your medication, Mr. Brandon," he said. "Go on into the bathroom and take it with a glass of water. Then I'll leave you alone."

Going through the main room into the bathroom, I put the pill down on the edge of the sink and ran some water into a glass.

"Fine, Mr. Brandon," Gilbert said behind me.

Turning, I saw he was standing in the bathroom doorway, watching.

"Drink it down," he said.

Putting the glass to my mouth, I drank the water down.

"I'll be going now," Gilbert said, turning and crossing the other room. "I'm locking the front door, Mr. Brandon. No wandering tonight, okay?"

Still holding the water glass, I went to the bathroom doorway and said, "I won't wander tonight."

Just before Gilbert closed the front door, he smiled at me, but his eyes weren't smiling.

He went on out, pulling the door shut behind him. I could hear him put the key into the lock, turning it in the lock.

Back in the bathroom, I put the empty water glass into its holder beside the rack for toothbrushes, and then I went back to try the front door. It wouldn't open.

Good! I couldn't possibly do any sleepwalking tonight.

Getting ready for bed, I quickly fell asleep.

A fist smashing into my face brought me awake.

Eleven

The punch sent me over backward. Stars and a half moon tilted in a dark night sky.

My back hit the ground. The breath whooshed out of my mouth.

It felt like soft sand under my back.

Blinking, I lay there, gasping, trying to breathe again, staring angrily up at the wide figure towering over me against the stars.

Rolling over, I tried to get to my knees.

"I warned you, Mr. Brandon. I told you not to pull any more of this sleepwalking."

Dimly, I recalled whose voice it was. Gilbert. The attendant, or keeper, or jailer.

Struggling, I got to my feet, both hands clutching fistfuls of sand. When I was standing up, I turned to face Gilbert in darkness lit only by moonlight.

Gilbert laughed.

"Don't even try it, Mr. Bran . . ."

Flipping sand into his face, I went in low, drove two up and into Gilbert's gut area. He bent over abruptly, wheezing. Bringing a right around, I clipped him in the side of his head.

Gilbert dropped and lay still on the sand, moaning softly.

Running footsteps approached out of the darkness.

"I couldn't find the other one," he started to say. Then he skidded to a stop. "Gil, you aint supposed to hit the guy!"

He stared down at the still figure of Gil lying in the sand.

I started over toward him. Halfway there, he looked up at me and cried: "You aint Gil!"

He fumbled for something. Moonlight glinted on whatever it was.

Slapping his gun aside, I clipped him, twice.

He wasn't nearly as big as Gilbert. He dropped without a sound or a moan.

Looking around, I saw the edge of the lake nearby. Where I stood was a sort of beach, but the sandy stretch ended against big sheer bluffs that climbed straight up from the water's edge.

I didn't know what to do or where to go.

Distant lights glimmered across the water, but they were too far to try to reach swimming.

"All right," I muttered into the night-silence. "Now that I'm here, what the hell did I want to get here for?"

No one answered, so I turned and tried to find a way along the shore, wondering who the other one was the second man had been unable to find.

Climbing up in a narrow crease between two huge shore-side rocks, I suddenly saw a figure standing above me, staring down at me.

My breath caught in my throat, and all I did was stare up at whoever it was.

"Daddy-O?" a girl's voice called. "Is that you?"

Swallowing hard, I managed to answer.

"Yeah. Who are you?"

"Bobbie. Don't you remember me? In that shack? With Mr. Mercator?"

Suddenly, I didn't have any trouble remembering anymore. I chuckled.

"Remember? How could I forget?"

"Come, let me help you, Mr. Brandon."

Taking her tiny hand, I climbed on up out of the crevice I had been balancing in so precariously.

"Bobbie, what are you doing here in the middle of the night?" I asked, looking around at the desolation piled up all around us, above the edge of the lake.

"Trying to get you away from them," she whispered. "Oh, Daddy, let's get away from those men. I don't want them to recognize me."

"They won't hurt you, Bobbie," I told her, trying to sound reassuring.

"But if they report me, I might lose my job. Hurry."

I scrambled after her through the jumble of sandstone bluffs and enormous rocks, but we didn't seem to be getting anywhere. Finally, I stopped and called after her retreating back.

"Bobbie, will you tell me where we're hurrying to?"

She stopped and looked back at me, then all around at the desolation and the lake water nearby, and she began to laugh, a light joyous tinkling sound that seemed to echo in the silence.

Hurrying back to where I stood, she put her arms around my waist and hugged me. Looking up, she stretched and kissed me, full on the mouth.

"I came here in a speedboat," she whispered. "It's just ahead. Hurry. Let's get out of here, before those two come after us."

That made sense. I had done a quick thorough job on both Gilbert and his buddy, but not so long-lasting a job that they wouldn't be coming to, fairly soon. I hurried along after Bobbie.

When she came up against what looked like an impassable wall, she turned and slid sideways down a sandy slope to the water's edge. I did the same. When I reached her side, she was already untying the bowline of a dark low-slung motor launch she had secured to a pointed rock.

Jumping aboard, she held out a hand to support me, when I floundered over the railing and tried to stay somewhere in the center of the thing. When she satisfied herself that I was settled, she busied herself with the motor, got it started, and we eased away from shore, first backward, then she swung us around, and we headed out into the vast lake.

"Won't they hear the motor?" I whispered in her ear.

To my hyped-up sensory condition at that moment, the launch's engine sounded as loud as a juiced-up jalopy with the cutout wide open.

"Hear this motor?" she asked, her eyes laughing up at me. "Herby says this used to go on smuggling runs, down in Mexico."

I listened to the engine. She was right. In actuality, it purred softly. I had simply imagined it was making an ungodly racket.

"Who's Herby?"

"Runs the boatyard where I rented this beauty." She reached over and squeezed my hand. "You'll meet him in a few minutes."

Looking back toward shore, I couldn't see a thing. No sign of Gilbert and his co-worker, no lights, no nothing.

Facing forward once more, I spent the rest of our short boat trip admiring the way Bobbie handled herself at the wheel. She was splendid, interrupting her concentration now and then to feed me information.

"The newspapers had you missing . . . the police seemed to think you were trying to avoid answering their questions . . . so when I saw you this afternoon, I knew what those people were doing . . ."

"What were they doing?"

She shrugged.

"Keeping you zonked out on pills, right?"

I thought about it.

"Right. Wiped out my memory, too."

"Different pills hit different ways," she said, sounding as if she knew what she was talking about. "Here we are."

She spun the wheel and the launch swung to the right and ran parallel to shore a mile away. After awhile of that, she made another right turn, heading in toward the distant shore again.

Now, for the first time, I could make out landmarks.

Southward, to the left, a big, lighted sign spelled out FLORIAN'S. Straight ahead was a small cluster of lights, but nowhere near as considerable as the Florian's sign.

Beyond Florian's and above the edge of the approaching shore, a wide glow of lights reflected from the sky. That would be the Strip.

"What's that Florian's sign doing over there?" I asked Bobbie. "Did they open another casino up here, too?"

She laughed.

"No, that's their yacht club. Florian's is turning into a pretty big operation."

"Is that where Herby rented you this boat?"

"Oh, no. He's got his own place. It's small, but I like to use his equipment. He takes good care of it. There's his dock now, dead ahead. See?"

I had already noticed the small string of lights she now pointed at. When she eased the launch alongside a wooden dock, a tall slim teenager in a peaked baseball cap came along it from the landward end and helped her tie up.

I managed to crawl up onto the dock without falling into the lake.

"Herby, this is . . . a friend I ran into."

I noticed she didn't give him my name. Herby noticed, too.

All he said was a casual, "Hi."

They strolled ahead of me along the dock, talking desultorily to each other.

"No word about your pal, Ben Crane?" she asked.

"Nuthin'," he replied. "It's weird. The cops tell me they sent some equipment down to the bottom, right about where they found his boat adrift, but they never could locate his body."

"The boat might have drifted," Bobbie offered sympathetically. "From wherever he went overboard, I mean."

Herby nodded.

"True. Coulda been anywhere."

A thought suddenly popped into my mind.

"How long ago did your friend Ben Crane turn up missing? That name sounds familiar."

I tried as hard as I could to recall where I had heard the name before.

They were both staring at me. After a moment, Herby spoke.

"Three or four weeks, I guess. He was gone a few days before I reported it, and another couple days passed before someone came across his boat adrift . . . out there."

He gestured toward the lake behind me.

Three or four weeks seemed a long time. Then I remembered something Belton had said when he first picked me up at my cottage, yesterday morning, something about telling me the same thing over and over, all last week . . .

"Bobbie, have you any idea how long I was . . ." I tilted my head back up the lake. ". . . there at the colony?"

She thought a moment.

"Let's see. Today's Tuesday. The news story about you being missing showed up, oh, not quite a week ago. I've still got it. We can check the date, when we get home."

Three or four weeks might have been just around when my friend Assault had gotten his working-over by persons unknown, before they dropped him in the desert where I had found him.

Finally I had a name: Ben Crane. But why did it sound so familiar? Damn, I wished my memory would straighten out!

Bobbie settled with Herby for the rented launch, and I followed her out of the boatyard to a little sports car parked at the side of the dirt road that gave access to the landing. The sign above the door of the wooden shack that served as an office said, Herby's Boatyard.

Simple enough and easy to remember. It was something I could pass along to Brode, in case I needed extra material to beef up my tale of being drugged out of my skull for most of the past week, during which period I seemed to recall vaguely that I was supposed to keep myself available, twenty four hours a day.

"How do you like it?" Bobbie asked, sliding behind the wheel and starting the car's motor.

"If it's yours, I like it."

Smiling up at me, she reached over and squeezed my hand.

"You like me, too, don't you?"

"Doesn't it stick out all over?"

She nodded, smiling, swung the car around in a sharp left, and drove up the dirt road, headed away from the lake.

"I can usually tell," she said.

"Most women can."

She went on smiling and driving until we reached the paved road. Turning left, she headed toward the distant glow in the sky.

I closed my eyes and tried to relax. Bobbie drove rapidly but smoothly. Once she made a right turn, and then shortly afterward, a left. Every so often I opened my eyes and looked around, then I'd close them again.

Before I would have thought it possible, the Florian's casino sign appeared ahead and approached swiftly. Just short of it, Bobbie glanced across at me.

"Daddy-O, would you mind doing me a favor?"

"Anything."

"Scrunch down so no one can see you. When we pass . . ." She nodded ahead toward Florian's. "Some of the people there know my car . . ."

I squirreled down as far as I could, until we were past the stretch of lights.

Up ahead, El Rancho Motel looked familiar.

"There aren't that many jobs I qualify for, in a town like this," she said, by way of explanation.

She drove past El Rancho Motel and then the string of stores in the brick building.

I looked at her curiously.

"You're not going to . . . your place?"

"My place?"

I jerked my thumb back toward the alley behind the row of stores.

Throwing her head back, she laughed, a rich peal of laughter, full of delight.

"No, Daddy-O, I don't live in that shack. I just . . . play there. Among other places."

Nodding, I faced forward, feeling ridiculous.

She lived in the new part of town, in a garden apartment with a parking area behind it. Locking the car, we walked toward the rear entrance, her hand in mine as naturally as if we had known each other forever.

"I'm going to slip you in quietly," she whispered, when we were inside, going up the stairs to the second of three floors. "Joyce . . . my roomie . . . well, it's best not to wake her up. She's . . . nosy. She might remember your face . . . from last week's newspaper picture of you."

"Makes sense."

We slipped into her apartment and along a hall past a closed door on the left, a living room, then a kitchen on the right, and finally a bathroom, also on the right, and the door to Bobbie's room on the left.

Inside there, we undressed like conspirators, which I suppose we were. Or at least I was. When I was ready for bed, I stood beside the only one in the room, a big double bed.

"Get in," she whispered beside me, giggling. "I won't hurt you."

I got between the sheets, and a moment later, she slid in from the other side. Then she was snuggled up against me, one arm wrapped around me. When she was comfortable, she sighed, as if she was finally home with the only person in the world who mattered.

I began to relax. I was so keyed-up and worried about what I was going to do next, that I didn't think anything could happen between me and this little friend beside me. But the old urge came out of nowhere, and she smiled with delight when I began making love to her.

"Daddy-O, you love me!" she chortled when I went in, sounding as if she was completely astonished that anyone could love her.

I couldn't help chuckling.

"You sound surprised."

She nodded.

"You're right. I'm not surprised. I knew you loved me."

When the lovemaking ended, she went out to the bathroom first. Then she was back and I used the facilities.

In bed again, she was snug up against me, whispering.

"Do you still love me?"

"It's only been a few minutes," I protested playfully. "How could I not still love you, Roberta?"

"All right, then," she murmured sleepily. "Just making sure. I want you to love me forever, Jimmy."

"I will. I'll love you forever."

"Promise?"

"I promise."

"Say 'I promise to love Bobbie forever,'" she insisted.

Very seriously, I said it.

"I promise to love Bobbie forever."

"There," she whispered faintly, stretching up and kissing me on the cheek. "Now I can sleep."

And she did, falling asleep almost immediately. And shortly afterward, around two or three in the morning, or whatever it was, surprisingly enough, so did I.

Twelve

Vaguely, I remember Bobbie whispering something in my ear about me phoning for a cab. Then she was gone, and I drifted off to sleep again.

Once I heard the bedroom door open. A young woman was standing there.

"Oh, sorry," she smiled. "I thought you'd gone already."

She left, closing the door after her.

It took a few minutes, but the message finally got through to me. I got out of bed and used the bathroom across the corridor. The wash-up felt good, but I could use a shave. It would have to wait.

On my way out, I passed the open door of Joyce's room. She smiled out at me.

"Sorry I rousted you out," she apologized. "But I've got to leave for work soon."

"It's all right. I've got places to get to, myself. What time is it?"

She checked a clock across the room.

"Two-fifteen."

"Wow! Later than I thought."

"Bobbie left a number beside the phone," she called, as I went along the corridor. "In case you want to call a cab."

"Thanks, Joyce. I'll get one up on the Strip."

The walk over to the Strip was more of a walk than I expected, but I was still accustomed to walking long distances, so it was no hardship.

First, I got a shave. That was a morale-booster. Then I had a late breakfast, right in front of a municipal bus stop.

Two-thirty or three in the afternoon would have been a strange time to be having breakfast anywhere else, but not in that kind of town.

I caught a bus down to the southern end of the Strip, before it begins making the big turn from southwest to due west. By some miracle, my car was right where I had parked

155

it, a short distance from the end of my street, beside the adobe wall fronting the non-existent sidewalk, just short of the front door.

Instead of going on inside, I hesitated beside the Ford.

There were three things on my list of priorities: get into a change of clothes, pay my respects to Sergeant Brode before he had me dragged in to pay them, and take care of what had been nibbling away at the back of my brain, waking and sleeping, since Bobbie and I turned in at three o'clock that morning. I was worried about Herby, and I couldn't pinpoint exactly why.

Finally, sighing with resignation, I slid behind the wheel, fished under the dashboard for where I hang the car key chain on a knob under there, out of sight, found the keys already in the ignition, and started the motor.

It was only afterward, at the corner turning onto the Strip, that I remembered I had failed to check the heap for a bomb.

Grinning, I shook my head. Apparently I was no longer much of a priority with the crowd who had arranged for my little sabbatical, up at the Arts Colony.

After the Strip had completed its big swing westward, I turned northward onto the road to Florian's, hurrying along, passing the lumber yard, then the dirt road leading back past the south end of the brick building containing the row of stores . . . a no-name fast-food place, a hardware store, a pawn shop (and what casino the size of Florian's wouldn't have at least one pawn shop within easy walking distance?), a deli with take-out for the lesser help up at the nearby casino, a dry cleaners . . . and at the northern end, the other dirt driveway giving access to the row of shacks back there, out of sight of the highway. Then El Rancho Motel fell behind, the stretch of brush and cactus, and finally the casino and hotel combination.

When all of it was behind me, I settled down to making mileage. At the east-west crossroad, I cut over past the northern end of the Strip to the lakeshore highway, opposite the lakeside state-park for picnickers. Making a left, I presently passed the yacht club, slowing to read the metal plaque, which discreetly revealed what was behind the wide-open gate with the guard's kiosk beside it: Florian's Yacht Club, S. Preston, Chairman.

Okay, nice and respectable. Respectable is good, like greed.

Finally, I reached the road giving access to Herby's Boat Yard.

Turning in, I went slowly and carefully along the dirt drive, until I nosed the Ford down the final slope to the flat stretch, where Herby's cabin was perched at the shore-end of his wooden dock.

A gentle evening breeze blew in across the water.

I got out of the car, peeling the shirt and T-shirt away from where sweat had stuck both to my back, in the drive up from town.

No one was about. A few launches were tied up to the dock, but there was no Herby anywhere to be seen.

I peered inside the open doorway of his cabin.

"Herby? You around, man?"

No reply.

I strolled out along the dock, and just as I did, far off to the south along the lakeshore, the Florian's sign was lit at the yacht club. It wasn't too impressive, with the last of the day-light still competing with it, but later, in the dark, it would look like something special.

One of the tied-up boats wasn't tied-up too well. Bending, I re-tied the line securing it to the dock post.

"Herby?"

Still no response.

I thought of my three priorities, and of having decided this was the one that was the most important. Now it looked as if I had driven all the way up here for nothing.

Turning to go back to shore, I noticed a line out at the end of the dock. It was secured to the last dock post on the left, but there was no boat beside the dock that it was holding.

Strolling on out there, I examined the line. Sure enough, it was taut, stretching at a steep angle down into the clear lake water.

"Don't tell me one of Herby's boats went under," I muttered.

Leaning over, I peered down into the water. It was so clear down there that you could see quite a ways. I followed my line of sight along the line until it revealed what it was tied to, twenty or thirty feet down: Herby.

I had sense enough to get out of my shirt, T-shirt, pants, shoes and socks. Then I went in and down, hurrying, trying to reach him, even as I realized there probably wasn't all that much of a hurry, not anymore.

I was right. When I got down to where Herby was, his empty open eyes told me Herby had all the time in the world now.

The line fastened to the dock above had been looped around his body, under both armpits. Another line fastened both ankles securely, and that one stretched down into the lake's depths, out of sight. Both his hands had been tied behind his back.

There wasn't anything I could do. I didn't touch him. I simply drove my arms furiously, trying to reach the surface, where I cursed steadily, while I got my shorts off and put on the rest of my clothes. Back in the Ford, I hooked the wrung-out, still-dripping shorts on a wall hook behind the seat back, on the passenger side.

Herby may have had a phone there, but I wasn't about to use it, not to call the police. If there were any fingerprints to be found anywhere in his cabin or out on that old dock, I wanted their forensics team to get nice clear copies of them, and find out whose they were, without any messing up from me.

The first phone I came to was located in the picnic area beside the road, some distance past Florian's yacht club entrance.

I called Florian's casino, asking for Joyce. They gave me the usual runaround they always do, when you try to contact one of the dancers, but I finally convinced them it was a legit call.

"Hullo?"

"Joyce?"

"Yes?"

"This is the man who slept too late this morning."

She laughed.

"Hello. Bobbie's friend."

"I've got two messages for you to get to Bobbie. Very important messages. Tell her the sailor she saw last night has left town and won't be back."

"What's this sailor's name?"

"Joyce, you don't want to know his name. Bobbie will figure it out."

"What's the other message?"

"Tell her to get down to the Hall of Justice and find a detective sergeant named Brode. He'll take care of her. Got that? The sailor is gone and won't be back, and she should find Brode. He'll protect her."

"God, this sounds heavy."

"It is heavy, Joyce. As heavy as it can get."

Hanging up, I called the cops, told them what and where and who I was, and got back in the Ford and headed north for Herby's boatyard again.

A police car passed me on the way. I saw him turn in out of sight along Herby's entrance road long before I could do the same.

When my Ford dipped down the last slope and I secured a parking spot there at the foot of the hill, where I could get back up and out of there without a lot of official vehicles hampering a quick exit, both cops were already out on the dock, peering down into the water.

Thirteen

It was long after dark before Brode could find enough time to get back to me.

I waited in the same little office next to the squad room where I had put in all those hours between line-ups. When Brode finally opened the door and waved me out into the big squad room, most of it was empty. Everyone was out following leads, trying to work out what and who had happened, up at Herby's Boat Yard.

"Sit," Brode said, slumping wearily behind his desk.

I took the seat facing him at the end of his desk.

"You look bushed," I observed.

He nodded.

"I am bushed."

Shaking his head, he sighed, then straightened and looked across at me.

"Funny," he said, "there were some days when I just wanted to get my hands on you and toss you into the tank . . . when you didn't report to Inspector McKenzie the way he wanted you to."

"I explained that," I said quickly. "Some of Wyatt's strong-arms stuck me full of drugs, and next thing I knew, I was pretending to be an artist or a sculptor at some artists colony, up near the northwest end of the lake . . ."

"I know, you told me," he interrupted. "But how could we know? McKenzie was having kittens, for awhile there." He stopped and stared at me curiously. "Are you planning on filing a complaint . . . about that artists colony?"

"You think I should?"

He shrugged.

"Hard to prove, kidnapping. Everyone you saw up there was either an employee or a guest. Not likely either sort is about to back up your story of being kept under some kind of mind-stopping drug. It'd be a lot easier for them to prove you insinuated yourself in there under false pretenses, like you were an artist or something . . ."

"Sure," I jeered. "And what was I doing with all this insinuating? Why was I doing it?"

Brode spread his hands.

"How should I know?" He grinned. "Maybe you always had a secret yen to paint, or sculpt."

"So I guess I won't be filing a complaint, then, right?"

"Might be best not to," he agreed. "It won't be a total loss. You've clued us in that there might be something a bit strange going on up there. We'll be able to keep an eye on them for awhile, see what happens."

After thinking about it, I had to agree.

"Maybe it's a new way people like Wyatt take care of people they don't want around too much, making noise," I speculated. "What better place for a potential witness to disappear in, for awhile, getting his pills and unable to remember his own name, unless people keep telling it to him every morning."

"Better than killing the witnesses," Brode observed.

"Oh, sure."

Grinning, he held up hand.

"All right, don't get ticked off about it. We might not be able to do anything about that place right now, but we know Townsend owns it, and it's a pretty good bet the hard knuckles who keep things under control at places like Florian's are tight as a tick, up at that artists colony."

"And they might be a lot closer than that to Herby's murder," I pointed out.

"I'll need clarification of that," Brode said.

"When Roberta and I took off in the launch she brought, we went straight out from shore, then we turned downlake. I was still half out of my gourd, so I didn't think about covering our tracks, and Roberta is only a dancing girl at Florian's. She wouldn't know the first thing about that sort of precaution."

"Meaning?"

"Meaning we left the running lights lit on the launch. Anyone back at the artist colony, one of those two I clobbered, all Gilbert and the other one had to do was watch our lights go straight across the lake partway, turn south two or three miles, and then turn back in toward shore."

Brode nodded, staring across the nearly empty squad room.

"I see what you mean," he said. "You practically drew them a map showing where you were going."

"Right. We went straight in to Herby's Boat Yard. Florian's Yacht Club is several miles farther down the shore, south of there. Except for Herby's, there was no place else we could have been going."

"And between the visit you and this Roberta paid Herby early this morning, and when you got back there late in the afternoon, unknown persons arranged for poor Herby to take a real long drink of water, right beside his dock."

"By the way, have you heard from Roberta yet?" I asked.

Pulling himself out of his thoughts, he frowned.

"Why? Should I have?"

"I phoned the gal she shares an apartment with, here in town," I explained. "They both work at Florian's casino, as dancers. Name's Joyce. I told her to tell Bobbie to get in touch with you, here, because of what had happened to Herby."

"You told this dancer about the murder?"

"I told her in code," I said quickly. "Something about the sailor Bobbie saw early that morning left town and wouldn't be back . . ."

"Oh," he said, settling back in his chair. "Okay. For a second there, I thought you were telling civilians about a murder case before you even reported it to us . . ."

"You never heard from Bobbie, then?"

Reaching for his message box, he riffled through it. Shaking his head, he put the messages back.

"Nothing from a Roberta." He eyed me for a moment. "You're really worried about her?"

I spelled it out for him.

"She works at Florian's. That means, they have access to her, whenever they want. They know where she lives, who her friends are . . . the works. The only one who can protect her is me, or you. Mostly you."

He grinned.

"You better believe it. Okay, give me her home address. I'll have a car drop by there and bring her in . . ."

"And don't forget the casino," I reminded him. "She's probably there at work right now."

"Casino, too. I'll get right on it. Be back in a minute."

He went out the door at the far end of the squad room. In a couple of minutes, he was back.

Seated across from me once more, he shook his head.

"Although why you're so worried about her, I don't quite understand. How could they connect her with helping you escape their artist colony up there last night?"

Astounded, I stared at him.

"Brode, they had all the time they needed to ask Herby any questions they wanted to before they sent him down into the lake tied up like a sacrificial capon."

Brode slumped lower in his chair, nodding his head tiredly.

"Herby was a good friend of Roberta's," I went on. "But from what I saw of him, I don't think he was tough enough to hold back any information they might have wanted out of him. Like who was it that dropped in on him at two or three o'clock in the morning . . ."

"You're right, Brandon. I didn't think of that. I guess I'm just tired. Things begin to slip past me, after a certain point."

"What about me? What do I do now?"

"Hell, go along home. Stay out of this. You handled the murder okay. Don't spoil it by messing around anymore. We'll give more than a simple looksee at that artists colony, now you've made the connection about them being able to see where your launch went, after you and your girl friend got out of there."

His phone rang. He picked it up and listened. His eyes began opening wider. Incredulous, he shook his head, even as he began taking notes.

When he hung up and stood, I stood up, too

"What was that about?" I asked.

"Big Sal Preston just got a rifle bullet through his face, up at Florian's Yacht Club. Staring out his office window at the lights across the lake, he gets it, boom! right in the kisser."

"Sounds familiar. Wyatt on the roof of the casino, the last time."

Brode's eyes were angry when he glanced at me.

"You're damn right it sounds familiar," he snapped. "It's that Ben Crane guy again. You wanna know what else went down, up there at that yacht club, awhile ago?"

"Isn't Big Sal getting whacked enough for one night?"

"That doesn't even start it," Brode snarled, coming around the desk and heading for the far end of the squad room, with me scuttling along beside him, trying to keep up. "When the security people ran down to the docks after whoever was out on the lake a few hundred feet, still blasting away with his rifle, one by one they jumped into the line of launches tied up there, and one by one they went tearing out of the marina after the bastard. And somewhere between the hundred and two-hundred foot mark, they blew up, one right after another. The son of a bitch must've rigged every one of those boats to blow . . ."

"That's why he stayed out a ways," I gasped, "taking pot-shots at them the way he did. He was drawing them after him."

"Huh?" Brode turned and looked at me as we burst through the doorway and hurried along the corridor. After a second's thought, he nodded, his mouth grim. "I wouldn't put it past that guy."

"This time it really looks like Ben Crane," I said. "Herby was a friend of his. Maybe this is his way of . . . expressing his disapproval of what was done to Herby."

Brode stopped and thought about that.

"Brandon, you may have something there," he muttered. He nodded, his eyes fierce, his face dark and angry.

"It all fits," I went on. "Crane went into those tunnels over in Nam, a work that certainly involved setting and defusing booby traps. Meaning explosives. Here you have . . . how many? . . . four or five motor launches being rigged to blow up, almost by the numbers . . ."

Brode started moving again, still nodding.

"You bet. Crane fits this modus like a glove."

"Okay if I go along with you?" I asked. "Maybe I can . . ."

"No," he yelled over his shoulder. "Stay out of it. I mean that, Brandon. Keep clear. You've done fine. We'll do what's needed, from here on."

"Okay," I agreed, stopping where I was and watching him disappear around a bend in the corridor, on his way outside.

I felt the letdown. I wanted to go along, to follow the hunt for Ben Crane. Then I shrugged. Brode was right. I was a civilian. I had done what I could to help. Now all I had to do was stay out of it and let the cops do their job.

I headed on over to Bobbie's place. No telling how long it would take the cops to get there to see if she was home.

It wasn't a long drive, but I found myself exhausted before I was halfway there. Maybe I was catching Brode's overworked syndrome. Or I could still be reacting to after-effects of those pills they'd been stuffing me with, up at the artists colony.

When I drove into the street where Bobbie and Joyce lived, a squad car was just pulling away. A woman in a housecoat was watching them drive off. As I eased in to the curb, she was turning away, headed indoors again.

"Was Roberta home, ma'am?" I called.

She turned and gaped at me. Apparently not impressed by what she saw, with a suspicious look on her face, she asked: "Roberta who?"

I got out of the car, trying to look harmless, but not too sure how to manage it.

"I asked Sergeant Brode downtown to check and see if your tenant was home," I explained to her. "I just now saw the police leave, so I thought perhaps they might have been the ones he sent to make sure she's all right."

Her suspicions somewhat allayed, she came a step closer to where I was standing beside the Ford.

"No one was home," she said. "Neither of the girls was there. Both of them are off working, at this time of night. They're good girls."

"You're sure they're not here," I insisted.

"Positive," she said. "I let the cops in. They wanted to be certain."

"Okay, then," I said, getting back behind the wheel. "It's best to be certain. I was worried. Glad to know the Sergeant got his officers out here this quick."

"Are they in any trouble?" she asked, approaching the car. "Joyce and Bobbie are both real nice girls."

"I hope they're okay. Thanks, ma'am."

Not wanting to have to give her any long-drawn-out explanations, I drove off.

The drained feeling was still with me, so I stopped and got some supper. That helped some, but when I parked the Ford at the end of my adobe walled building and got out, I still felt as if I'd been dragged behind a herd of stampeding buffalo.

Blowing at the top of the flight of stairs as if I had just climbed a rock face, I unlocked the door to my room and stepped inside.

Smiles was standing off to one side. When I shut the door behind me, he jammed a short-barreled revolver into my ribs, hard.

"Oooph!" I blurted. It was all I could think of to say.

"About time you got back, Brandon," he said. "You kept us waiting in this dump of yours a lot longer than I like."

"Just once," I gasped, rubbing my side, "I'd like to come in here and not find your smiling face waiting for me."

He grinned cheerfully and said: "Don't worry, big guy. This'll be the last time."

There was another one in front of me, a hard, pale, almond-eyed face. Its owner held a big .357 Magnum, which he seemed to be able to handle.

"Elephant season doesn't start till autumn," I grunted.

"Huh?" Ridges and knobs under the new one's skin stretched it taut, all over his face, so that it seemed to have no flesh, just bone and knotted muscle and ligaments. He looked from me to Smiles.

"He means your cannon," Smiles explained. "He's a comic."

"Oh, that's it?" He turned back to me and his left fist lashed out and clipped the side of my jaw. I hardly felt it.

"Easy, Val," chuckled Smiles. "They don't want any marks on the body."

"If that's the hardest he can hit," I said, "they've got nothing to worry about.'

"Oh, you want some more?"

Val stepped closer, peering up at my face, tense as a pulley cable, his peculiar eyes flashing.

Behind me, Smiles gave me a shove toward the door.

"Come on, let's blow," he growled. "I'm sick of this hovel. Check him for metal. He carries under the arm."

Val took my .38 and tossed it onto the bed. Sneering at me, he spat on the floor.

"A character!" he piped. Turning, he went out onto the landing and down the stairs.

"Follow along," Smiles instructed cheerfully. "Don't do any yelling."

I followed along.

The entire scene felt as if I had been through it before, and with almost the same characters playing the various parts. Except for Val, of course. He was new in the cast.

When I stepped out into the same evening I had thought I'd left behind me, two minutes earlier, there was the same sedan from before, with Jeff behind the wheel.

I couldn't help but laugh.

"Now the original cast is complete, almost," I chortled.

For some reason, I felt giddy. Everything seemed funny.

"Except the budget's gone up. The backers have given us Val as a spear-carrier for this out-of-town production."

Jeff got out, glanced quickly up the street toward the Strip, opened the back door and motioned me in.

"Move it," he told me.

Inside, I sank back on the soft, comfortable seat. My eyes closed. The door slammed shut and my eyes opened.

Smiles went around the car and crawled in through the doorway on the right side, shoving me over on my side of the car.

"You take up too much room, Brandon," he said good-naturedly.

Jeff swung the car smoothly around and headed toward the Strip.

Absently, I examined the back of his thin head with its dark gray straw fedora tilted just slightly to the left. My eyes closed again.

From what seemed like a great distance, Smiles said mockingly: "That's the way, Brandon. Just relax and enjoy the ride. It's gonna be a long one."

I took his advice. I fell like a stone into something less than sleep, in which I was somewhat aware of the car going along smoothly through the night, and, at the same time, I seemed several removes from being one of its occupants. I would wake fitfully, lifting heavy eyelids now and then, to check and see where we were, as if I was taking a bus trip, and didn't want to miss my stop when I reached my destination.

The Strip went flitting by first, a kaleidoscope of lights whirling past. But I was used to the Strip. I saw it every day and most nights. I was used to it . . . wasn't I?

In my quarter-coma, I smiled wisely. Could anyone ever get used to it? All that glitter slathered over the greed and grime of humanity?

On my right, Smiles sat holding the snub-nose gun with his right hand resting on his knee. He didn't seem specially alert, but with a single twitch of that hand, he could turn that relaxed-looking pistol and blow a hole right through me.

"Where we headed?" I murmured sleepily. "Florian's?"

"Not this time," Smiles replied. "Down Mexico way."

"Cut the talk," Jeff growled. "The less he knows, the better."

Smiles laughed.

"Why? Who's he gonna tell?"

Sure enough, when Jeff stopped for the light at the highway junction, and it changed to green, instead of making a right turn up to Florian's, he made a left, which led down past the gas station where Ben Crane had begun his war against these people.

"All roads lead to Florian's," I pronounced, letting my eyes close again and drifting off. "Almost."

When Smiles commented delightedly, I heard his voice as if it was coming from a long way off.

"Hear that, Jeff? The guy sounds like a press agent for the casino, don't he?"

The next time my eyes floated open, I stared through the haze of my eyelashes at the highway arrowing ahead, straight through the open desert, the darkness sliced far ahead of us by the headlight beams.

Up in the front, Val's flat mid-western voice was going as a kind of permanent undertone, punctuated occasionally by the lower voice of Jeff. Most of it I heard clearly, but I paid no attention to any of it, not consciously, until Val brought up how Big Sal Preston had been killed.

"That I don't get," Val said, puzzling over it. "After what happened to Wyatt on the roof of the casino, here Preston is, like the rest of us, on the watch for some guy, and he gets it from out on that lake, right there in his office, admiring the view. If I'd 'a' been in Preston's shoes, I wouldn't 'a gone anywheres near a window, *any* window. Not till they nailed that bastard. Him and his rifle!"

"Maybe Big Sal forgot," Jeff suggested.

"Forgot?" Val shook his head, baffled. "Back east, they'll never believe it, when I tell them."

His harsh laughter sounded not unbearable, inside the car. I wondered if there was some sort of sound-proofing built into the interior, or sound-suppressing system.

"They'll wonder how you guys manage to run things out here at all," Val went on.

"Okay, okay, Val, lay off," Jeff muttered. "We know how hotshot you Big City boys are, on account of you keep telling us."

"Oh, hell, Jeff," said Val. "I'm not razzing you, but don't it sound like one of them cowboy movies they used to make? Don't it? Be honest, now. Lone cowboy goes after the cattle rustlers, just him and his gun, all by himself! Hah!"

If Jeff replied, I didn't hear it. Time for my instant nose-dive into oblivion again.

Way back in my conscious mind, I suspected that all I was going through here was withdrawal from the pills I had been taking, up at the artist colony. There was also a hazy awareness that I ought to do something about this ride I was being taken on. What was it Smiles had said: this was the last time? Why wasn't I concerned about that?

Leaning back into the comfortable seat as the big car tore southward through the night, I filled my lungs with air. Every so often, I came out of my peculiar torpor, perhaps for only a second or two, and I would watch the ghostly sage fleeing past beside the road, and up in the sky, the stars remaining as far away as they always did.

Like a continuing refrain, which seemed hugely amusing to me, I would wonder how Jeff and Smiles and this Windy City windbag Val and all his out-of-town friends they'd pushed the panic-button for and brought in as reserves, how had they all managed to avoid getting stood up in those line-ups the boys at the Hall of Justice had kept me staring at, through a night and a day, a week ago?

I couldn't help thinking of all the special deputies and state police roping in everyone within fifty miles who wasn't

carrying a sign saying Jesus Saves! while all the real specimens they were looking for were probably eating meals
prepared by an imported slum-gullion of a cook, probably
whelped on stone waterfront steps at *Le Havre* and now calling himself a French chef. They weren't hiding in alleys, or
crouching in cheap motels, not anymore. Now they were in
the houses of the rich and famous. Some of them were rich
and famous themselves. They didn't worry about line-ups
anymore. They had too many lawyers platooned in front of
them, taking care of that sort of thing.

My mind kept soaring off and circling around and then
returning to that picture of the law running around, roping
in jackals and coyotes, while the wolverines looked silently
down from the heights, well above timberline.

For some reason, I could not seem to stop enjoying the
humor of that picture.

The two men in the front seat droned on.

"How're those other creeps making out?" Val was asking.

"Most of them were nothing," Jeff replied. "The cops did
the work for us, marching them around in circles. Probably
bounced half the bastards out of the state, by now."

"What about that Mercator guy? I hear he's a shrewdie."

"He's probably been dusted already," Jeff said. "I heard it
was tonight."

Val laughed.

"DeMerra don't like Mercator. Got a screwing from him
once, up in Dune City. Never forgot it. He in Wyatt's shoes
for keeps down here?"

"If they want him there."

Eyes wide open, now I was completely awake. No
more drifting off into my dream world. Through my entire
body, something wet and colder than liquid ice flowed and
swirled.

Val laughed suddenly.

"I wonder if that Lanson guy uses a chopper on them in
that shack they're holed up in?"

"In the alley, you mean?"

"I hear Lanson's been dying to break in that juice gun on someone. I bet he uses it on them."

"Hell, no," Jeff scoffed, almost under his breath, sounding exasperated. "How much do you characters think you can get away with out here?"

A sheet of flame went roaring through me. I swung the left around in a hard tight loop, smashing it into Smiles' breast-bone, where the nerve is. His scream sounded like it was trying to tear his throat apart getting out. He cringed against the seat cushion almost hard enough to push his back right through it.

"Hey!" Val asked, glancing over his shoulder. "What gives back there?"

Smiles had tried to swing his gun around, but the pain from the punch stopped his hand in mid-air.

Both my hands grabbed his wrist and half his gun hand. Sliding down in the seat corner on my side of the car, I kicked out with my left leg over the top of the front seat. The heel caught Val in his forehead and snapped his head back. Without a sound, he dropped out of sight.

Sliding my left hand down from Smiles' wrist, I got hold of his snub-nose. The thumb of my right hand crunched savagely down into the rope of muscle between his thumb and forefinger, where it hump-stretches over the back of the gun-butt. His hand sprang open. Both my hands fumbled desperately with the gun. From the corner of my eye, I could see one of Val's hands clawing its way over the top of his seatback, trying to get a grip on it.

Jeff was braking gradually, in an attempt to slow smoothly and not screw things up for Val. It worked. The snout of Val's Magnum came up, outlined against the head-lit road beyond the windshield. Then his face appeared, streaming blood down from his forehead, where I'd kicked him. His voice was snarling incoherent sounds, thick with pain and fury.

Finally getting my hands on the .38 I had taken from Smiles, I leaned forward and shot Val twice through the seat-back. Both reports sounded muffled. The car's interior filled with acrid cordite fumes.

Val disappeared.

Beside me, Smiles came at me with a lunge. I slashed the snub nose at his face, and felt bone crunch under the impact. Smiles spun away, groaning, and fell off the seat.

Leaning forward, I shoved the still-smoking muzzle of the snub nose against Jeff's right ear.

"Wanna bet I can't put one in through this ear and bring it out the other one?" I whispered to him.

Jeff swallowed and licked his lips. His right hand froze, half out from under his jacket. The dash light glistered on metal in his hand.

"No bet," he growled.

Reaching my free hand over his far shoulder, I plucked a long-barrelled .32 from his frozen hand.

"Turn this load around and head back," I ordered.

What was left of Val was sprawled every which way down on the floorboards beside where Jeff's foot was braking.

Beside me, an occasional grunt came from Smiles, down on the floor next to me.

Jeff slowed enough to swing the car around. Before he could get it moving again, I told him: "Open the door across from you and boot that bastard into the road."

Jeff turned his head and looked at me with what may have been reproach, but he did as I told him.

"And make damn sure," I said, as he was shoving Val out the open passenger doorway, "that you don't come up from down there with his .357. Right now, Jeff, I'm two-gun Brandon, and one of the guns is yours."

"I'll make sure I don't, Brandon," he murmured.

He had to wrestle to get Val unstuck from the narrow space beneath the dashboard, but he finally tilted the last of Val out onto the concrete pavement and pulled the door shut again.

I stuck Jeff's .32 into my belt.

Jeff began picking up speed, heading northward toward the pink glow in the sky made by the lights along the distant Strip.

Reaching across Smiles on the floor, I opened the door on his side of the car.

Glancing over his shoulder, Jeff began reducing speed.

Swinging the snub nose at him, I snarled: "Faster. Speed it up."

Jeff stared at me in the dim dashboard lights, shrugged and faced forward. He started to pour highway under us.

I sweated getting Smiles up from the floor. He was big and blocky. His face would never again look like it was smiling.

Shoving his head and shoulders backward through the partly open door, I used his body to try pushing the door wider open against the wind our forward speed poured relentlessly against it.

I was panting. A hot hating fire burned behind my eyes like a blowtorch.

It was no use. The outside wind, pressing against the door, held Smiles jammed in the opening. No matter how hard I shoved against him, I couldn't budge him.

Finally, furious, I lay on the back seat, braced the hand that wasn't holding the gun, and straight-kicked out at him with both feet.

Smiles was still alive, and conscious. When my feet punched into him, he grunted.

The double-kick did it. His body shoved out through the open doorway over nothing, and then he was gone. A single sickening slap when he hit the pavement was the last I heard of him.

"Okay, Jeff, faster. We've got a little girl to find alive up there under those pink lights, and you'd better pray we do find her alive."

Still panting, reaching for air, I realized sleep and exhaustion no longer crowded in on my eyes or dulled my mind. I felt keyed up to the highest pitch, and I stayed that way, all the way back to town.

First I gave Jeff directions to where Joyce and Bobbie lived, but when he reduced his speed in among the side streets, I told him not to.

"I better slow down or cops'll stop us," he protested.

"Don't worry about cops, Jeff. You've got me to worry about."

"Suit yourself."

He had to screech the tires a bit, to slow enough to make a turn. He was a good wheelman.

"One more block, then right for half a block," I whispered. "Turn into the rear parking area."

He saw where I meant and turned in, moving slowly now.

I had him park in the slot where Bobbie had parked her sport car.

Inside the building, I told him, "Open the door," when we reached her apartment.

His mouth crimped in slightly, but he didn't say a word, got out a pick and went to work. He had it open in twenty seconds, faster than I could have.

Inside, we found no one in the apartment.

"They're both at work, around now," he suggested.

"Let's hope they're both at work," I said. "Let's go. There's one other place, isn't there, Jeff? A shack in a block-long alley, just this side of Florian's."

Back in the big sedan, we got out onto the northwest highway again, headed toward the distant Florian's sign.

An eighth of a mile short of it, Jeff turned off between the northern end of the row of brick stores and El Rancho Motel. When we had driven the block in from the highway, he was about to turn into the alley when I stopped him.

"Just park right here, next to the end shack."

He went straight ahead and slid the car to a stop.

"Third shack in?" I asked.

"Yeah."

There was light coming from inside the paper-covered windows. I hoped that was a good sign.

"Keep your hands where I can see them, Jeff."

He nodded.

"Off with the motor. Give me the car keys."

Switching the motor off, he handed me the ignition key ring over his shoulder.

Raising the snub nose with my hand wrapped around the barrel end of it, I clipped Jeff behind his right ear. The blow made a cracking sound I didn't like and hadn't been trying for, but maybe his head was harder than it looked.

Breath expelled from his lungs with a soft, drawn-out "Ugh!" His right hand leaped away from the steering wheel, down toward the seat beside him.

His sudden move startled me. I gave his head another one with the gun butt. This one did the job. His head sagged, then the rest of him tilted gently forward against the steering wheel.

Quickly, I reached over and grabbed him, pulling him back and to one side. I didn't want him falling onto the car horn and waking the entire area with the noise.

Leaning forward over the seat-back, I groped around under Jeff's loose form until I found Val's big .357 Magnum where it had settled in the crack between the seat cushion and the seat-back . . . or where Jeff had managed to ease it, somehow. A tricky guy, Jeff!

Taking the Magnum along, I climbed out of the car, leaving Jeff where he'd slumped against the door.

Making noise was unavoidable, getting through the tin cans and other junk spread over the third shack's front yard, but I kept it down as much as I could.

Listening at the front door, I heard no sound inside.

The night wind was as gentle as a zephyr on my right cheek, but I shuddered from its touch. My own sweat made it seem like an icy blast.

An insect buzzed around my head. I nearly ducked.

I felt as if eyes were on me, from all along the row of flimsy huts and shanties in the alley. But I saw no one, heard no sound. And the lights inside Chavez's shack, which Mercator was using as his base, were the only illumination nearby.

At least I had enough firepower. More than I could handle.

Leaving Jeff's .32 stuck in my belt, I pocketed Smiles' snub nose and held Val's .357 ready. With my left hand free again, I eased the front door open an inch and punted it softly inward with my foot.

The door swung all the way around, bumped gently against the inside wall, rebounded from it a few inches, and stopped moving.

Standing just short of the threshold, the Magnum cocked, I found there was nothing for it to shoot at.

I stepped inside. The room was empty, except for the body of Mercator sprawled on its back, over by the right-hand wall. His serious eyes, prominent nose and determined jaw all pointed up at the ceiling. If his mouth had remained closed and his eyes hadn't been fixed in an empty stare, he might still have seemed alive. No, there was a single minute thing that was out of whack on his face: a thin line of blood had trickled from the side of his mouth. The blood had dried on his cheek.

Directly across the front room, the door to the rear half of the place was partly open. Swinging my own door shut behind me until the latch caught, I crossed the room and very cagily eased into the opposite doorway.

Chavez lay halfway between where I stood and the mattress over by the right- hand wall. One of his legs was stretched out behind him, while the other was bent high up, the knee of it almost tucked into his armpit. Both his arms were stretched along the floor in front of him. The point of his jaw was the only part of his head that touched the floor: the muscles of his upper arms touched both sides of his face and propped his head up. He looked like a man trying carefully to climb up a steep roof. A wide pool of blood extended from beneath him and had spread across the floor on both sides of where he lay.

Bernard was nowhere in sight.

Roberta lay on her right side on the mattress, curled up in a fetal position, both forearms folded tightly across her stomach.

Going over there, I stood looking down at her. I felt empty. Too late. Always too late for the most important things in life.

The big handgun swung from my hand, and I remembered that Jeff was right outside in the car, out like a light.

My hand tightened on the gun. It wouldn't do a damn bit of good, not anymore, but that didn't matter to me now.

I was half-turned away when Bobbie's eyes opened.

I sat on the floor beside her.

For a second, she stared up at me as if she couldn't remember who I was. A look of terror filled her eyes. They widened until the whites showed all around the washed-blue clarity of her eyeballs.

"It's all right, Bobbie," I whispered. "It's me, Brandon."

It got through to her. The fear went out of her eyes, and she murmured: "Oh, Daddy-O, you came. Much too late . . . much . . ."

"Where are you hit, kiddo?"

My voice sounded like the voice of someone else, hoarse, harsh, a voice I had never heard before.

"Tummy," she gasped softly. "Doesn't hurt now, but . . . it did . . . just after they . . . but now it doesn't . . . not anymore . . ."

With a slight frown-wrinkle in her forehead, she stared up at me.

"Don't cry, Brandon Daddy. I don't care. I don't m-mind . . . dying."

For an instant, her eyes became deep dark-blue. Her face squeezed up. She looked about to cry, but she didn't. She had cried already: tear-streaks had dried all around her eyes, and had left their glazed residue on her pale white skin.

Then her gaze returned from wherever it had gone for a moment.

She grinned defiantly.

"This living isn't so much!"

Both her hands pressed against her stomach, one hand against the back of the other, both held there tightly.

"Roberta, listen to me," I said, trying to clear my throat. "I'm going for a doctor. Don't move from exactly the way you are. I'll be back with help before you can . . . before you . . ."

Once more, her eyes widened, but not as much as they had earlier.

"Brandon Daddy," she begged, "don't leave me alone. I don't want to die alone."

Tears spurted from her eyes and poured sideways down her face into the dark patch on the mattress where her earlier tears had fallen.

I tried to reassure her, tried to think of something to say, tried to make myself get up from where I sat on the floor beside where she lay on the mattress. Then it all went out of me. I slumped back and stayed where I was, and didn't say anything more about going for help. I knew there was no help.

Her skin had always been white, but now it was whiter than any skin ought to be, chalk-white. Her eyes had returned to the pale blue-green of a chlorinated swimming pool. There wasn't enough blood left inside her to give them the deep dark-blue they had been when she was still alive.

One of her hands groped toward me. Her eyes squinted, trying to see through the tears filling them.

"Daddy-mia, don't leave me alone," she said in a faint soft voice.

I put my hand on hers. She grabbed my fingers and hung on.

"I won't leave you, Bobbie-O. I'll stay with you for the rest of your life."

"Forever," she sighed. Her eyes closed. She looked happy.

Twisting, I used my other hand to get out a handkerchief, using it to wipe around her eyes.

She kissed the inside of my wrist, whispering something. I had to lean down to hear what she was saying.

"I'm a good girl, Jimmy. I'm really a good girl."

"Yes, Roberta, I know you are. You're a good lovely girl."

Her eyes popped open and struggled to open wider.

"No, I mean it," she cried sharply. "That . . . the other time you were here . . ."

She glanced toward where Chavez lay dead on the floor nearby.

". . . I was just teasing you."

Her lips smiled at me, and her eyes smiled, too. The skin at the outside corners of her eyes crimped up. She watched me through the slits with eyes softer than any eyes have ever been.

"I know you were," I grinned. "Just getting me jealous."

"You like me, don't you?" Her eyes remained crinkled up, eyes full of mischief.

I nodded.

"You love me, too, don't you?" A sly little gleam peeped out of the crinkled-up slits.

"I think so."

"I thought you did," she whispered with satisfaction. "I can always tell."

Then she stiffened. Her eyes closed. She waited, listening to her own pain.

Slowly, her face relaxed again, but her eyes remained shut, and her hand in mine was limp. It no longer gripped my fingers.

I sat there and watched her face.

Suddenly, her eyes flew open, looked around desperately, filled with fright until they found me.

"Oh, Daddy-O," she whispered, her voice so soft that I had to lean my head close to her mouth to hear her.

"Yes, honey, I'm still here," I assured her. "What is it? Don't be frightened. I'll stay right here with you."

"Daddy-O, kiss me goodbye," she wailed. "Oh, I don't want to die."

Her lips were warm. They spread under mine.

I don't know when she died. After awhile, I realized that the hand I held was the hand of a tiny little dead girl.

For the first time, I could make myself look away from her face and down at the mattress.

Her other hand no longer pressed against her stomach. It had fallen limply. The knuckles and the backs of her fingers rested in the blood on the mattress. The palm of the hand was red with blood, too.

Her fingers were so tiny, compared with mine!

I hardly glanced at the three or four bullet wounds across her stomach. It didn't matter anymore.

Next thing I knew, I was out under the night sky once more, with the gun again in my hand.

I strolled across the littered front yard as if I had all the time in the world. My feet made an awful ungodly racket among the tin cans, but that didn't matter, either.

When I saw that the car was gone, I just stood there at the end of the alley, staring at where I had left it, with Jeff inside, unconscious . . . but apparently not unconscious enough.

It didn't bother me, particularly. There was plenty of time to do what I had to do now.

I don't really know how long I stood there, staring off at the back wall of El Rancho Motel, and beyond it at the lights of Florian's. I just couldn't seem to think what to do next. I knew there was something, but exactly what it was eluded me.

Finally, without thinking about it, I turned, went past where the car had been parked, past the end shack and out into the desert, in among the sage bushes.

I walked quickly, smelling the fragrant night-odor of the sagebrush high up inside my nostrils, feeling the wind blowing against me, once I was clear of the buildings.

I kept going, weaving in and out among the clumps of brush, squinting up at the high-flung stars.

Occasionally, aloud, I said, "Roberta?"

Fourteen

Sunlight streamed through a window.

Rolling over in bed, I tried to get back to sleep. When I realized I couldn't do it, I wondered why, until I opened my eyes and saw the room wasn't my room, and the sun wasn't coming through my eastward-facing window. It wasn't a morning sun, either, but a late afternoon one, and it poured at an angle through a big picture window that hadn't been cleaned in awhile.

I wondered if this was the next day or two days later. Lying there, I let it all come floating back to me, wondering how I could kill two men and not feel a trace of guilt about either of them.

Somehow, I had made a wide swing south of town and approached my rooming house through the desert. Some people had been waiting. I stayed out there in the brush, and watched whoever it was. The .357 I had taken from Smiles hung from my hand while I watched.

It turned out to be the police. A second car joined the one already there. When the car door of the new arrival opened and its inside light went on, I recognized Brode getting out. His being there didn't make any difference to me. I remained where I was.

Lying now in the strange bed, I realized what had been in my mind, while I sat out there in the brush. If they spotted me out there, and had come on out after me, I would have shot them, Brode first, then the others.

Shuddering at that realization, I sat up in bed and swung my legs over the side. I didn't like thinking that about myself.

Gazing around the motel room, I was about to get up and cross to the window, to see if I could find out what motel it was, when I remembered.

I had gone all the way back through the sagebrush to El Rancho Motel and gotten a room, and this was the room.

At the time, in the strangeness of last night, it had seemed enormously important to reach El Rancho Motel. Thinking about it now, sitting on the edge of the bed, I wondered why it had.

I remembered Roberta's face. Then I forced myself to stop remembering it.

Getting to my feet, I went into the efficient little bathroom and used it. Surprisingly, they had a razor and a new, or at least an unused-looking, razor blade.

Refreshed after a shower and shave, I got dressed.

The three handguns sat on the seat of the chair where I had thrown my suit coat.

I shook my head at sight of them. The guns complicated things.

At the side of the picture window, I peeped carefully out past the Venetian blind at the U-shaped motel court. A lot of cars were parked out there.

My unit was halfway back on the south row of rooms. There were five units directly across from me, five at the western end, and five more on my side, including my own. Three units almost closed off the eastern end of the square, leaving room for the entrance driveway and the corner office beyond it to complete the rectangle.

The sun went down below the roofline of the western row of units, but it was still daylight.

I wondered why I hadn't thrown the three guns away in the desert. Now that I was relatively sane again, I had no idea what to do with them. In the words of Sheriff Carroll, I was by way of being an indirect officer of the court, a licensed private detective. I couldn't see myself getting rid of evidence, even evidence against myself. Maybe especially evidence against myself.

Parked over in the northwest angle of the court was the familiar old gray Chevy sedan, unmistakable because of the big smooth crunched-in two-foot-long dent in its left rear fender, well behind the wheel. El Rancho had at least one old resident besides the manager.

Perhaps all the newcomers were just trying to get as close as they safely could to the scene of the recent trouble out at Florian's, both the casino with Wyatt getting whacked, and at their yacht club farther north and east, by the reservoir, with Big Sal's dispatching.

Drinking some tap water, I sat near the picture window, smoking unsatisfactory cigarettes with a mouth parched and bitter-tasting.

I knew I couldn't leave the motel until after dark. Even just sitting there, watching late afternoon light gradually fade, and feeling the intense heat of the day slowly lessen, I had a hunted feeling.

And why shouldn't I feel that way? Jeff had witnessed the two killings. Even if he hadn't reported them to the police, somehow they must have connected me with the two bodies, out there on the highway to the south, or they wouldn't have been staked out at my rooming house the night before, waiting for me.

There was no way I could avoid taking the rap for wasting Smiles and Val, but there was one more thing to do before I could walk into the Hall of Justice with my fists full of dead hoods' guns.

I went on smoking and waiting for night to fall.

When it was dark enough for me to leave, I put the snub nose into a coat pocket and tucked the other two bigger handguns into my belt.

Watching at the window until a couple out there got into their car and drove out of the court, I slipped out my door and closed it silently, just as I heard another door open and close across the court.

I remained as I was, facing my closed door, as if I was fumbling with the key. I didn't want anyone to see me. But as the seconds passed, I heard no footsteps. After waiting long enough, I looked quickly over my shoulder and scanned the court. No one was visible.

Maybe I was still punchy from those pills, imagining I heard doors opening and closing.

Keeping close to the side of the court, I hurried around the court's inner square and down the driveway out the highway exit, glad no one was inside the manager's office. That was unnecessarily foolish, because he must have seen all of me he would ever need to see, whenever I had registered, the night before.

Very hazily, I recalled speaking to the man, a thin-haired, open-faced character who talked too much in a rambling, pointless way.

Now, out by the highway, I walked toward town until I was opposite the nearest end of the dirt driveway entrance to the alley behind the row of stores. I waited there until an empty cab came along, after it dropped a fare out at the casino.

As I climbed into the cab, I couldn't help wondering if the police had yet found the three bodies in the shack. And for some reason, I wondered what had become of Bernard. Had he been tagged by Lanson's machinegun, too?

Getting rid of the cab near the southern end of the Strip, I again approached my rooming house through the desert. I still did not want to find policemen waiting for me when I arrived home.

There were no policemen there.

Upstairs, I fixed something to eat and put the three weapons in separate paper bags, writing Smiles, Jeff and Val in ink on the appropriate bags. Then I locked all three in my leather suitcase, and took my time eating supper.

My own Police Special was still lying on the bed where Val had thrown it the night before. Stowing it in the sling under my left arm, I went back downstairs and got into the Ford.

Instead of turning right onto the Strip and going up through town, I hung a left. Where the road begins to swing

toward the west, I turned straight east onto the first road going that way and stayed on it until I cut the lakeshore road
going north, toward the upper dam. There might still have
been law hanging around Herby's Boat Yard, and especially
around Florian's Yacht Club, and I wanted to avoid them.
The law could have me, but not quite yet.

The gate to the yacht club was closed and locked. Driving past, I saw no police cars in there, but they might have
been farther in, close to the clubhouse, down near the water's
perimeter.

Pulling onto the shoulder of the highway, I spent some
time watching stars and an occasional light far off across the
water reflected in the motionless lake. There was almost no
wind. The mountains ahead seemed closer than they should,
appearing to hang over my head, when I got out of the car.
After locking the car, I walked back to Florian's gate.

Just inside the gate was a little kiosk with a miniscule
porch covered with a pointed shingled roof. A bright white
light shone down on the porch from up beneath the steep
roof.

No one was in sight. Insects made crazy swoops under the
light, flashing down in swift whipping circles, then climbing
back up toward the light, out of sight under the angle of the
pointed roof.

There was a metal rectangle with a big black button in it,
attached to the wire fence beside the gate. When I pushed a
thumb against the button, a buzzer sounded inside the little
hut. Its door opened, and now the inside of the kiosk was lit,
too. A heavy-set man stepped onto the porch, putting on a
military-style garrison cap and straightening his tie. Leaning
out of the light above his head, he peered out at me.

"Yes, sir," he called. "What can I do for you?"

"I'm looking for Mr. Townsend, Brockton Townsend. I
understand his yacht is moored up here. Is he around?"

Descending the two steps from the porch, he came over
toward me. A revolver in a holster swung at his right hip.

"Mr. Townsend isn't at the club tonight."

Past him, I could see along the curving private road beyond the gate. Above nearby trees, I could see window lights in the upper floors of the big clubhouse.

"How about on his yacht?" I asked. "Would he still be aboard?"

"What did you say your name is, sir?"

"James Brandon. An associate of Mr. Townsend, Ted Fenton, hired me for him."

He nodded, watching me impassively.

"I'm a private detective," I added.

Again he nodded, but after a moment he asked: "Will you wait here, Mr. Brandon? I'll give Mr. Fenton a call."

"I'd rather see Mr. Townsend himself," I called, as he turned away toward the kiosk.

Smiling over his shoulder, he climbed on up the two porch steps imperturbably.

"You say Mr. Townsend isn't at the club, either?" I asked a second time.

"No, sir. He rarely spends nights on his yacht. He has his own ranch up in the mountains." He gestured to the north.

"All right," I said. "Don't bother Mr. Fenton. I'll try to contact Townsend himself. He's the one who hired me. Where is that ranch of his? How do I get there?"

"Best way is . . . You got a car?" He squinted past me, up and down the road, then back at me, his eyes narrowing.

"I left it parked up the road a ways," I said, adding by way of explanation: "Thought perhaps the club wouldn't want . . ."

I let it trail off a moment, before adding: "Being a private investigator, you tend to handle clients with kid gloves, after awhile."

He thought about it. I hoped he went for the line. I was getting tired of making people do things at gunpoint.

He went for it.

"Townsend's ranch," he said, coming back down the porch steps and approaching the other side of the gate. "You stay on the highway to the upper dam, make a right across the dam onto the county road. Turn left on that past the blinker light and go up into the foothills to the first left turn. There's a sign there, Toaquilla Springs. Make your left and go on up to the gas station, just below the pass. It's open all the time, Pete's Place. Just bang on the door, if old Pete doesn't hear you drive up. He'll tell you how to make the rest of the trip."

"Thanks," I said. "How's the fishing? I've never tried, up this way."

"I wouldn't know," he grinned. "I'm a gun club man, myself."

His hand flicked. The big pistol wasn't in his hip holster any longer. He pointed it at the sky somewhere behind me, sighted along the barrel, grinned again, and put it away.

I thought of myself trying to get my Police Special out from under my arm quickly enough to make him do something he didn't want to do. The hairs on the back of my neck stirred slightly.

"Well," I chuckled heartily, "if you can hit as well as you can pull, you should be in the Nationals."

"I have been," he laughed. He turned back toward his miniature cabin. "Careful of those turns, up in the mountains," he called over his shoulder. "They can be tricky at night. Or anytime, for that matter."

"I'll watch them," I said. "Thanks again."

Following his directions, I reached the sign that said Toaquilla Springs, with an arrow pointed north. I followed the arrow. The road began to climb. My headlights picked up fewer clumps of sagebrush near the roadside.

It was a well-paved county road, and that was just as well, because in a car as light as my Ford, some of the turns I had to negotiate higher up could have been really dangerous ones on a poorly paved and -banked road surface. I kept my speed moderate.

The dashboard clock no longer told time, so I dug out my pocket watch. Almost midnight.

I was beginning to feel sleepy again, and I wondered what the hell kind of pills those bastards like Hancock had been feeding me at the art colony.

The road climbed on. In the deep black night, the stars were diamond-brilliant. The air was getting thinner, too. Not too thin, but getting there.

I wondered how high these mountains were.

The Ford's motor was sounding funny. Too much fuel going into the carburetor for the thinning air joining it.

Stopping at a wide spot in the road, I took a flash and a screwdriver and turned the screw that regulated the amount of gas being pumped into the carburetor. It helped. From there on, the motor didn't sound so labored.

Now the heights were closing in on both sides of the road. Timber silhouettes stood up clearly against the lesser darkness of the sky. The wind punched against the car fitfully, hitting suddenly when I would top a rise over a pass, or round a curved stretch and emerge from the lee of a slope onto its windward face.

Presently, the road left the heights and swooped back down into sheltered timberland. The air had gotten cold and penetrating. I could smell the pungent odor of pine and spruce and the dry night air. Just when I was about to turn on the heater, I spotted lights ahead.

It turned out to be the gas station.

Slowing, I pulled into its graveled clearing and stopped beside the pump.

A sign over the frame building said *Pete's*.

I tapped the horn. When no one came, I climbed out.

The cool mountain air bit through my lightweight suit, and the breeze, blowing through the hot seat of my pants, felt like a sudden dousing of ice water.

Going over to the cabin, I peered at the office inside through small window-panes in the top half of the door. Talking animatedly into a pay phone attached to the wall was a leathery little old guy. He saw me. His eyes smiled, crinkling the skin around them like a piecrust cracking.

The air up there was blowing too cold to suit me, so I opened the door and went on inside, just as he said into the phone: "Call you back, Ed. Customer." He hung up.

"Welcome to Pete's," he said. "You want gas?"

"Yes. Better fill it up, Pete's."

He went out grinning.

Shoving money into the cigarette machine, I got a pack. No matches came out the slot with the cigarettes, so I fished around in the breast pocket of my suit coat and found a book that still had a few matches left in it.

Out at the pump, Pete finished up with the gas and checked the oil and water under the hood.

Two bright fluorescent lights outside lit up most of the cleared space, but beyond, everything was black, far blacker than it ever was down in the desert. Up here, there were no other lights to see, in any direction you looked.

Pete came back inside.

"Your oil's okay. I gave her a little water. The climb up here gets it heated, some."

"What's the damage?" He told me and I paid him. "How far is Townsend's place?"

"The fancy ranch? 'Bout ten miles farther along. Just stay on the road you're on. There're no turnoffs. Trees, most of the way down, but they thin out enough so's you'll know when you're hitting low rangeland again. When you're running along the face of a mountain ridge in a long curve, you're near his place. Watch for the turn to the left, off the county road. You won't be able to miss it. Your lights will pick up the bridge."

"What bridge is that?"

"His bridge," Pete snapped. "Townsend's bridge."

The bridge seemed to make Pete mad.

"Couldn't just cut himself a drive down the side of the ravine and across the wash and up the other side, no. He had to build him a whole bridge. Wanted privacy. Huh!"

He looked about to spit, but he didn't. His bright little black-button eyes studied me.

"You a friend of his, mebbe?"

He didn't look especially worried if I might be, but when I shook my head, no, he nodded with satisfaction.

"Kinda late to be goin' up there, aint it? Townsend sometimes has some odd-lookin' friends up there, lately . . ."

"Odd-looking how?"

"Aah, city boys. Tough guys. Think they're tough . . ."

"If they're like some I've seen lately, they'll be tough, all right."

"Hey, that's right," he cackled. "I heerd they's been some fancy shootin' goin' on, down to the Strip. That right?"

"Too much shooting."

Slapping his hands together, Pete howled with glee.

"Sure wisht I coulda seen some o' that shootin'. I was just hearin' about some of it, talkin' just now to Ed Granger. He's down on the dam. Reminds me."

He went over to the phone.

"Wait!" I called. "Have you got a book of matches?"

While his coin clanged down into the phone box, Pete pointed to a little cardboard boxful of book matches on top of the tall cigarette vending machine. I hadn't noticed them up there. I took two books.

Brandon the detective.

"That's funny," Pete said, staring at the phone in his hand.

I opened the door to leave.

"What's funny?"

"Line's dead. Wires must be down."

He plunked the receiver prong down and up a few times, before giving up.

"She's out, all right."

We stepped outside. Pete examined the dark sky.

"Don't seem all that windy," he muttered absently.

"Your lights are still on," I pointed out.

Pete shrugged.

"Got my own generator. Kicks in like that . . ." He snapped his fingers to emphasize his words *like that*. ". . . whenever there's trouble."

I pulled open my car door.

"You notice if there was much of a wind, on your way up?"

I shook my head, holding the door open.

"Not too bad. It was pretty windy in the gaps."

He nodded.

"Mighta been what done it. I oughta get me one o' them cell phones. Been meanin' to. Goldang, now I won't be able to hear about the rest of them shootin's from Ed. You see any? Gunplay, I mean?"

"No," I lied, sliding behind the wheel. "I live a quiet life, for the most part."

I didn't want to be there for the rest of the night, telling him about all the shootin's.

Waving, I drove out of the bright canopy of light there at his gas station into the high mountain darkness again, following my headlight beams in a long winding drive that went down and down until my ears popped.

When the road ran along the side of a mountain in a long easy descending curve, I sat up and watched for the turn Pete had told me about.

At the bottom of the descent, the headlights picked up a small sign with an arrow pointing left. Slowing, I negotiated the turn. Just ahead, my lights revealed a bridge built of oak-beams bolted together with steel connecting plates. It spanned a steep-sided dry wash about forty or fifty feet wide at that point, and maybe a little deeper.

Slowly, I drove across, the solid planking thumping beneath my tires. Just beyond the far end of the bridge, a steel gate stretched across the private road. There was so little space, that when I stopped at the gate, my rear tires were still on the planks at the end of the bridge.

Nothing moved. Beyond the chain-link gate, my brights showed that the road ahead swung to the right past a cabin and disappeared upward. My hand was on the door, ready to open it so I could see if I could get past the gate, when I caught a movement out of the corner of my eye.

Off to the left a few feet, a man wearing a dark suit, with a cigarette dangling from the corner of his mouth, stood well out of the beam of my headlights.

"Keep your hands in sight," he called.

I left my hands where they were, on top of the steering wheel.

On the passenger side of my car, another man appeared. He wore dark clothes, too, but there was no cigarette in his mouth. I could tell the difference between the two of them that way, but I couldn't tell any difference between the sub-machine guns each of them held pointed directly at my head.

Fifteen

Midmorning sunlight shone through the open cabin door when one of them shook me awake.

Shivering in the chill mountain air, I watched him put a key into the big padlock that tightly held two links of the short chain with which they had held me secured to the steel cot I slept on through the night. The chain had been twisted just tightly enough above my left elbow-bones to keep me from sliding my arm out. Since one of the machinegun men had always been in the room with me through the last third of the night hours, I hadn't even tried. The first rattle of the chain against the cot's steel frame would have wakened him, anyway.

My left forearm tingled when the chain's pressure was removed. Holding that arm with my right hand, I sat up on the cot. The machinegun was under his right arm. He stood well away from me. His eyelids drooped, he had swarthy skin, and he hadn't shaved yet.

"I think they're going to give you breakfast," he said, grinning mirthlessly. "Up at the main house on top."

I glanced around at the cabin.

"I thought this was the main house."

"Nah!" he scoffed. "This is where the hired help stay, when there's a dirty job that's got to be done. Come on. Get up."

I got up. While I slept, my coat had fallen off me and the cot, both. Picking it up from the floor, I went through the open doorway, out into the sun.

The air was chilly and thin with altitude, but the sun warmed me in an instant.

Fifty feet downhill from the cabin, the solid-looking beamed bridge spanned the ravine. Its far end was still in shadow.

No cars were in sight. Nor was the second guard.

"Get in your car," he directed me. "It's around in back."

He followed me around the cabin to where they had pulled the Ford off the road, just this side of the now-open gate.

When I got behind the wheel, my keeper climbed in behind me with his juice gun.

"To your left," he said, "up the hill."

Although it was a well-maintained road, I drove slowly, climbing up the side of the rock-strewn ridge in a gentle grade until I reached the top, perhaps a quarter mile north of the bridge. There, the road swung left and went straight across the top of the mesa to a wide, rambling, ranch-like building, where it ended in a circular graveled drive.

Stopping my car, I got out on command and walked up a path paved with tiny white stones, which looked as if they were oval seashells, but weren't.

The path ended at the foot of redwood stairs. At the top of the short flight of steps stood Jeff, staring down at me. He nodded to my guard behind me. I heard the man's footsteps receding down the pebbled path as I climbed the stairs toward Jeff.

I was surprised that I reached the top of the steps alive.

Jeff must have noticed. He chuckled at the look on my face.

"Relax, Brandon," he advised quietly. "Everyone makes mistakes."

Turning, he went back across a wide flagstoned patio, out of the sun beneath the shade provided by a calculatedly frontier-type lodge-pole roof, which was cantilevered out over the patio from the front of the ranch-building itself.

Jeff wore no hat. There were no bandages on his head where I had slugged him two nights before, but something glistened under his thinning combed gray hair.

Stopping beside a table laid for breakfast, he beckoned me over.

"Better get in out of that sun, Brandon. You know better than to go around without a hat in this country. Haven't you got one?"

"Maybe it's in my car. You want me to go get it?"

He chuckled.

"Always with the joke. Come over here. Mr. Townsend will be out in a little while. Better eat while you get the chance."

Following him into the shade, I felt the morning chill again, the instant I was out of the sun.

Silver cozies covered the various dishes, keeping the food warm.

"Dig in," Jeff urged. "And don't bother trying to leave. The way you came up just now is the only way down from this mesa."

"Jeff, why would I want to leave? I came all the way out here to see Townsend. He sent Teddy-boy for me, awhile back."

Jeff's scar-stitch of a mouth twitched. Turning his face away, he crossed the patio to go through the wide-open front doorway.

Hearing a splash, I glanced along the front façade of the house and noticed for the first time the aqua shimmer of pool water below patio-level, on the north side of the ranch house. As I watched, Jan Thornton swam lazily into sight, across the stretch of pool I could see, and then out of sight.

On the table, there were strips of crisp bacon, still warm. Two of the three eggs' yokes had not yet hardened. The coffee was hot.

I dug in.

When I was full, I refilled my coffee cup and tried not to think about condemned men and last meals.

I kept an eye out, but I didn't see the girl again.

Her skin had been bronze looking, but perhaps it only seemed that dark because of the contrast made against her skin by the white bathing suit she wore.

I smoked, drank coffee, and studied the gradual slope of the mesa, north of the ranch house. The slope ended at the edge of the mesa maybe half a mile away. Beyond it, far below, distant desert was the next thing you could see, spreading for miles until it washed up against the foothills of a range of mountains whose sharp peaks formed the northern horizon.

Absently, my right hand massaged the upper part of my left arm near the elbow, where the chain links had pressed into the muscles and ligaments through the last part of the night in the cabin down by the bridge.

A short, stocky Indian-looking servant came, put the dishes on a tray he brought, and took them away. A few moments later, he returned and took whatever dishes he hadn't been able to remove on his first trip.

After watching him disappear through the open front doorway into the inner gloom, I rose and crossed the patio to the waist-high adobe wall that ran along the northern perimeter of the patio. Leaning on the top of the wall, I saw that the ground fell steeply away for fifteen or twenty feet, then leveled off to fine-graveled poolside territory, spotted with an occasional table sheltered from the sun by multi-striped canvas or plastic umbrellas, on poles sticking up through the center of the tables.

To the right, a stepped path descended the slope along the side of the patio to the pool area.

No one was down by the part of the pool visible to me, so I went back and sat down at the breakfast table, where I stayed until Brock Townsend came out and crossed the patio to me.

I got to my feet.

"No, Mr. Brandon," he said, "keep your seat."

His voice was low-pitched. His face looked grave and was somewhat lined, although he had gotten desert sun shining on it recently enough to give it a tanned healthy look. He wore an open-necked white shirt under a light-blue wide-checked sport jacket, dark blue slacks, and black comfortable-looking shoes.

He was not as tall as I am, nor as wide and deep in the shoulder area, but he carried himself well. He was a much more impressive man than size alone could have made him, although he had enough of that for convenience.

"Sit, please," he said again, standing across the table from me, watching as I sat once more.

His full head of hair had a touch of gray sprinkled all through it, not just dabbed on where he wanted it gray and the rest blacked out. His eyes, though dark blue, appeared startlingly light-blue in the tan surround of his face, much as Jan Thornton's white bathing suit had contrasted so strongly with the bronze of her skin. His nose was straight-boned, with a medium nostril-spread. His mouth and jaw were set forcefully, as he watched me.

It went like that for a spell, the pair of us staring at each other.

Finally, he half-turned, and his eyes roved out under brows squinting against the nooning sun, gazing across the sage-spotted mesa-top.

"Why have you come here, Mr. Brandon?" he asked quietly.

"Your man, Ted Fenton, told me you wanted to see me."

"But that was several days ago." He turned and stared down at me intently. I was beginning to see why he had insisted I sit. "And you refused to see me then."

"I don't like Mr. Fenton," I said. "And I didn't like the way he handled it. I've changed my mind . . . not about Fenton, but about coming to see you."

"Why?"

"Conditions have changed, Mr. Townsend."

"They have," he agreed grimly. "They have indeed changed, and so drastically that there isn't much point in my seeing you at all. Not anymore."

"Why did you send for me in the first place?"

He shrugged.

"At the time, it seemed a precautionary measure. Now . . . alternative precautions have had to be taken." His eyes narrowed as they watched me. "I may say, Mr. Brandon, that you are very lucky to be alive, particularly since you were reckless enough to approach this place the way you did, unannounced, in the dark of night. I marvel at the restraint of the men on guard, down at the bridge."

"So do I. And I also marvel that there is any reason for them to be on guard here."

"Any reason?" He stared at me, disturbed. "After the way Mr. Wyatt and, more recently, Mr. Preston were murdered, you can ask why I have seen fit to guard my ranch."

I stood up, tired of being looked down upon.

"Actually I'm asking why you are here at all, and why the young Thornton woman has been kept here? Just how many different kinds of damn fool are you, Mr. Townsend?"

His eyes became bleak.

"Ah, the woman," he murmured. His lips tightened against his teeth, in what may have been a savage smile. "Always the woman. She's really the reason you came up here, isn't she, Mr. Brandon?"

"Part of it," I said, "but not for the reason you seem to think . . ."

"Spare me your interpretations of my thoughts, Brandon," he interrupted.

Striding across the patio to the north parapet, he peered over it toward the pool for a moment before turning to face me. He remained there by the wall, watching me.

"She's what started all this, isn't she?" I asked.

"What?"

He had been staring at me, but thinking of something else. Now his attention was on me again.

"That's what began this whole deal, isn't it?" I persisted. "The young woman, and you, and the way you feel about her, and about any man who . . ."

Under the tan, his face paled. He strode toward me, and his eyes were no longer bleak. They were ablaze.

"I'm going to tell you this only once, Brandon," he hissed, from no more than two feet away. "Keep your cheap private cop mouth off the subject of Jan Thornton . . ."

"Do you want her dead, too?" I howled. "Is that why you've got her holed up out here? You think those two machine gunners of yours are going to keep that Ben Crane guy away from here?"

"He doesn't know we're here," Townsend said flatly. "He *can't* know . . . unless you led him here."

"Why can't he? Nobody has had to tell him a thing throughout this entire blood bath . . . except maybe Fats, when he needed basic information. Like a few names: Fenton's, for one, and maybe yours, for another."

I waved an arm out at the sea of sage spreading away under the sun.

"He could be right out there, this minute," I said, trying desperately to get through to this man. "Neither of us would know what hit us. He moves through brush like that as if he was born in it. Maybe he was."

Taking a deep breath, I kept my eyes locked on his, trying to get past the anger behind them.

"Mr. Townsend, this may sound foolish to you, but I'm trying to help you. All of you. Yes, and Jan Thornton, too. Her, most of all. But I can't be much help if I don't know what happened. What caused all this killing Ben Crane has been doing?"

For a second, I waited. When he didn't reply, I went on.

"I don't know whether he's going to kill her, too. By now, he might be crazy enough to kill any of you he can get in his sights, including her . . ."

Drained, I stopped. I watched him, waiting, wondering how he was taking it.

It took several long minutes, but finally I knew I had gotten through to him.

At first, a touch of doubt appeared in those furious eyes of his. Gradually the doubt increased, the anger seemed to lessen, and suddenly a frightened look appeared to crumple the very bones under the flesh covering his face.

Trying to conceal it, he turned half away, lowering his head. He sank his teeth into his lower lip, in an attempt to stop its trembling. He bit down hard enough to make me flinch.

Forcing my glance out across the flat mesa top, I watched the midday breeze frisking across it and rippling the tops of the bushes.

"All these years," he said softly.

I returned my attention to him. He was staring across the mesa toward its eastern rim, where the road turned out of sight at the start of its course down the ridge side to the guarded bridge.

"All the precautions I took," he went on, "keeping myself in the clear, in my dealings with them, all of them, all the different kinds of them! The so-called legitimate business-men, and the other kind, too, Wyatt's kind, and Preston's." He waved a negligent hand, dismissing them. "All those years!"

On the last words, his voice rose in a shriek of fury and frustration, broke, and then he stood there, choking, furi-ously trying to clear his throat.

When he was reasonably composed once more, he stood there in the deep cool shade of the patio, staring out across the sun-beaten mesa, but apparently seeing many other things.

"To have been so careful of them!" he whispered, almost with wonder. "If I had been careless, and let them do me all the favors they're so good at, then I could understand. But I was so careful never to get too involved with any of them, in any deal . . . and now to have it end like this!"

He laughed, but it was laughter without joy, bitter as bile, harsh, angry laughter, as his eyes were angry when he raised them to the sky, as if he was staring into the face of a malig-nant fate only his eyes could see.

"It's almost as if all this was planned," he said quietly, shaking his head, baffled. "That's the eerie joke of it. It's as if all the Wyatts and Prestons and Ted Fentons I have dealt with so carefully through the years had been preparing me for that . . . that lunatic animal!" He waved a hand out at the shimmering brush.

He spat the last words out, and then he stopped speaking, his eyes downcast, staring at the flagstones of the patio be-fore him.

It was as if he were examining the words he had just poured out of his mouth with such bitterness, and the hatred he felt for whatever had made him say them, forced him to spit them out.

"What happened to bring it on?" I asked, trying to keep my voice as gentle and unobtrusive as possible.

Sighing, he nodded.

"Oh, I started it," he admitted, his voice husky. "I can't deny that. Of course, at the time, I wasn't aware I was starting anything. When I first heard what Wyatt had done, I wanted to . . ."

He raised his arms in front of him. Both his sun-brown hands clenched convulsively into fists.

His eyes closed. His face became weary, resigned. He shook his head from side to side.

"Wyatt!" he snapped, saying the name as if he hated it. "The cheap alley-fighting fool. He did me a favor, he said. He thought he was doing exactly what I wanted him to do."

Again he shook his head in exasperation. Then he shrugged, as if it was hopeless to regret. When he went on, his voice was quiet, almost devoid of expression of any kind.

"I saw the two of them together, Jan and the boatman. A young man and a young woman, laughing, happy for a moment, the two of them. In the evening, you could hear their laughter for a considerable distance. They weren't trying to hide it. Why should they? There was nothing to hide. They were just fooling around on a boat at dockside.

"But when I heard that laughter of theirs, in my heart I hated the sound of it. I must have said something. Even Wyatt couldn't tell me later exactly what I did say. The only thing his dirty little gutter-snipe instinct knew was precisely how to handle a situation like that. He was used to doing that sort of favor for his associates. He told Ted Fenton to handle it. And Ted did. Oh, he handled it, all right. A stranger whose face I had only seen at a distance, in the dusk of evening!"

In quiet despair, he threw his hands up

"What can I say? They beat him. And now he has been killing them, one at a time. And I see at last that he will kill me, too, unless he can be stopped before he reaches me."

"And maybe he'll kill her, too," I reminded him.

Gloomily, he nodded.

"Oddly, I never thought of that possibility. But yes, I can see that happening. To him, Jan might appear to be a part of it, instead of an unknowing cause."

"Perhaps he won't," I suggested. "Trouble is, by now I don't think Ben Crane can be considered altogether sane. Not surprising, after what he was put through, and now after what he has put himself through . . ."

"Why should he be sane?" Townsend asked. "How can I deny him the right to vengeance?"

"I guess you can't," I admitted. "I'm just surprised to hear you admit you can't."

"But not vengeance against Jan," he said emphatically. "She has never been involved in any of this. I was the cause. I'm responsible for all of it. Oh, don't worry, Brandon. I'm not going to stand up and wait philosophically for him to mow me down. I want to go on living. I'll do everything I can to protect myself, whether I'm right or wrong, responsible or not. But I want her safe. I can't take the chance he won't harm her, too. She's got to be safe."

"She's not safe here," I insisted.

"Then I'll take her away from here."

"Wherever you are isn't safe, as long as Ben Crane lives."

With eyes that were suddenly hopeless, he stared at me. His eyes hated me. He turned away to conceal the hatred. I was telling him what he already knew, but he wouldn't let himself believe it.

"Mr. Townsend, you're the target," I said, pressing it home. "You and Ted Fenton. It was Fenton you turned him over to, wasn't it?"

"Of course," Townsend said disgustedly. "I presume Ted wanted in on it. He wanted to see how professionals handled something like that. At least he wanted it for a little while. Ted Fenton is one of those folks who believe in trying everything at least once. Sensation is his karma."

His smile was without mirth.

"Are you saying Fenton is crazy? I mean, legally crazy?"

Townsend snorted.

"Of course not." But he paused, uncertain for a moment.

"If you had seen the shape they left Ben Crane in," I said, "you might not scoff at that idea. From what I have seen of

Fenton, he is a somewhat unhappy man, one of the people who like being unhappy, who are at their finest when they're miserable, the kind who sometimes take things out on people around them. Their unhappiness bursts out. It's got to, I suppose. With Fenton, perhaps he had to hold it in too long because of you. He wasn't able to take anything out on you, so he had to keep it bottled up inside. And every so often he would come across another outlet, some situation in which he could really cut loose."

Townsend was staring at me, his face grave, thoughtful, even slightly surprised.

"Do I sound as if I'm describing Ted Fenton?" I asked him. "I'm not. I'm describing other people I have known. He reminds me of them. He is . . . probably capable of doing anything, to anyone. The things he did to Ben Crane, and to that poor teenager Herby, who ran the boatyard until Fenton reached him, are pretty clear measures of what Ted Fenton can do, when he has the opportunity, and sets his mind to it."

Impatiently, Townsend turned away from me, gazing off toward the mountain wall to the southeast, looming beyond the ravine separating the mesa from the county road that ran along the base of the mountain, headed toward the wilderness area to the north.

"I'm somewhat surprised," he said thoughtfully. "You show more penetration than one expects from a man like you, Brandon. You're right. Ted is almost a brilliant man, but he lacks control of himself, and therefore of others. Life must be a special kind of hell for those with considerable talent, but who lack that . . . that crucial something which would enable them to implement their talent. He should have been a great film director, but when he tried, they always had to replace him partway through the shooting schedule. Anything he tried to do, he should have done so well. But he never did. He couldn't. Partway through, something inside him would collapse."

Shrugging, he spread his hands helplessly.

"To someone like myself, a man like Ted is invaluable. As long as I was there to control him, all went well. But on his own?" He shook his head. "What a waste! I suppose you're right in your analysis of him, Brandon. I'm not too tender a man, myself. Subtleties, shadings of character? Many of them escape me, even though they might be all around me, every day. As, indeed, they are, in Fenton himself. But things like that never disturb me. Perhaps if they had, none of this would have happened. I've been aware of them, but because I knew they didn't bother me, I could ignore them. I'm accustomed to dominating people, of contending with them, in a business way. In all ways, really. In short . . ."

"In short," I helped him by saying it bluntly, "you use people."

His smile was rueful.

"Someone always will, Brandon."

"You could use Fenton's various talents, so you did, and probably still do. Whatever he was like in his private time was none of your business, was it?"

"Exactly," he said, watching me as if he wasn't certain how I had meant what he was agreeing with. Shrugging away the moment of uncertainty, he asked: "Will you take Jan . . . Miss Thornton . . . away from here for me?"

"Miss Thornton will take herself away from here, Brock, my love."

The nearness of her voice surprised both of us.

She stood at the top of the flight of steps that led down to the pool. She wore a white, calf-length terry-cloth robe, belted at the waist with a terry-cloth rope. A towel casually draped one shoulder. Blue and white sandals covered her feet.

Her eyes were fixed on Townsend's face. They were as remote and cold and impersonal as any eyes could be.

For a moment, Brock Townsend seemed to be about to say something, but the expression on her face stopped his words before he could speak them. A whicker of pain fled across his face and was gone. Squaring his shoulders and standing straighter, his jaw set. When he did speak, his words were casual.

"How was the swim?"

Ignoring that, she continued to stare at him. The silence between them stretched out, like an electric cable that carried too much energy for the insulation at either end to handle.

At last, she broke the silence.

"You've done quite a job, Brock. For some time, now, I've felt something strange going on all around me, but you have managed to conceal it from me quite nicely. You're such a considerate man, Brock. Aren't you?"

He stood braced, as if he was waiting for anything she could throw at him, his lips pressed together, firmly set, saying nothing.

"Answer me," she cried. "Now, at last, you don't have anything to say. Now you can keep your mouth shut tight, can't you? But you couldn't when it counted, could you? You sent that filthy mobster after that poor young man just because he and I could enjoy working together on a little sailing boat."

"I sent no one after him, Jan," replied Townsend quietly. "Wyatt took it upon himself to . . ."

"Don't tell me that, you poor fool," she hissed. "You wanted him to. He knew you wanted him to do what he ordered his garbage people to do. You simply can't admit it to yourself. Oh, shame on you, Brock. You disgust me. What a terrible thing to do to anyone."

"I couldn't help myself," he said woodenly. "I love you. I can't help that. Yes, I suppose you're right. I did want them to . . . do what they did to him, in my heart. I couldn't help it, wanting them to hurt him. I love you."

She nodded, her head thrust forward fiercely. When she spoke her next words, it was through gritted teeth.

"And I can't help despising you, now."

She laughed, briefly and bitterly.

"You see? We can both use this I-can't-help-it line of yours. How dare you imagine that you owned me? I don't love you. I told you that. I wouldn't marry you because people like you think you can own. I wouldn't give my life to you. I'll never give it to anyone. I own myself. I'll talk to anyone I please. I'll laugh with anyone I want to laugh with. Yes, and I'll sleep with anyone I wish to sleep with. God damn you and your grabbing, owning kind of love. Look what it's brought you."

When he still refused to defend himself, she swung her raging eyes at me.

"Tell him, detective. Tell him how many people have died because of one dirty little favor just one of his many dirty little gangster friends did for him. Tell him the count up to now."

"I stopped counting awhile back," I replied. "Around twelve, directly or indirectly, that I know of . . ."

"That he knows of," she spat at Townsend. "And maybe there are more. All because of . . ."

She stopped, unable to go on. Turning, she ran into the house.

Townsend stood like a man facing a firing squad.

A sudden drumming noise took my attention away from Townsend. It was made by the hooves of a horse Ted Fenton rode past the pool below.

He went out of sight behind the patio's north wall, reappearing a moment later, riding into view again at the foot of the front patio steps, where he viciously pulled his lathered horse to a clattering stop.

Frantically, the horse stomped on the fine gravel, tossing his head, trying to ease the unnecessary pressure of the bit in his mouth, caused by Fenton's too-tight grip on the reins.

When Fenton saw me standing there on the patio, he pulled a small semi-automatic pistol from the side pocket of his brown leather and cloth riding jacket. The weapon didn't want to come out. He cursed it, and when it cleared the pocket, there was a sound of cloth ripping.

His mount refused to stand still, turning away under the heedless pull of Fenton's left hand on the reins, so that Fenton looked ridiculous as he tried to keep me in sight, while the horse kept turning away. That left Fenton's back to me. His twisted face tried to keep watching me over his shoulder. Continuing its turn, the horse went the rest of the way around, causing its rider to whip his head the other way until he was able to see me once again, still waving his pistol.

If it hadn't been for that pistol, the sight of his antics might have been funny.

I glanced at Townsend. He hadn't noticed any of it. He still faced the open front door of the ranch house, with his back to Fenton.

Stepping behind the breakfast table, I gripped my chair with both hands. I didn't have much faith in its stopping power, if Fenton began shooting, but it was the only thing within reach I could lay hands on that I could throw.

Fenton looked gaunt, wild-eyed. He had the inflamed look in his eyes of a man who hadn't slept in days. Unshaven, his whiskers weren't too noticeable against the taut brown of his skin, stretched too tightly over the narrow-boned face.

There was a look of desperation about the man. He was hovering on the edge of something, all set to go over the edge, too.

"So, Brandon, now you come up here," he panted. "Does that mean you've brought along that murdering buddy of yours?"

Jumping down from his horse, still clutching the pistol, he bellowed: "Mano!" The cords in his throat stood out like ropes, when he threw his bead back to yell.

The Indian servant came out in a soft shuffling run, moving across the patio almost without sound in his straw sandals. He went down the stairs, took the reins from Fenton, and for a moment, he stood there, gentling the animal, talking softly into its ear.

"Answer me, Brandon," snarled Fenton.

His voice cracked. It was hoarse and harsh. He had done too much drinking recently for it to have done his voice much good.

"God damn you, Brandon, I told you to answer me. Is he out there? Did you bring him here, too?"

"Calm yourself, Ted," Townsend told him, turning and facing us again. "Brandon's leaving soon."

Silently, the Indian servant led the horse along the front of the ranch house and around the corner to the south side of the building, out of sight.

Fenton's too-bright eyes didn't leave my face. He ignored Townsend.

"How many more of us," Fenton asked me in a voice little louder than a whisper, "is that bastard going to butcher?"

"I've advised Mr. Townsend to leave here," I said. "Just get out of the entire region. Take a train, a car, or a plane, but go. And soon. Otherwise, you're all helpless. He knows you. You don't know him. He can pick you off at his leisure, here or anywhere. If you had any sense, you would at least make it difficult for him. You wouldn't just squat here on top of a mesa, waiting for him to come and get you in his sights"

Fenton went on staring at me, panting. He seemed to be waiting for me to say more. When I didn't, he roused himself, glanced over at Townsend, and said, "He's right, Brock. We should do what he says. Leave here. We can change our names, disappear, just the way he did . . ."

Without saying a word in reply, Townsend turned away in disgust.

"Brock, what else can we do?" Fenton screamed. "He'll slaughter us the way he did Wyatt and Preston. We'll never know when or where it's coming from . . ."

"That's why I'm staying," Townsend replied coldly. "To finish it here, one way or the other. Either we'll get him, or we'll take our medicine like men."

"Medicine?"

Fenton was astounded.

Trembling, he stood at the foot of the steps, the pistol hanging from his right hand, his mouth open, slack, his hair plastered to his forehead by his own sweat. He stood there in the beating midday sun, squinting, still panting, his breathing labored.

I wondered how long he had gone without eating, without being able to sleep.

"Brock," he whispered, then stopped, apparently unable to think what more he could say.

For a moment, as the silence dragged out, it didn't register.

I was watching Fenton's face. His eyes sprang open, the whites showing all around the irises. Then the single report reached my understanding, repeated in flat, soon-gone echoes bounced back by the mountain wall, east of the mesa.

Townsend's head came up. His mouth tightened purposefully. Listening, he squinted across the field of cactus and sage bushes to where the private road turned at the edge of the mesa and dipped out of sight down toward the bridge spanning the dry wash ravine.

Fenton spun around, too, when the distant pop-pop-popping sound of one of the guards' sub-machine guns reached us faintly.

Then that stopped.

After the faint echoes died, all we could hear was the sound of the wind blowing from the northwest toward the source of the distant shots, carrying them swiftly away from us.

"Mano!" Fenton suddenly shouted.

Townsend went over to the open front doorway and called inside.

"Jeff, get out here."

Jeff emerged from the dim shadows inside. He wore a dark-gray straw fedora but no jacket.

"I heard them," he told Townsend.

Jeff's right hand held a long-barreled revolver, which could have been a twin of the .32 I had taken away from him, two nights before. The leather straps of his gun harness looked strange against the impeccable white of his shirt and his neatly knotted patterned light-blue tie.

"Think you'd like to chance a look down there?" Townsend asked him.

"Okay if I take him along?" Jeff flipped the pistol in my direction. "Kind of backup."

Smiling, Townsend glanced briefly at me, and nodded.

"Why not?"

There was the sound of another shot, followed by a burst of faint-sounding machinegun fire, then a final single shot.

The three of us stood there, listening, gazing off toward where the road dipped . . . although whatever was happening was taking place out of our sight.

"What do you think?" Townsend asked Jeff.

"Can't tell much, this far away," Jeff said, shrugging.

The sound of machinegun fire began again. Burst after burst, longer bursts than before.

"They'll jam the action," Jeff said, pursing his lips in disapproval, as if to himself.

The sound of the machinegun firing stopped. We stood there, motionless, waiting.

A moment later, the machinegun fire began once more, this time coming in one long continuous burst.

Long after the firing stopped, I found myself holding my breath, waiting for another single rifle shot. It never came.

"That might have done it," Jeff said to Townsend. "I'll go see."

Turning to me, he waved me ahead of him downstairs to the circular drive.

"Okay, pistolero," he told me, as he followed me down the steps. "We'll take your car. You drive. I'll ride shotgun with this." Grinning meagerly, he brandished his .32. "I'm your protection."

At the foot of the stairs, I crossed the fine gravel drive and slid behind the wheel of the Ford. Jeff got in back, slamming the door shut before the motor caught.

Feeling like a convict walking the last mile on death row, I drove along the road to the turn at the edge of the mesa, and was about to drive on down when Jeff snapped: "Stop!"

Braking, I turned to see what the problem was.

Jeff was looking over his shoulder, back toward the ranch house. For a second or two, I couldn't see what it was that bothered him, but then I picked up a glimpse of something flitting across the sage flat a hundred yards from the driveway we were on.

Once more, Ted Fenton was on horseback, taking a shortcut to the rim of the mesa farther down, where he would be nearer to the bridge and the shack down below, where the guards had been posted.

"Ride 'em cowboy!" Jeff snickered.

Turning back to me, he ordered: "Move it, Brandon. Drive down there, but slow. Be ready to stop on a dime. And when you stop, stay stopped, or I'll stop you, real sudden. Get going."

I got going.

Driving slowly and carefully, we descended the eastern face of the mesa to the shack and the gate and the bridge beyond it.

Behind me, Jeff hunted with his eyes, ahead and on both sides of us, watching for movement of any kind.

As the road neared the bottom, it angled slightly away from the nearly perpendicular side of the mesa, and just short of the shack, Jeff muttered: "Stop here."

The shack was on our right, and beyond it, the bridge spanning the dry wash.

"Now let's get out," Jeff said. "We'll look around, but careful. I don't like all this quiet."

We both got out of the car. The sun felt like a flat hot smothering fist beating down on the top of my head. Glancing back inside the car, I tried to find my hat, but it wasn't there.

Jerking his pistol, Jeff indicated for me to move ahead of him, and he followed me along the road down to the front of the shack.

One of the guards was sprawled face down across the porch with his head hanging over the edge, turned sideways, his left temple resting on the top of the step below. His eyes were wide open. He was dead. His machinegun lay on the ground near the foot of the porch steps.

Jeff followed me up onto the porch. The dead man's body had been raked from head to foot by machinegun bullets. He was a mess. So was the wooden porch around him. Bullets which had missed his body had torn into the thick planks in short curved lines.

I glanced at Jeff. His thin lips were invisible. His face was pale. But his eyes, though bleak, were always alert.

"Some piece of work, that guy is," he said. "Empties a machine gun clip into a dead man. Go on inside, Brandon."

No one was inside the shack. I found my hat on the floor in a far corner of the main room. Dusting it off, I put it on.

Jeff motioned me outside again.

"Take a look around," he ordered. "Don't go near your car. That other guard must be somewhere nearby."

All the while he spoke to me, his glance roved back and forth. He stepped back and squinted up along the face of the mesa.

I glanced up there, too. Close to the edge, up top, Ted Fenton rode his horse, which picked its way carefully along the edge. The slope below where he rode was steep, but a bit farther south of that point, the high ground swerved back to the west, and the incline in that area was not as steep as the rest of the eastern escarpment. That section was also littered with outcropping rocks and boulders, though. They looked bone-white in the sun.

Jeff and I separated.

I stayed away from the bridge, went past it into the dry wash south of its near end.

The ravine was choked with cactus and mesquite and dwarf-trees, and an occasional withered sage bush clinging to life in there, somehow.

Down in the wash itself, my footsteps raised dust from the hard ground. I could feel the heat of the ground through the soles of my shoes.

"Okay, Brandon," Jeff called from above.

He stood near the end of the bridge, waving me up toward him.

Picking my way back up through the tangled undergrowth, I climbed up the slope to where he stood on a slanted rock face, his legs spread wide apart for balance. His slitted eyes still ranged endlessly back and forth on the rock-covered slope above.

On the far side of the rock he straddled, in a natural nest of boulders, lay the second guard.

He had been dealt with summarily, much the same as the first one we had found dead on the porch of the cabin. This one's sub machine gun lay nearby. It had been emptied into his body.

I was beginning to feel slightly sick. I could taste the bacon-and-egg breakfast I had eaten, up on the ranch patio a little earlier.

A sharp crack sounded on the rim above us.

We both looked up. Fenton sat his restless horse, his right arm extended downward toward the more gradual slope of the area below the edge where he was now. He was firing his semi-automatic, and he kept firing.

Running my glance quickly down along the face of the slope, I tried to see what he was shooting at.

Beside me, Jeff said something sharply, but I couldn't make it out. He raised his gun, but he held his fire.

Then I saw the other man up on the slope, too.

He was outlined against the pale sky. He ran up the rock-littered slope as if he was moving across level ground. His legs worked like pistons. His face was raised, up toward Fenton on his horse, up there on the rim.

The running man never looked at the ground. He kept his head thrust fiercely upward, never taking his eyes off his target, Fenton. He ran bent forward a little at the waist. His right hand held a rifle. On his head he wore a long-billed baseball cap.

Both he and Fenton were so far away from us that when the pistol Fenton had been firing was empty, we heard no other sound from either of them.

The man running up the rocky slope did not raise his rifle to reply to any of Fenton's shots. He didn't have to. He was still well beyond the range of the little pistol. He just went plunging on upward, in long furious leaps.

My stomach turned cold as I watched Fenton fumble with his handgun, trying to get a fresh clip into it. The horse he sat wouldn't stand still. All the shooting had panicked the animal, and perhaps the rider, as well.

As I watched Fenton trying to handle his horse and reload the pistol, I almost felt sorry for him. He showed much courage in being able to remain there at all, in full sight of the man racing up the side of the mesa toward him.

Fenton had probably been the one who enjoyed it most, when he and Smiles and Fats had worked over Ben Crane, before they left what remained of him in the desert for me to find, all those weeks ago. Fenton would have been the type who prolonged the victim's agony. That was why Ben wanted to get his hands on him. No quick rifle-shot would do for Fenton.

Thinking along those lines of probability, I gagged and had to turn away.

Beside me, Jeff chuckled.

"It's about time the damn fool took off."

When I felt I could, I looked back up at the rim of the mesa.

Fenton was still having trouble with his mount, but now he was urging it away from the point of the rim from which he had been firing downward. The horse plunged, once or twice, tossed his head from side to side, but finally moved, gathered speed going along the edge of the rim for a moment, and then both horse and rider were gone from our sight.

Surprisingly close below the rim, I caught a final glimpse of the man on foot, just as he, too, went up and over the top of it and out of sight. He had almost reached the top at the same moment Fenton got away from there.

Jeff shook his head.

"No wonder the little creep is scared," he commented casually.

I nodded. I still felt unable to open my mouth for fear of what more might come out of it.

"Come on, Brandon," Jeff said, sounding weary. "Back to the car."

He hustled me along the road to the Ford. I turned it around, and we drove back up the mesa ridge road, turned at the top and leveled off.

Nothing was in sight across the sage flat, which stretched out ahead of us, to and beyond the ranch house, due west. I kept flicking my eyes off the road ahead, trying to locate Fenton on his horse, but nothing moved out there.

"Where'd he go?"

"What difference?" Jeff said laconically. "He's done for. They're all as good as dead. I can't stop a guy like that, not with just a handgun. Probably not with anything less than a battery of mortars, and I'd need a squad of trained men to handle them. And even then, I wouldn't be sure I nailed that bastard, no matter how much we pounded each grid out there . . ."

"Doesn't Townsend have any hunting rifles out here? Is he just going to sit and take it?"

"How should I know?" Jeff snapped. "Stick to your driving."

At the ranch, I swung my car around at the foot of the patio steps just as Jan Thornton came out the front door carrying a soft carry-on bag for air travel. Dressed in a powder-blue suit, she wore no hat. Her light brown hair was combed and held by a powder-blue plastic clip on the left side of her head.

Walking right past where Brock Townsend stood, she stopped on the top step and put the bag on the flagstones beside her, just as Jeff and I were getting out of my car.

"Will you have Mano bring my car, Brock?" she asked, without looking at him.

Townsend ignored her.

"How does it look, Jeff?" he called.

"The sumbitch got both guards. Sprayed them with their own juice guns, after he'd put them down with his rifle."

Townsend's eyes closed. His head sank, and he stood for a moment like that, silent.

The girl's eyes widened. She stared down at Jeff, swung her gaze from Jeff to me, then looked across the flat field of sage behind us. Her lips trembled, briefly.

Townsend's head came up. His face was calm again, as he told Jeff: "All right. Get her car, Jeff. Drive her out of here . . ."

"I'll drive myself," Jan Thornton said, but now her voice was no longer strident and sure of itself. It was low, uncertain. She kept staring off into the distance toward the wall of the mountain, east of the mesa.

As if she had not spoken, Townsend continued issuing orders to Jeff.

"Get going now. Perhaps we can cut the casualties and end this, right here. I'm tired of it. Tired of all of it."

His gaze ranged above our heads in a wide sweep, taking in the mountain and the endless desert wasteland to the north, and the line of faint purple jagged ranges of hills beyond.

Jeff went inside, and a moment later reappeared wearing his suit coat. He stopped beside Townsend.

"You don't want me to stay on here?" he asked. "Maybe the two of us can handle this . . ."

Townsend chuckled.

"Not a chance. We haven't got a prayer against someone like . . . that. No, Jeff, I've had enough. I've got a Mannlicher inside. What has to be done from here on, I'll do myself."

"I mean it," Jeff insisted. "I'll stay, if you want."

He didn't look at Townsend when he said it, and there was no expression in his flat voice.

Glancing down at Jeff, Townsend almost smiled.

"Thanks, Jeff. No. It's over. Get them both out of here. Where's Ted?"

Vaguely, Jeff waved out toward the southern part of the mesa, without saying a word.

Townsend waited a moment for him to elaborate, seemed to understand when he didn't, and let it go.

Mano drove Jan Thornton's car around the corner of the ranch house and stopped it beside mine.

Jeff pointed at me, and then at my car. I got in and had trouble getting the motor started again. As I whined away at the starter, Jeff picked up the woman's bag and came down the steps to her car, putting the bag in the trunk in back.

Listlessly, Jan descended the steps. Jeff opened the door on the passenger side for her, and afterward went around her car and got behind the wheel.

Jan was almost seated inside the car when she stepped back out. Glancing up the steps at Townsend, she turned and faced the sweep of sage flat stretching away in front of her. The wind blew her hair forward on both sides of her face.

Putting both hands up to her mouth, she cupped them and called out strongly across the emptiness.

"Benny, what have they done to you?"

Her voice choked on the last word.

Her cry seemed so pitifully small. The wind swept the words across the flat land, seemed to disperse the very sound of them, to reduce all her anguish to something of no meaning under the immense pale blue sky.

When the words were gone and silence remained, she stood there, swinging her glance back and forth across the wind-ruffled clumps of sage bushes.

Tears streamed from her eyes, but she didn't sob, nor did her face twist from crying. It was as if only her eyes wept, without her knowledge or consent.

She tried again. Using all the strength she could put into her voice, she cried down the stream of wind.

"Let them go. Not one of them is worth it. They have nothing but hate in their hearts."

She stood then, beside the open door of her car, listening, waiting. But no answer came back to her. The only sound to break the early afternoon silence was the two motors idling, and even that seemed muted, raveled by the wind-sound.

Jeff leaned across inside her car and said something.

Impatiently, she shook her head, but a moment later, her shoulders slumped, shaking now with her weeping. Now her face was squeezed up. She stumbled into the car, pulling the door shut after her, and buried her face in her hands.

Jeff touched his horn, pointed at me, then straight ahead.

With a final glance at Townsend standing up there on the top step, I drove off, with Jeff at the wheel of Jan Thornton's car right behind me.

After descending the mesa, we passed the cabin with the body of the dead guard still stretched across the porch, partly in shade now, drove across the bridge with the planks under the car wheels sounding like shotguns going off, as the tires bounced over them, and around the bulge of the rock outcropping to the county road, where we turned right and began the long climb.

A quarter of an hour later, around one o'clock, I glimpsed something in my rear view mirror, after we had climbed through the first pass over the mountain. Sticking my hand out, I brought the Ford to a halt and got out.

Jeff stopped the other car and stuck his head out to yell at me.

"What are you stopping for? Get moving."

"Take a look," I yelled.

Twisting in his seat, he looked back the way we'd come.

A thick column of smoke rose from somewhere far below. From where we were, we couldn't see the base of the column, and up as far as we were, in among the mountain's ridges, we were looking down at the top of the column from high above it.

Even as we watched, the thick smoke column was quickly being dispersed by the wind, but to have reached as high as it did in that strong a wind, the smoke must have been very thick and dense at its base.

I found myself wondering which was burning, the cabin at the bridge or the sprawling ranch house, up on the mesa.

I also wondered if Mano would be killed, too.

Jeff faced forward again. His mouth was tight when he waved me on.

Taking one last look at the smoke, I got back in the Ford and drove on.

We didn't stop at Pete's gas station. We didn't stop anywhere until we came to Florian's Yacht Club, and there, only the other car stopped.

I slowed, and in my rear view mirror watched Jeff get out of Jan Thornton's car and cross the road to the gate leading past the gateman's kiosk to the clubhouse farther in.

Sliding behind the wheel, Jan started her car moving again. A moment later, she flashed past me. I noted her license number, wrote it down, watched her vanish toward the city far ahead, and took my own sweet time getting home.

Showered and shaved, I put on a change of clothes and lugged the suitcase with the three captured handguns in it down from my room and stuffed it inside my car. After a moment's thought, I opened the suitcase and took out the two larger caliber guns and stuck them in my belt, out of sight under my suit coat. Then I stuck the suitcase back inside the car. I left the shoulder holster hanging from the nail behind the dresser. They had taken the Police Special away from me at the bridge cabin.

At a restaurant whose food I knew was good, I had an excellent meal, took my time reading today's newspaper over coffee afterward, and finally realized the police had arrived.

I looked around. Except for me, the place was empty. In front of me, on the white tablecloth beside the glass of water, was the snub nosed revolver I had gotten from Smiles, and beside the plate, on the right, was the .357 Magnum.

Behind the customers gathered in the entrance foyer and peering in at me were two uniformed cops. Both had guns in their hands, as they worked their way through the knot of people.

"Get Brode," I told them and went on sipping my coffee.

They took a step toward me.

Shaking my head at them, I picked up both handguns and pointed one at each of them.

"Get Brode," I repeated.

I had no idea why it had to be Brode, but it did.

One of them quietly told the other: "Hold it a minute." To me, he said: "You mean the detective downtown? That Sergeant Brode?"

"That's the one."

Turning to his partner, he said, "Radio for Brode."

His partner looked at him as if he thought he was nuts, but after a moment, he went out through the crowd in the doorway.

Putting both guns down, one on each side of the plate, I had some more of the excellent coffee. They didn't have coffee like that where I was going.

The remaining cop stood there, still holding his revolver, watching me.

In a little while, his partner returned and nodded to the one who had stayed.

"Brode'll be here in two shakes," I heard him mutter. "Although why you let this . . ."

The other one shrugged.

"Look at his eyes," he said quietly. "He's on cloud thirty-seven. We're just lucky he doesn't want to see the governor."

The other one still didn't look happy about any of it.

"Relax," the first one told him.

The next time I looked up, Brode was standing on the other side of my table, looking down at me curiously.

"Citizen's arrest," I told him, nodding at the two guns on the table. "This is evidence."

Brode was grinning. Glancing over at the watching cops and the restaurant's customers and waiters, his grin widened.

"All right, citizen," he said, gathering up the two handguns. "Come with me. It's not an official arrest until we're in the Hall of Justice, where the jail is. Who should we arrest?"

"Me," I told him, finishing the last of my coffee. "I meted out justice unlawfully. Summary justice, and it ain't even summer."

"Well, actually it is," Brode murmured, "but why spoil a so-so pun, right?"

Getting up, I paid the bill, left a generous tip on the table, and followed Brode out past the two cops. Beyond the doorway, the crowd of onlookers melted before us.

Sixteen

They didn't keep me busy watching lineups that night. They gave me a nice clean cell, all to myself. I was the only inmate in that section of the jail, so it was nice and quiet. I slept more than twelve hours.

Three days later, after my fourth session on various carpets, Sergeant Brode was admitted to my cell. Sitting on the edge of the cot, I looked up at him. Brode waited until the turnkey was gone before he told me the news.

"They didn't get him."

I nodded.

"I'm not surprised. You got any extra smokes?"

Absently, he handed me an almost full pack.

"Was it him? Ben Crane?" he asked.

I shrugged.

"It could have been him. The guy was a long way off, the only time I got a glimpse of him. It might have been him. Who else would it be?"

Brode grimaced.

"That buddy of yours, Jeff, wasn't much more help. He couldn't identify who it was, either."

"You holding him?"

"Who? Jeff?"

I nodded.

"What for? What did he do?"

"He helped kidnap me. Twice. That's what for."

"Where's your witnesses?"

"My . . ." I stopped.

"You killed those two guys. Upstairs, they don't like that."

"I don't blame them for not liking it. I'm not crazy about it, myself. But I told them why I killed them. I was trying to save some lives. A man named Mercator, a chorus girl named Roberta from Florian's, two clowns . . ."

"I know, I know," Brode broke in impatiently, "but they don't like you shoving Smiles out of a car going over sixty. To a grand jury, it won't look elegant."

"By then, I was probably a little crazy. Can you blame me? Did you see that little girl, Roberta? One of those bastards stitched her right across the middle with a juice gun . . ."

"Brandon, what difference does it make whether I can blame you or not? It's can *they* blame you? They're your problem, not me."

Lighting a cigarette from Brode's CARE package, I dragged a couple of lungfuls of smoke in and dropped the butt on the steel floor, where I watched it smolder.

"How about Jan Thornton? Did they pick her up?"

"Yeah, they did. There, you were lucky. She was halfway to Dune City in her car, belting away at a fifth of Teacher's as if it was the last bottle on the planet."

"Did she back up my story? About what went on out there at the Townsend ranch?"

"Oh, yes, she said the same as you, for all the help that was. The guy still hasn't been turned up. He could've driven his car out of there after it was over, turned north on that country road, and he could be anywhere up in that wilderness area. No one but tourists and forest rangers ever go up there, not in this kind of weather. It's like a furnace up there now."

"What about Townsend and Fenton?"

"Both dead. All they found of Townsend was bones in the embers of the ranch house. They identified him, though. The other one, Fenton, he was at the bottom of the west wall of the mesa. He might have been thrown over the edge, or he could have been trying to climb down from the top and slipped. Anyway, when he hit the rocks at the bottom, anything that might have been done to him before was pretty well covered up just from him landing. They didn't find him until yesterday."

"How about Ben Crane?"

Brode shrugged.

"The highway patrols are still looking, of course, but . . ."

He didn't finish. He didn't have to.

"Did he kill the Indian, too?"

"The servant at the ranch? No. Townsend told him to stay with the horses. He did."

"Well, that's something, anyway," I muttered.

Standing, I stretched and yawned.

"Now what?" I asked. "What about me?"

"That's up to the grand jury. And them." He jerked a thumb vaguely upward. "You'll be lucky if you don't have to kiss that P. I. license of yours goodbye."

I started cremating another of the cigarettes out of the pack he'd given me.

"Hell with the damn license," I said. "I just hope I don't have to forfeit the bond I had to post to get the damn thing."

Chuckling, he stared at me.

"You don't turn a hair about knocking over two guys, but you worry about some crummy dough that you might lose . . ."

"Hold on," I snapped. "Don't start sneering at crummy dough. You're on a salary. I'm not. I had to turn in that hundred bucks Mercator paid me to keep my eyes open for him. That leaves me with well below a hundred of my own money left."

"Then you shouldn't have turned in Mercator's hundred. It didn't have any bearing on the rest of it."

Impatiently, I tried to explain why.

"How could I keep it? I didn't earn it from the man."

Brode's face was a study in perplexity.

"You blow away two hard knuckles, just like that." He snapped his fingers. "But your conscience would hurt if you kept a bill you don't think you earned. Brandon, you're too fragile for this world we live in."

"How do you know I could kill those two just like that?" I snapped my fingers back at him.

Brode threw his head back and laughed.

"Okay," he said. "Forget I said that. Maybe they won't hang you, after all."

Crossing to the cell door, he yelled for the jailer.

While we were waiting, he turned and asked: "Anything I can get for you? In case they keep you here awhile?"

"Newspapers, I guess. Something to read."

He nodded and left soon afterward.

For awhile, though, it looked as if they really might hang me.

They dug into the whole thing from the beginning. They looked up my previous record, which wasn't spotless, I admit, but it wasn't previously littered with casual killings, either.

In the end, they let me off, making allowances because Val turned out to be a known no-good from Chicago with a long string of unproven, or unprovable, felonies on his arrest record, and Smiles had been up for assault on two previous occasions, for both of which his lawyers had gotten him off with plea bargains.

They didn't take my license, either, although I had been certain they would. That didn't help me any. I got no clients.

My money disappeared, as money tends to do. I couldn't maintain even the desk-space pretense, and it wasn't long before I was scrounging around for another bacon-and-bean job. I found one shortly, unloading trucks at a shipping terminal.

However, I still had the Ford. When the whole thing had slid imperceptibly into the past, and people became less likely to remember seeing my picture in the papers in connection with all of it, I began to drop in at El Rancho Motel, out near Florian's casino.

I never hung around long, just a moment or two, while I bought cigarettes, or talked about local scenic stuff. One day when I stopped by, Chester, the manager, was busy with a family who were renting one of the units in mid-afternoon.

"Be right back," Chester told me.

When he was out of sight, I went into his empty office and around behind the counter, where I got his registry book and quickly looked back through it, until I came to a page with the date I was looking for: the day I had found Ben Crane, when he was thrown from a car in the desert, southeast of town.

I skimmed down the names fast, looking for a Ben Crane. I got about two weeks prior to my starting date when I saw one of the pages had been very neatly razor-bladed out, close in at the binding.

It was far enough before my starting date to have gotten past any police who might have been looking for a man who had registered on or before the night of the assault in the desert.

Closing the register, I returned it to its place and got back out from behind the counter. There was no hurry. Chester was busy for a good fifteen minutes, settling the family in.

I hadn't discovered anything, really. But there was a remote possibility that El Rancho Motel was where the assault victim had been holed up before the crucial night, and perhaps even afterward. He could always have gotten another room in the place, if he suspected his attackers might have known about the one he had been staying in, prior to running afoul of Townsend, and whatever ill-advised wish he might have expressed, which had started Wyatt and his people on the opening move that had gotten all the mayhem going.

Strolling out of Chester's office, I looked across the inner court. The gray Chevy with the smooth two-foot-long dent punched neatly into its left rear fender, behind the wheel, was no longer parked in its usual spot, back in the northwest angle. It hadn't been there since the final windup of the whole thing, up at Townsend's ranch.

Watching the traffic pass both ways along the highway, I was thinking that Ben Crane certainly had his nerve about him, if he'd stayed that close to Florian's. Maybe he wanted to be able to look out the north window of his motel room and be able to see the Florian's sign, to remind him . . . like he'd need reminding!

I wondered if he had picked off Wyatt on Florian's roof from the motel itself.

I wouldn't have put it past him.

Shrugging, I drifted back to town, feeling as if none of us would ever know how he had managed it, or where he had been holed up, all through it. The only thing I could do was guess.

That was until three months or so later, when I ran into Brode, over on the Strip.

"Seen today's paper?" he asked. Without waiting for a reply, he handed a copy over. "Front page. Chuck Macy's byline."

It gave me a jolt. The story contained a photo of the gray Chevy sedan, instantly recognizable to me because of the big smooth dent in the left rear fender.

"They got Crane?" I blurted.

Brode blinked.

"Man, you're sure a quick reader," he said. "Yeah, it looks like your friend came to the end of his rope, up north of that ranch of Townsend's he burned down."

I read the front page story.

It was brushfire season. Up there, the brushfires were all over the place, here and there in the wilderness area and national forests. The day before, a helicopter attached to a firefighting outfit spotted a car in the middle of nowhere. He couldn't investigate right then, but later he went back, landed, and instead of finding a damn fool camper who had gotten himself lost in the desert, it turned out to be . . .

I looked up at Brode. He was watching me, waiting, grinning.

"A skeleton!"

Brode nodded, delighted to be the first to sock me with the news.

"Well, he's been up there three months," he pointed out.

Suddenly, I felt empty. Handing the paper back, I observed: "After all that, to have him run out of gas and die like a careless tourist!"

"It may not be so simple," Brode said. "That's what it looked like, at first. But they handled it by the book, once they got the brushfire under control yesterday evening. They sent in a forensic team. And guess what they turned up?"

"I wouldn't have a clue," I grinned. "And I also wouldn't want to spoil your story for you by accidentally coming up with the right guess."

He laughed sheepishly.

"They found a bullet," he said, "on the seat underneath where the skeleton was still propped up behind the Chevy's steering wheel."

"A three-month old slug?" I was skeptical. "What good would that be . . .?"

"It's in perfect shape, though. Not a mark on it. As clean as if they shot it into cotton for a ballistics check."

"Okay, could be," I admitted. "Which would mean he caught one of the shots Fenton fired at him from the rim of the mesa."

"Could be," he echoed.

"Well, Fenton sure fired enough of them."

I shook my head in wonder at the way it seems to have turned out.

"Funny, that's the last thing that would have occurred to me, that one of Fenton's shots actually hit the guy. While I watched him going up the side of that mesa, he was never anywhere near within range of the handgun Fenton was blasting away with, from up top."

Brode nodded.

"Maybe shooting down could explain it? One of the bullets went further than it should have, and by some miracle, it connected."

I grinned.

"Okay, a miracle I'll buy. Nothing less."

"Anyway, nothing's been proved yet. We'll have to wait for the ballistics report. At least we've got the gun that Fenton guy was shooting with. That will clinch it, for certain, either pro or con, with a bullet that clean."

Brode was busily reading the news story again.

"They still don't know how he could have gotten that far," he marveled. "This Chuck Macy was up there. He could hardly believe a regular car could make it through the kind of terrain that old Chevy was put through."

"We should have brought Chuck in on the case," I said. "Maybe he could have figured out what we should have done back then, when it mattered."

Brode laughed.

"Macy's good, but he ain't that good. And as for whether it matters, it's always good if we can bring in a case that's solved. I like it when we can wrap things up nice and neat and get on to the other ones . . ."

"The ones that end like most cases," I put in. "Unsolved."

"Right," he admitted. "All right, we'll see what ballistics tell us. And the skeleton, too. His teeth should reveal whether it's Ben Crane from those medical records the Army came up with."

It turned out pretty much that way. The slug they found with the skeleton, up there in the Wilderness Area, was a perfect match with Fenton's handgun. One of those many shots he had fired at his pursuer had somehow found a mark. It hadn't been enough to stop Ben Crane on the spot, nor to prevent him from doing what he ended up doing, to Fenton himself, and to Townsend and his magnificent ranch house, but it had been enough to kill him, thirty or forty miles north of there.

Sergeant Brode got his wish. They identified the skeleton found in the broken-down Chevy up in the wilderness area as that of Ben Crane.

Chuck Macy milked the story and the follow-up for all it was worth, and maybe a little more, and for him, it paid off. He got a ticket to Reno, and a job on a newspaper up there, with the extra bonus of a connection with the local TV news outlet. He was on his way. Or still on his way.

As for me, eventually work began to drift in. Not a lot of it, but enough for me to be able to quit the truck-loading gig and hire desk space and get a telephone again.

Now, every so often at night, I sit on the adobe wall at the end of the meager terrace outside my room. I go over it in my mind, trying to figure out how I should have handled things so little Roberta wouldn't end up dead in that shack in the alley near El Rancho Motel.

Bobbie-O, the girl who wanted to be loved forever.

She was buried somewhere out there, under the distant night. Her folks had come down and reclaimed her body and taken it away for proper interment, somewhere in northern California . . . much as I had reclaimed my .38 Police Special after the police found it locked in a metal file cabinet in the shack at the bridge, below Townsend's mesa.

I don't know where Roberta is buried. I don't want to know. I prefer to keep her the way she is in my memory, along with the night and the desert wind, the line of distant lights along the east-west highway, a mile or two north of my adobe perch. Even the nearer, harsher glare of lights thrown up to the high night sky by the Strip was a part of it, and the smell of the sagebrush nearby, musky and pungently aromatic, especially at night.

All those things still bring back my few brief memories of Bobbie-O. They left me with the one thing that counted, besides the memory of the desert, and the distant mountains, and the high, clear, star-filled night, where she rested somewhere safely in the ground: all of it left me with the memory of her delightful impudent face, a face I can never forget.

Maybe it's enough.

THE END